NEARLY DEPARTED

NEARLY DEPARTED

LUCAS OAKELEY

Bedford Square
Publishers

First published in the United Kingdom in 2025 by
Bedford Square Publishers Ltd,
London, UK

bedfordsquarepublishers.co.uk
@bedsqpublishers

© Lucas Oakeley, 2025

The right of Lucas Oakeley to be identified as the author of this work has been asserted in accordance with the Copyright, Designs and Patents Act 1988. All rights reserved. No part of this book may be reproduced, stored in or introduced into a retrieval system, or transmitted, in any form or by any means (electronic, mechanical, photocopying, recording or otherwise) without the written permission of the publishers.

Any person who does any unauthorised act in relation to this publication may be liable to criminal prosecution and civil claims for damages.
A CIP catalogue record for this book is available from the British Library.
This is a work of fiction. Names, characters, places, and incidents either are the product of the author's imagination or are used fictitiously, and any resemblance to actual persons, living or dead, businesses, companies, events or locales is entirely coincidental.

The manufacturer's authorised representative in the EU for
product safety is Easy Access System Europe, Mustamäe tee 50,
0621 Tallinn, Estonia
gpsr.requests@easproject.com

ISBN
978-1-83501-294-9 (Paperback)
978-1-83501-295-6 (eBook)

2 4 6 8 10 9 7 5 3 1

Typeset in Bembo Std by Palimpsest Book Production Limited,
Falkirk, Stirlingshire

Printed in Great Britain by CPI Group (UK) Ltd, Croydon CR0 4YY

To Ron and Julie, with love, forever.

Unable are the loved to die, for love is immortality
—Emily Dickinson

PART ONE

Beth

Beth woke up before the sun. She'd been dreaming of flying – blue skies, ant-nest cities, the wind in her ears and the clouds on her clothes – when the alarm yanked her out of bed. Some people can hit the snooze button three, maybe four, times before succumbing to the whine of their iPhone. Most do it with a full-body shrug. Not Beth Lewis. Beth was up the second she heard the opening chimes of her five-thirty wake-up call.

Her fingers fumbled in the dark until they found the reassuring touch of her diary's cool, supple leather. She moved her pen across the lined paper, her thoughts running a mile a minute as she scribbled down a dispatch of her dream. Her therapist had told her keeping a dream journal would be 'helpful'. She wasn't entirely sure what that meant.

As the sun slowly climbed the rungs of the horizon, the world outside the window shifted from a a bruise-coloured palette of greys and purples into an endless wash of gas blue. With the gentle soundtrack of birdsong in the background, Beth set her daily intention ('I will make it through the day without accidentally saying "cheers" in a non-cheers situation') and ticked off a substantial portion of her Wednesday to-do list. She was ruthlessly efficient. A pleasure to have in class. The sort of person capable of saying, 'Once I'm up, I'm up,' and somehow, miraculously, making it charming.

Summer was at its sweaty peak and Beth knew she could jerk back her forest green curtains and have plenty of light to work with as she fumbled with her Reeboks and multivitamins. Unfortunately, doing that would risk waking up her boyfriend, Joel, who was safe in the clutch of his own flight-less sleep. Joel didn't keep a dream journal but, if he did, his entry for the day would have contained an eerily vivid description of a crumbling country manor.

The covers rustled softly as Beth slipped out from under them, and she held her breath, listening for any signs of movement, but Joel didn't stir. His mind was still walking down a long gravel drive. Beth let out a sigh of relief and gathered up her things for the day.

Laces tied and teeth brushed, she patted herself down like a festival security guard to make sure she had her keys and wallet before wheeling her bike out of the hallway and gently shutting the door behind her with a soft click. No matter how quietly Beth closed the door, the subtle handshake between the latch and door frame would always wake up Joel. His eyes would flutter open for a moment or two before closing again like a drowsy clam, heavy and content at the thought of Beth's existence in the world. The knowledge of her being out there – not doing anything special, just answering

Nearly Departed

her emails and living her life, really – made Joel's extra two hours of rest until his own alarm even sweeter.

She made her way down the stairs and out into the street, taking a deep breath of the morning air. The city was just starting to wake up, the stuccoed buildings were still quiet and peaceful and rubbing sleep from their eyes. A fox sprang out from a bin in a flurry of rusty orange, nearly toppling Beth off her bike. She regained her balance, just, and watched as the creature's bushy tail vanished into a nearby shrub. Beth gripped the bike's handlebars, the harlequin texture biting gently into the soft flesh of her palms. She couldn't help but smile. This, thought Beth, will be a good day.

As Joel dreamed of oak panelling and cornices, Beth sweated to the sounds of two lifestyle journalists arguing about the latest period drama on Netflix. Was it anachronistic to have a gay storyline? Was it homophobic if it didn't? Beth knew you weren't supposed to listen to podcasts or music while you were cycling but she couldn't help herself. Wearing a helmet was a given, of course. She wasn't a complete idiot. But even the thought of having to listen to her own internal monologue for forty minutes as she raced from Hackney to Clapham, her right trouser leg tucked snugly into her bamboo sock, seemed like a fate worse than death.

Beth didn't hate Clapham. She simply hated everything it stood for. Like boat shoes. And rugby. She hated spending too much money at the Little Waitrose near Clapham Common every day and she hated how her colleagues earned so much more than her that they didn't have to worry about dropping £4 on a prawn mayo sandwich. Beth had worked out the other month she was spending roughly £12 a week on kombucha. She didn't even like kombucha. She drank them 'for health' while her brain craved the cool, caffeinated hit of a Diet Coke.

She'd tried a handful of true crime podcasts out for size but found the murders too grisly and the hosts too American. She wasn't fussy about who she listened to, in all honesty, as long as they passed the Bechdel test and there wouldn't be a danger of anyone saying 'arugula'. Anything related to business, however, depressed Beth even more than hearing about prolific rapists and serial killers. 'Please tell me more about how hard you had to "hustle" after your parents gave you a £150,000 loan,' she grumbled to herself. 'It must have been *so* difficult for you.' Beth would voice these gripes out loud to Joel while, internally, she battled with the ethics of the grammar school she'd attended growing up. It was unfair to say she resented her parents for the comfortable upbringing they'd provided her with, but would it have killed them to have given her more of a tragic backstory?

Like, sure, her dad had walked out on them when she was fifteen and that was sad. But her mum had replaced him with a much better-looking and much more capable man within about ten months of his departure. So what right did she have to complain? Beth blamed her longing for a more heartbreaking narrative on the chokehold Jacqueline Wilson had on her childhood. Good old Jackie – now there was a woman who'd never have to worry about the price of a prawn sandwich, thought Beth as she clunked between gears and careened along Silverthorne Road.

Beth had been at the same company for about four years now, designing and redesigning endless single and double-page spreads for clients that ranged all the way from high-end olive oil brands to high-end tahini brands. She had always wanted to be a 'real' artist but it turned out doing 'real art' required you to network from the age of ten and Beth simply didn't have the patience for it. Not anymore, at least. She was twenty-six now, edging closer and closer to the reality of blowing out thirty candles on a Colin the Caterpillar in a pub charging £15 for 'cakeage'. Beth had resigned herself to a life as a graphic designer rather than a Pre-Raphaelite after university and it wasn't long before she actually learned to love her job – rote as it may have been. Waking up on Mondays wasn't the worst thing in the world. And it was that, combined with the fact she couldn't be arsed with scrolling through LinkedIn for hours every night, that had kept her at BoldType Studio for so long.

Joel had often told her she should try looking for another job so she could 'spread her wings'. But maybe Beth felt fine with her wings slightly clipped. Maybe she was okay with her little lot in life. Yeah, it'd be nice not to stress about the price of supermarket sandwiches but it wasn't like she was struggling. She and Joel lived in a nice-ish flat in a nice-ish area of London rapidly being gentrified as more nice-ish couples like them moved in. She gritted her teeth and pumped her legs to overtake a suited Santander cyclist. She was happy. The price of a flat white was scrawled on the chalkboard at her local coffee shop as '3.50' and the lack of a pound sign made it seem like it wasn't real money she was spending every Saturday morning. She was happy. Her body, which had felt loose and baggy on her bones as a teenager, was finally starting to feel like it fitted. She was happy.

She should have seen the cement truck. If she'd seen the cement truck, she might not have died.

(Almost) Three Years Later

You find solace where you can; Joel sought it in the dark blue veins of the Piccadilly line. The thought of growing accustomed to the way it purred, juddered and screeched like some sort of big mechanical cat had seemed an alien concept to him when he'd first moved to the city. But that's exactly what had happened. A couple of months into his forty-five-minute commute and Joel Foster felt just as at home on the tube as he did in his own flat. He probably spent just as much time there, too.

If he got a seat, he'd read. Preferably fiction, something light and forgettable with an ending he could predict after the first twenty pages suited him down to the ground, but he'd happily settle for the Showbiz section of the *Metro*. If he was forced to stand, music was his distraction of choice. The more ambient, the better. He didn't want lyrics, he wanted tinkly background noise he could let his ears take a rest on before they got assaulted by London's din. There was a comfort in the knowledge that regardless of where his mind wandered or which avenues it explored, he could always rely on the tube to get him from A to B. It remained, in spite of the occasional Saturday-night chunderer, almost spookily dependable. If Joel was honest with himself, it might be the only consistent thing left in his life.

Tinny music blared from someone's phone speaker down the carriage. Joel looked up and rested his eyes on an advertisement for a Muslim dating app: 'You had me at halal'. He smirked, briefly, before the reality of his loneliness whooshed through his chest like a freight train. It was the same hollowed-out feeling he got when he cracked up watching comedy shows alone. Whenever a solid punchline landed, his reflex was to whip his head towards the empty seat on the right side of the sofa where Beth had always sat. Where she'd always left behind a trail of biscuit crumbs and loose strands of hair.

The three-year anniversary of Beth's death was coming up in a few weeks – forty days, to be exact – and he was already dreading the chunky wall of text his mum would trebuchet to his phone on the day. She'd ask him if he was 'doing okay', which meant 'Are you seeing anyone yet?' And he'd say 'I'm fine,' which meant 'Of course I'm fucking not.'

Three years. That's exactly how long he'd given himself to fall in love again after she died. Which was absurd. Because who sets an internal deadline for something like that? Love isn't a half-marathon. But there he was, ticking off the weeks, haunted by a promise he never should have made.

Thoughts of that deadline had been simmering at

the back of Joel's mind every morning for the past week. They tended to barge in when he was mid-way through his bowl of Shreddies, slowly fogging the corridors of his brain with the stale scent of death and week-old cereal. It was no surprise, then, his emotions had been all over the shop at work. That's what happens when your girlfriend is wiped out in an incident involving a very large, very unyielding truck. Your life changes. You get a little shaky. One minute, he'd be as melancholic and morose as a wartime poet. The next, he'd be humming along to Coldplay.

In the moments where Joel did catch himself singing, smiling or exhaling sharply out of his nose at something funny – which, he had to admit, was starting to happen more often lately – a cold elbow of guilt would slam hard into his stomach. His conscience would kick into gear and broadcast a message of 'Oh, so you think it's fine to smile, do you? While Beth is dead. And buried. And never coming back?' throughout his entire body.

It seemed so cruel to Joel how the person he'd known to cry tears of joy at the sight of a butterfly at Kew Gardens, or his gap-toothed smile in his Year 3 class photo, had had her life ended before it ever really started. But the distinct flavour of guilt he felt that morning didn't have anything to do with a feeling of personal responsibility for Beth's death. He didn't blame himself for not telling her to take the overground instead of cycling in, and he didn't even feel guilty that he hadn't woken to kiss her before she left him for what turned out to be the very last time.

Joel was too rational to worry about the 'what ifs' of Beth's death. What if she'd stayed at home that day? What if she hadn't been going so fast? ? What if the driver of that truck had been held up in traffic? All of those hypotheticals were just that: hypothetical. What Joel did feel guilty about was that he didn't, no matter how hard he tried, wish it was him who was dead instead. He'd have loved to be able to wail at the top of his lungs that it should have been Beth who had to attend *his* funeral and hold *his* mum while she sobbed. But he couldn't. As much as he wanted Beth to be alive, he didn't long to be dead in her place. That's what ate him up every time he woke up in the morning: the sinking feeling of guilt that chased his violent relief at being alive.

He used his debit card to tap out at Hammersmith and considered, as he did every day, whether it was worth paying a sizeable chunk of his wage just to get into work. He exited the station, took a left turn and let his body switch onto autopilot. Joel had made this journey so many times he reckoned he could do it with his eyes shut.

One of the few benefits of long-term bereavement was Joel could arrive at work at nine on the dot and leave exactly at five without anyone saying anything obnoxious like, 'Didn't know it was a half-day?' He'd even managed to avoid the ire of his boss for the most part.

Joel peered up at Sabine through his glasses and leaned back against his desk chair, absent-mindedly toying with the wheel of his mouse. She was busy chewing out Michael for putting their pronouns in their email signature. He busily opened and closed the emails in his inbox without digesting their content, while Sabine screeched, 'It's unprofessional!' across the office, threatening to terminate Michael's temporary contract. Sabine was constantly threatening to let people go. Yet throughout all his years of working for her, Joel had only ever seen her fire one person for the 'gross misconduct' of spilling an Americano on the carpet. Everyone else who'd left had, unsurprisingly, walked out on her of their own volition. Joel imagined pulling out a cigarette and exhaling a plume of smoke into her devastatingly pretty face.

Sabine possessed an almost ethereal beauty, as if each of her features had been crafted in a lab. Excellent bone structure, sculpted eyebrows, and plump lips that sent teenagers googling for fillers. Beyond that façade of perfection, though, was a stone-cold bitch. Eight years past her chance of ever making the *Forbes* '30 Under 30', Sabine was a playground bully in Prada loafers, a sociopath dead set on gaslighting her way to the top of the LinkedIn mountain.

Filling up his water bottle simply so he could have something to do with his hands, Joel took the moment to consider how much longer his immunity from watercooler chat would last. He reckoned he could stretch it out to at least another half-year. By that point, there'd probably have been enough staff turnover that no one would even know what had happened to him. Or Beth.

Joel had significantly upped his use of the office coffee machine since Beth's death. Partly due to lack of sleep, partly out of rebellion against a company that clearly had no compassion for the people who worked there, and partly because it was free, so — fuck it — why not?

He'd kept things together for the most part but only getting four hours of sleep a night had slowly started to gnaw holes in the fabric of Joel's day-to-day life. Just as he'd never expected to grow fond of the tube, he had never anticipated he'd miss Beth's relentless snoring. Every night, without fail, he'd been woken up at least once by the erratic symphony of her snuffles. She didn't have a Disney snore. When Beth was properly asleep, it sounded like a clutch of piglets was being squashed inside her chest.

Now, Joel slept in the complete and total silence he'd always yearned for. There was no more having to listen to *The Archers* until Beth dozed off. No danger of going for a pee in the middle of the night and returning to a bed vibrating in time with her staccato inhales.

And he missed all of that. Desperately.

Trust Your Gut Or The Algorithm

'You need to get back on the apps,' said Sam. 'It'd be good for you.'

Sam had been Joel's best friend since university. They'd met in the second term of their first year and swiftly bonded over a shared desperation to be liked. The year passed in a drunken blur of toffee shots and regret, yet their friendship held firm. Which is why, when Sam told him, 'You'll never move on unless you try,' he actually listened.

He might have set himself a three-year deadline to get loved up, but Joel had made little effort to actually start a romantic relationship with anyone since Beth's passing. As far as his friends were concerned, he'd made none at all. Sure, he'd had women try to strike up a conversation with him when they were four pints deep, but a mixture of Joel's general state of depression, combined with his historic lack of self-worth, meant he often read those encounters as polite gestures rather than genuine romantic interest.

He wasn't completely hopeless with the opposite sex, though. Before he'd met Beth, Joel had had a bit of success in 'the scene' at university. He'd had casual sex with enough women (three) to warrant a visit to the campus sexual health clinic to make sure he hadn't accidentally caught 'anything serious' (just thrush). But the thought of building his entire dating profile from the ground up filled him with dread.

Joel hit the 'Create Profile' button, offered up quite literally all of his personal information, and started sweating profusely from his palms. He stared at his pint and felt his anxiety seep into the bubbles.

'Should I mention that I'm a widower?'

'What?'

'Like, do you think I should mention that I'm a widower on my dating profile?'

'No,' said Sam, 'because you're not a widower.'

'I mean, I practically am.'

'No, you're practically not,' said Sam with a finality that made Joel feel like he was getting told off by his teacher for picking his nose.

Sam had been one of the best rowers the University of Manchester had ever seen — a cult figure around campus, one of those men who other men swarmed to whenever he entered a room. An injury to his right shoulder might have curtailed his rowing career but it didn't put a dampener on his popularity. He was a king for those three years. A revolving door of women — all beautiful, all vaguely interchangeable — clung to him like burrs. Joel still found it hard to believe they were friends.

Since his university years, Sam had grown slightly softer around the middle. The calluses on his hands had softened, too, but not even the baggiest XL T-shirt could hide the size of his broad shoulders. He was big and placid, like an overgrown golden retriever, and had to duck through roughly forty per cent of the doorways he encountered. By the age of thirteen, he'd been taller than half of his teachers at school and he hadn't stopped growing until he was the largest human in just about every room he entered. Thankfully, all Sam needed to do to dispel any notions of him as a comedic André the Giant-like figure was open his mouth.

His voice was clipped, like a hedge, which added to the impression he was always trying to race to the end of whatever he was trying to say. There were people who heard him speak and assumed he wanted to be somewhere else – and there were people who resented him for that – but the truth was that Sam was in a constant battle with himself to fit in as much life as possible.

'Yes, you and Beth were in love,' said Sam, 'but that doesn't mean what you two had was so precious and perfect and one-of-a-fucking-kind that you won't be able to find that ever again. And, besides,' he added, picking his glass back up, 'you'd have to have been married to be able to call yourself a widower.'

'What if I told you I was planning on proposing to her the year she died? Would that change whether or not you'd consider me a widower?'

Sam paused mid-sip and a look of profound contemplation clouded his face. Joel strained to recall if he'd ever seen Sam look this serious, and it brought him back to the time they'd visited the Sistine Chapel during their second-year summer holiday. In that hallowed space, burdened by kilos of Catholic guilt, something transcendent had seized Sam and shook him by the shoulders. It wasn't the fleeting awe he had experienced while dining next to a B-list celebrity in Soho, but a beatific wonderment which started in his feet and rose right up till it was hot and throbbing at the roof of his skull.

'No,' said Sam. The doubt lining his face slowly transformed into casual confidence, filling Joel with a feeling of warmth and kinship, 'because I know there's no fucking way you were going to propose to Beth before you turned thirty.'

Joel looked sheepish but felt seen by the man at the table opposite him. Not counting Beth, Joel was fairly certain Sam was the greatest love of his life. 'Yeah,' he sighed, 'that would have been a terrible idea. But still,' he took a nervous swig of his own pint, 'where do I start?'

'It's easy. Dating in your twenties is just taking turns asking the other person whether they've seen the show you're currently obsessed with and saying, "No, but I've heard good things," until one of you eventually gets bored and decides to do it all over again with someone new.'

'As magical as that sounds, I hardly think I'm hook-up material. I've barely got any photos of myself from the last three years. And the ones I do have are all with Beth before she . . . went.'

'That's not a problem,' said Sam, 'we'll start taking some right now.' He whipped his phone out of his pocket and started doing his best paparazzo impression, taking an endless stream of photos until Joel was eventually forced to crack, grabbing Sam's phone off him and letting out a high-pitched, almost falsetto, laugh. For a brief moment in Joel's life, he felt as if things had returned to normal.

Having deleted five pints each, the two left the pub and stumbled like toddlers towards the nearest underground station. Sam was heading west – back to the flat he lived in with his fiancée, Holly, which sounded awfully adult – while Joel was due back east for an appointment with some relatively tasteless pornography.

Sam hugged Joel and told him he loved him before he plugged his black kidney-bean-shaped wireless headphones into his ears and jolted into the nearest carriage. That was that then. Joel was left on the platform, drunk and alone, waiting for his own pumpkin to come and take him home. He had forty days left to fall in love, and his phone, now loaded with three dating apps he'd heard of and one he was fairly certain was banned in a handful of countries, burned a hole in his pocket. He'd have a scroll as soon as he could get a signal, he thought. There'd be no harm in having a look.

'After all,' Sam had said, 'what's the worst thing that could happen?'

Days left to fall in love: 40

Agnes

Joel's first date from the apps was with Agnes. He sat in a bar near Old Street, clammy hand latched onto a glass of beer, and drank as if he was trying to drown himself while he waited for her to show up. The music was loud. And lousy. People couldn't possibly enjoy music at this volume. It was too loud to think. Too loud to talk. Too loud to do anything aside from suck down sugary cocktails and nod furiously at whatever was being shouted at you. Perhaps that was the point.

Although he'd been out of the dating game for some time, Joel was stunned at how efficiently the process worked. A few emoji-laden texts back and forth, a nervous yes, and 'It's a date!' – that was all it took.

Agnes arrived twenty minutes late and Joel awkwardly introduced himself, trying to ignore that she didn't look anything like her profile picture. It was the same her as in the photographs, all right, but Agnes looked to be about twenty years older than her Lisbon holiday snaps had suggested. Still, thought Joel, as Agnes told him about how lonely she'd been since her divorce, what's the worst thing that could happen?

Sophie

His second date was with Sophie – a twenty-four-year-old trainee investment banker who couldn't shake off the shade of 'horse girl' she'd picked out for herself when she was eight. Joel could deal with her passions for dressage and equity but he couldn't help but be concerned when she told him she'd almost drowned on three separate occasions. Once was terrible. Twice was unfortunate. But three times? Surely you'd have learned your lesson by that point, thought Joel, as he said, 'That's just awful, Sophie,' and patted her gently on the hand.

Preet

Joel couldn't quite believe his luck when he matched with Preet. She was so funny and charming it almost felt like a mistake – as if the all-seeing algorithm had felt sorry for Joel and thrown him a bone in the form of one of the most gorgeous women he'd ever laid eyes on.

They met for an overpriced coffee and hit it off right away, bonding over their shared love of McFly and a mutual feeling of late-twenties ennui. She left a gossamer-thin trace of Carmex on his lips as they kissed goodbye. 'I'd love to see you again,' he texted her, immediately. She texted back a fortnight later.

Preet: Joel. It's not going to happen, honey. P x

Plenty Of Fish

Chloe looked perfect on paper. She had style. She had an interesting job. They went out for dinner at a smoky ocakbaşi, swiftly realised they had nothing at all in common, and were forced to make stilted conversation over their plates of congealed hummus and labneh for an hour and a half.

Joel met Daisy at a house party and ended up going back to her place (a warehouse she shared with two visual artists, three DJs, and a primary school teacher named Dean) for a coffee (two lines of ket) and a one-night stand. They made love tenderly behind an IKEA room divider. Joel stared at a rose of damp on the ceiling afterwards, feeling empty and unsatisfied. He listened to the gentle scratch of Dean's red pen as the sun came up and elbowed the city awake.

And then there was Cynthia, a massage therapist, who Sam had set Joel up with. She was a friend of Holly's, with firm, plate-sized hands and a grating way of ending every sentence with a stress that made it sound as if she was constantly asking the world a question. Cynthia was a nice person, mostly. She had opinions. Taste. Her arms were peppered with fine-line Matisse tattoos that danced whenever she moved them. But what Holly had failed to mention to Sam was that Cynthia was already in a polycule with three other people.

She scrolled through her phone at the bar, showing Joel photos of her boyfriends as he gazed sadly into her screen. They were all in tremendous shape. Overwhelmed by their Adonis belts and calculator abs, Joel's eyes welled with tears. She offered to give him a hand job under the table to cheer him up but he told her he couldn't think of anything he wanted less. Cynthia left in a huff and the bartender, feeling equal parts bemused and sorry for Joel, let him drink for free all night.

Days left to fall in love: 24

Human Resources

Joel jiggled his key into his door and, as gently as he could after drinking too much lager and cheap whiskey, shut it behind him. The neighbours were notoriously cranky and complained whenever he had Radio 4 on slightly too loudly in the morning. Other than that, he'd had no real issues living where he did. The door frame, etched with the scars of countless comings and goings, bore witness to his six-year tenure: three years of solitude, two with Beth, and before that, one shared with Sam until he'd abandoned their lager-soaked sanctuary for a one-bed in Hammersmith.

Without anyone to split the costs with, roughly sixty per cent of Joel's salary each month was getting eaten up by bills and rent. He dreaded thinking about how much money he'd handed over to his landlord in more than half a decade. Best not to even try and work it out, he thought, flicking on the light.

He trundled down the hallway, too numbed by the alcohol sloshing in his veins to gauge if the noise pollution of his boots would leak through the walls. He'd known going to the party would be a bad idea, but he'd done it anyway. One of their clients had just closed a seed round of funding for their new fitness app and wanted to celebrate. Which meant, according to Sabine, he was contractually obliged to celebrate with them. By midnight, a bag was getting palmed around between the account managers and Joel decided to leave before things got out of hand. He'd have made a clean getaway, too, if he hadn't been intercepted by Sabine and dragged into the women's toilets.

'You don't leave this party,' she said, using her company card to portion out two fat slugs of powder on her phone screen, 'until I say you can leave.'

Shortly afterwards, he was standing over the toilet bowl with his feet spread shoulder width apart, contemplating whether or not to make himself sick, when his phone vibrated in his pocket.

Squinting with his good eye, his left, Joel was surprised to see a fire-engine-red notification dangling on the corner of a dating app. He unlocked his phone, slamming zero four times on the keypad until it let him in, and thumbed the icon screaming for attention. His screen was taken over by a pop-up.

You've got a match! Go get 'em, tiger!

His pulse started to race.

Joel tried to manage his expectations, but his heart refused to cooperate, doing an excitable two-step behind his ribs. Had any of his previous dates gone exactly as planned? Absolutely not. But he only had twenty-two days left to fall in love. And, besides, the idea of 'dating around' had a nice ring to it. The part of him that wasn't watching the weeks peel off his calendar with dread rather enjoyed the prospect of kicking his habit of diving headfirst into long-term relationships.

All his life, Joel Foster had believed he'd never be truly happy until he fell in love. This conviction, inspired by a steady diet of sentimental mid-2000s indie music and a misguided obsession with Brangelina, shaped his unwavering faith that one day he'd find 'the one'.

Before Beth, there'd been Jo. She had long, thin legs and an Australian accent. Things ended with her over cortados when they mutually agreed that eight months of tedious dinner dates and park strolls had run their course. Prior to Jo, there had been Noor, a stunning Dutch woman who commanded every room she entered. Joel was in over his head with her and, predictably, she shattered his heart. And before Noor, there'd been Soyeon Kim, whom Joel had pined for over five long years of secondary school maths lessons. She was unaware of his existence, and he never found the courage to speak to her about anything but algebra.

Through each failed relationship, Joel had come to the profound realisation that love wasn't just about fireworks or the uncontrollable urge to tear another person's clothes off. It was about learning what to do with yourself once the fireworks display had finished – what to do when the eggy smoke was swirling in the air, and it was time to go home. You've got to grab your person by the hand and not say anything too dumb that'll break the spell of what you just saw together.

That's what love is, thought Joel, as he swayed and stared at his phone.

'I've got about a month to find it,' is what he said to Alice, his oldest friend, as they nursed drinks before his date with perfect-on-paper Chloe.

'Find what?' she asked.

'Love,' he said.

She looked at him with a mixture of amusement and concern, as though he'd just announced he was planning to become a professional wrestler or the prime minister. It was a reaction he'd grown accustomed to; it was the same look the bartender had given him just this evening when he'd ordered his third whiskey. But Joel was undeterred. He was a man with a plan, and nothing was going to stop him from channelling his inner Hugh Grant circa 2002.

His plan for the night had been built around a brief and intimate session with an incognito window on his browser but now, suddenly, his mind was awash with endless fantastical possibilities. If he was quick, brash and confident with his chat could he – perhaps – spend the night with an actual honest-to-God human instead of his laptop screen? Could he give them an orgasm and make them breakfast in the morning? Probably not. Sam had told him this was one of those apps where people were actually looking to make 'a real connection, Joel,' and he figured the most he could feasibly hope for in that case was a conversation over a flat white in a week's time. Whatever. It was still good news.

He brushed away the pop-up and looked at the profile of the person responsible for the interruption.

Nina
Age: 27.
Likes: watching cute videos of dogs.
Dislikes: how I spend every waking second of my weekend watching cute videos of dogs. Please save me from myself.

Nina, who Joel felt he was safe to assume was the woman in the first photo on her profile, was wearing a Breton top and holding a glass of white wine. It looked like a photo taken during a holiday to a place like Cyprus or Malta. Somewhere hot. She was smiling. She had a slightly lopsided grin which made her instantly more endearing. But what should he say?

'*Favourite breed of dog?!*' is what Joel's fingers eventually decided on as his opening gambit, pressing the enter key and immediately regretting his use of an exclamation mark the moment that message left his hands and travelled down an invisible telephone line into the mobile of Nina, 27, who lived in Stoke Newington. Was it too needy? Should he follow it up with something more nonchalant? Would following up before she responded be even more needy? Joel figured the best form of damage control would be to leave the message as it was – if she wasn't going to reply to his message because of an over-excited exclamation mark, then he wasn't confident she was the type of person he wanted to hang out with anyway.

At least, that's what he told himself. In reality, he cared more about whether or not she responded than he cared about every single email he had sent that month.

Ten minutes passed. Joel felt the adrenaline of the match slowly seep from his body. Twenty minutes passed. He sat on the edge of his bed in his underwear contemplating whether he should go to sleep and see if she responded in the morning. Maybe it would be like when you go to the bathroom in a restaurant and it somehow, as if by magic, made your food arrive quicker. He took one last look at his phone screen before pressing its temple lightly and sending it to sleep. Then he manoeuvred his head onto his pillow, too sad to worry about doing his night-time skincare routine, and switched off the light.

How Do You Like Your Coffee?

Joel didn't bother checking his phone when he woke up. It was a Saturday. He was physically incapable of sleeping in past 10 a.m. so he knew it would be some time between 8 a.m. and 9 a.m. He sat up in bed and ran the idea of making a coffee by his id. Maybe that would help, he thought. Caffeine made it easier for him to arrange his thoughts; it made his eyeballs less foggy, and plunging the cafetière gave him a sick satisfaction, like seamlessly peeling the label off a beer bottle or biting off a perfect half-moon of fingernail. He got up, made a half-hearted attempt to straighten out the S-curve of his spine, and padded barefoot towards the kitchen, where he kept his coffee accoutrements.

Joel was aware he was just one of many Joels in the world. He had a certain middling quality to him, a colourless mediocrity that made him worry he might one day blend into the background completely. His music taste was the kind nobody would object to but nobody would bother Shazam-ing at a house party. His clothing choices were dictated by targeted ads and he was funny enough, sure, but not to the extent he'd ever make anyone laugh until their sides ached. If it wasn't for the constant Cartesian rumble of I-am-ness rattling around his head, Joel would be worried about bumping into another Joel in the street one day and fusing into him like one identical cell subsuming another. He was that distinctly undistinctive.

Beth was, without a doubt, the most interesting thing that had ever happened to him. Before he met her, he'd never watched a French film, never read Virginia Woolf, and never known couscous came in sizes like 'giant'. Galleries were just dusty buildings you were dragged to on school trips. The day she came tumbling into his life was the start and end of everything. All of a sudden, he had an opinion about Jean-Luc Godard. He had a favourite David Bowie album. He could happily kill an hour in the Tate Modern gift shop.

He had fallen into the trap of thinking what they had would last forever and now, pitifully conscious it hadn't, he was liable to break down in the middle of the street whenever he caught the spoor of her perfume on someone else's skin or heard a twenty-second snatch of 'Life on Mars'. People say grief gets easier, but it doesn't. Not really. Not ever.

Spooning out three hefty quenelles of medium-grind into the beaker of his cafetière, Joel wondered why no one ever asked him about the provenance of his coffee. Today, he was drinking a wild single-origin coffee from Tanzania. It tasted faintly of almonds. He'd love to have someone in his life he could bore to tears with mundane observations like that.

Nearly Departed

While he waited for his coffee to steep, he watched the small hand of his clock do three full laps. He swirled a spoon in the coffee's dark mist and felt the granules tug and resist before eventually acquiescing and gliding in a small tornado inside the cafetière. He liked the moment those particles stopped resisting and all just decided to go with the flow, as if they'd hopped onto lilos in a lazy river and simply accepted their fate. It made him feel powerful: like he was an all-seeing, all-hearing, all-powerful god. It was the only time in the day he ever felt in control of his destiny.

Joel squinted as the twister inside his cafetière settled down. He thought about storm chasers. He plunged. He considered comparing this act of plunging his first coffee of the day to an orgasm but felt like that was probably a bit much. It was an experience that teetered towards orgasmic but failed to attain that unfiltered level of ecstasy, plonking itself firmly in the camp of 'very, very nice' instead. Cleaning his ears with cotton buds, and digging into the ear canal further than is generally recommended, was another experience Joel would put in the 'very, very nice but not orgasmic' category.

There were no milk or milk alternatives in the fridge so Joel told himself he preferred his coffee black anyway. This was a lie. It was a lie he'd been telling for years, trying to convince himself he was a character in a Raymond Chandler novel who could subsist on black coffee and cigarettes, and not the kind of person who enjoyed the velvety kiss of whole milk and got a sore throat from Marlboro Golds.

Thinking of cigarettes made Joel think of lung cancer. Thinking of lung cancer made him think of death. Thinking of death made Joel think of Beth, which made him sad. But his coffee was hot and woke his tongue up with a bitter hit of frangipane. That, combined with the synapse shock of caffeine, made his brain momentarily happy, ironing out any wrinkles of anxiety until he remembered that cyanide smells and tastes a bit like almonds. This meant Joel was still thinking about death when he received a message from Nina, 27, who lived in Stoke Newington. Not the best omen, he thought.

Mixed Messages

The following messages were exchanged on the app over a two-day period:

Joel: Favourite breed of dog?!
Nina: It's got to be a vizsla. You?
Joel: Probably a boxer dog. Love 'em. Undocked tail though. Obvs.
Nina: Obvs.
Joel: So, what else are you into? Apart from dogs.
Nina: Idk. Music? Films? Television? I'm actually not sure I'm into anything that a billion other people aren't already into. I'm like the least niche person on the planet. [grimacing face emoji]
Joel: I can relate haha – I'm pretty sure that my fave album of all time is *Now That's What I Call Music! 64*
Nina: I was more of a 69 girl myself
Nina: Wait
Nina: No
Nina: That came out wrong
Joel: Lol
Nina: I just really like 'Work' by Kelly Rowland . . .

Joel: Who doesn't?!
Nina: [prayer hands emoji]
Nina: So . . . do you really know the best place for margaritas?
Joel: Huh?
Nina: It says that on your profile hun . . .
Joel: Oh!
Joel: Lol my friend wrote that! Sorry!!! He said it'd make me sound 'fun' . . .
Joel: Did it work?
Nina: Kmt . . . I sort of hate that it did?
Joel: He's much better than me at this sort of thing haha. Can confirm I am actually fun though! I just don't know much about margs apart from they taste . . . lime-y?
Nina: Lime-y? Wow. Are you a mixologist?
Joel: Part-time
Nina: Maybe don't give up the day job just yet . . .
Joel: Trust me, if I could afford to give up my job, I would!!
Nina: How very *Das Kapital* of you
Joel: Can I be honest with you?
Nina: Yeah, shoot
Joel: Do you also find making small talk like this unbearably awkward?
Nina: Unbearably. It takes me about 45 mins to decide which emoji is going to make me seem the least cringey. But they're all cringe.
Joel: All of them?
Joel: [zany face emoji]

Nearly Departed

Nina: That one's the worst one
Joel: Isn't it just
Nina: This one is also terrible: [biting lip emoji]
Joel: I'll avoid it like the plague
Nina: Wow, you are a charmer
Joel: [biting lip emoji]
Nina: Fuck sake haha
Joel: I know this is forward but do you want to chat on something that's not this app?
Nina: Are you asking for my number?
Joel: Yes x
Nina: Then ask me for my number x
Joel: Can I have your number? x
Nina: No x
Nina: [zany face emoji]
Joel: [biting lip emoji]
Nina: 07700912945 [dancing woman emoji]
Joel: [dancing man emoji]

Sacred Texts

Texting is odd. It can make you feel empowered and bold one second, and then vulnerable and naked the next. If all you've got to fall back on are sentences, and your entire sense of self is reduced to a puddle of words and emojis, then you best be sure you're using the right ones. And presenting them in the correct order. And not sending them too often.

> **Joel:** What are your plans for this weekend then?

The beauty of texting, to Joel, was that it gave him more time to think. It was less spontaneous, more pre-planned and structured. There was nothing he hated more than spontaneity. For as long as he could remember, Joel had needed a plan and, once a plan was made, he had to stick to it.

> **Nina:** I've got a mate's 30th tonight . . . or maybe it's an engagement party?
> **Nina**: Or maybe it's a 30th AND an engagement party? I honestly can't keep track haha

It wasn't that he *couldn't* relax, it was simply that he felt more at ease when he wasn't trying to.

Joel: Can relate. I've already used up half my holiday allowance for the year on the weddings of people I don't even like that much lol

His phone blipped. It was too soon for Nina to have replied; she always took at least thirty minutes to get back to him. He wasn't yet sure whether that delay was something she did on purpose to make it seem like she was busy doing other things, or whether she genuinely was, in fact, busy doing other things.

With Nina mathematically ruled out of the equation, Joel figured it had to be Sam sending him some esoteric meme he'd plumbed from the depths of his photo library. He reached out to grab his phone from its resting place on the arm of his ratty maroon sofa, and smiled when his prediction proved spot on.

Joel squinted at the message.

Sam: Imagine the Tweenies smoking lol
Joel: What
Sam: Milo and Fizz and Jake just ripping cigs
Joel: Good

He fired over a GIF of the Tweenies wearing sunglasses and dancing before closing the chat with a satisfying click. Most of their text exchanges followed a similar pattern of disconnected sentences and inside jokes that would have been almost impossible to decipher without at least a forty-five-second explanation. Or a ten-minute YouTube video. Despite the near-psychic connection that tethered them together, Joel still couldn't shake a quiet anxiety that settled in his stomach whenever he was alone with Sam. He knew he shouldn't care so much, but the question of whether Sam would choose him as his best man lingered like a stubborn cloud over their friendship, casting a shadow over every shared pint and piss.

Although Sam and Holly had only got engaged in June and planned to wait at least a year before tying the knot, Joel was already feeling uneasy about the tight-knit group of friends Sam had made since moving out west. Men with faces and names and jobs he didn't care to remember.

He was happy for him, obviously. That went without saying. But there was a not-insignificant part of him that was afraid of losing his best friend. He didn't want Sam's wedding — a day supposed to be all about happiness and love and rinsing the open bar because Sam's dad was fucking minted — to be the nail in the coffin that affirmed to Joel, and everyone else at the inevitably quaint church the happy couple would have picked out, that the two men weren't as inseparably close as they'd used to be.

Nina: Lol
Nina: Where do you actually want to go on holiday tho?
Joel: Portugal

Waiting for a reply was always an excruciating experience. It was stupefying, if you thought about it too much, how a simple sentence or two could dictate your emotions for days, weeks, months or even years. But it was natural. Human, even.

'Texts are the closest thing I've got to poems, okay?' – that's what Beth had told Joel after he'd teased her about the length of time it took her to compose a simple message. With a furrowed brow, and the tip of her tongue peeping from her lips, she treated each text as if it were a weighty, wax-sealed letter. Joel had taken to writing Beth haikus on a weekly basis in the wake of that information, 'text poems' as he liked to call them, and it was a commitment he'd upheld with unpredictable dedication.

They weren't exclusively haikus of passion and love. Sometimes they were about doing the weekly shop or the near-sexual satisfaction of scratching an itch. He had all of the haikus he'd ever written for Beth saved on his phone in a section of his notes called 'Haikus For Her'. Before he could even think about dusting off those haikus, his phone trembled with an uncharacteristically quick reply from Nina.

Nina: Why Portugal?

Joel read the message over four or five times as he thought about what he wanted to say. It didn't take him long – it was only two words and eleven letters to get through. But what he didn't know was if he was ready to tell Nina why Portugal. The idea of drinking vinho verde and eating *pastéis de nata* under the warm Lisbon sun was still so tied up in his mind with Beth it felt impossible to justify it without digging up an old grave.

Beth's old grave, to be exact. He tapped out a limp three-sentence explanation before he obliterated it with a flurry of swift backspaces and switched over to the haunted notes section of his phone instead.

He could remember exactly where he'd been when he'd written each and every one of his 'Haikus For Her'. Which probably sounded a lot more impressive than it was, since he only ever wrote them on the train.

When Joel had been particularly moved by the small divot Beth's recently departed body had imprinted into the mattress topper, he'd written a text poem about it as he was catapulted to work, thumbing out as much truth as he could muster into seventeen syllables over the whinny of the rails.

<u>Tempur Haiku</u>
My mattress misses
You. I guess that's why they call
it memory foam.

He'd also write them at night, drunk. He'd haiku on the journey home from a trip to the pub with his colleagues, having spent the whole night wishing he was back in the flat with Beth, watching trashy reality television instead.

<u>Thoughts Haiku</u>
I can't stop thinking
About if you're thinking of
Me too. I hope so.

Nothing profoundly life-changing, thought Joel. But they made her smile and they let her know he cared. Haikus were his version of buying flowers. And they were a lot more affordable than rushing into the supermarket and grabbing the least dead-looking bouquet you could find.

Joel had made the mistake of buying supermarket roses for Beth once before a date and had spent a good fifteen minutes peeling off a £4 sticker while sitting on the oddly squidgy seats of the Bakerloo line. The look of pity on her face when he presented her with the wilting roses let him know he should never do it again. He stuck to the haikus after that. He'd contemplated writing a haiku for Beth's gravestone but couldn't find the right words in time.

<u>Miss You Haiku</u>
They say you shouldn't
Rhyme in a haiku but who
Are 'they'? I miss you.

Joel placed the phone on the table with a clack. His lock screen stared up at him, glaring, waiting for him to reply to Nina's text. With a deliberate flip, he turned his phone onto its stomach and silenced its judgement, reassuring himself that he simply wasn't ready to get back to her yet. After all, he thought somewhat unconvincingly, he was the one who'd been properly ghosted.

Those Who Run Away

London Fields isn't the best park in London for a run, but Joel liked how he could do laps of it and count them as he went along. Kilometres and heart rate were fine metrics, to be sure, but nice round whole numbers were what made Joel's brain light up.

The perimeter of London Fields was about 1.6 kilometres in total and the satisfying attrition of doing one, then two, then three, then four loops of the park kept Joel's attention as rapt as it needed to be. It did, at times, get a bit like those old Hanna-Barbera cartoons where the same background tree or car would reprint itself in his peripheral vision over and over again, but that relentless consistency was actually one of the pleasures he got from running. Joel had been eight when he'd realised he could tell when an object in the background of a cartoon was about to be used by a character because it was slightly lighter in colour than everything else. He wished every object he was eventually going to have to interact with stood out from the rest of the world like those painted cels.

It would have been handy to be able to tell the

difference between the objects destined to remain in the background of his life, and those that were soon going to be making the all-important jump into the foreground. If Joel's life had been styled after an episode of *Scooby-Doo* then maybe he'd have seen the baseball-sized rock on the path coming from a mile off, and not – as he had done – fallen flat on his face in front of two papoose-wearing women.

Joel brushed himself off and picked grains of gravel off his hands. He wasn't hurt. Not badly, at least. Three people had paused their weekend to try and help him back up and check if 'he was okay, mate,' but Joel had simply nodded and grunted a spartan 'thanks' as he shrugged them off. His face still burning scarlet, he walked towards a Wimbledon-green patch of grass where he could sit and squint at the sun.

London was a different animal in the summer. She was more herself, and everyone inside her was warmer and friendlier, sniffing for any opportunity to break out into a smile or sink a pint. Even the birds sounded happier. Joel's head still throbbed faintly, but a few swigs of lukewarm water from his water bottle would have him feeling right as rain, he thought.

It was then, when he was cocking his head back to let the water slide softly down his throat, that he got the feeling he was being watched. He placed his bottle back into his bag in slow motion, as if a policeman with a megaphone had just squawked at him to 'put your weapon down', and pretended to stretch his neck in a wide circle.

His far left was all clear – just a couple lying on a blanket, enjoying a punnet of red grapes. The best kind. To the right of that couple, positioned at about ten o'clock, was a bulldog on a thick rope leash. Straight in front of Joel was a group of men playing Spikeball. He slid his eyes swiftly to the periphery of that platoon before watching them try to shirtlessly outdo each other gave him second-hand embarrassment. Towards his right hand, positioned at about two o'clock, was a slim, sallow-faced man with tired eyes, reading in a folding camp chair.

It was so far, so good until Joel's head owled as far as it could go and he spied a familiar-shaped smudge. The profile of his nose was blocking his view so he shut his left eye for his right to focus, and the moment he did it, the smudge disappeared. He looked to his left. He looked to his right. He looked up to the sky, hoping for an answer. No dice. Whatever it was – or whoever it was – had gone. But he was left with a disconcerting feeling; a chill ran under his skin and threatened to seep into his bones. He wasn't one of those people who thought they had a sixth sense or anything like that. He simply couldn't ignore the feeling there was a pair of eyes boring into the back of his skull.

He was about to puppeteer his body back up to standing when he was startled by a voice that sounded like it came from directly behind him – perhaps because it did, in fact, come from directly behind him.

'It's Joel, right?'

Joel pivoted around and looked directly upwards, ineffectively blocking the sun with one hand and trying to work out why the silhouette standing above him knew his name.

'Yeah, it is,' he said, 'how did you know that?'

'I'm Nina, from the app,' said Nina, from the app.

'Oh. Wow,' said Joel. He unfolded his legs and got up, standing straight to make himself taller. His eyes widened as he confirmed it really was the same Nina he'd left on read for the last two days.

'Fancy bumping into you here,' he said, inexpertly forcing a casualness into every word he uttered. He already felt as if he knew her. Even though he didn't. Not properly, at least. They'd exchanged lengthy messages covering everything from the discomfort Nina felt in all-white social settings to their respective death row meals. And then he'd gone and fucked it all up.

Joel read Nina all the way from her feet to her head in the least creepy way he could. Her Birkenstocks told him she was functional, yet fashionable. Her burnt orange jumpsuit said she hadn't predicted today to be quite so warm and the tight coils of her dark hair – combined with her smile – made him instantly stressed out about how sweaty and bedraggled he looked in comparison. Joel fidgeted with the sleeves of his T-shirt.

'I'm sorry I didn't reply to your message the other day,' he spluttered. 'Like really sorry. I just—'

'What?'

'You asked me where I'd like to go on holiday and—'

'Did I?'

'Yes, and then I couldn't think of how to tell you that . . . wait, what do you mean "Did I"?'

'I mean, I don't really have any vivid memory of that,' said Nina, whose lips were pursed in amusement. 'I'm actually texting a lot of different men right now and they all blur into this one big homogenous toxic mass.'

'Ah, yeah. Right,' said Joel. He ran his finger over his chin and watched as the dimples in her cheeks deepened. 'You're fucking with me, aren't you?'

'Yes, Joel,' said Nina. 'I'm fucking with you. You don't need to apologise for not responding to a message I sent . . .' she paused as she pulled out her phone to verify its version of events, '. . . forty-three hours ago.'

'God, yeah. No, of course. You probably think I'm a bit of a maniac,' he said, trying his best to sound as sane as possible while acting the exact opposite. 'If you're wondering why my face is so red right now, it's because I've been running. Not because I'm, like, nervous about seeing you in person or anything.'

'Red?' said Nina.

'Red,' nodded Joel.

'I'm not sure about red,' said Nina, 'I'd say it's more of a . . . ghostly white? Kind of like a Victorian child that's suffering from consumption. That's actually why I came over to say hi. I thought I recognised you, and my friend, Aisha' – Nina thumbed out a woman sitting roughly twenty metres away who was eating crisps and staring intently at Joel – 'bet me five quid you would pass out if I came and confronted you.'

'I'm glad I didn't,' he replied, returning Aisha's daggers with his own scimitar of a stare. Nina, who seemed suddenly unsure of what to do with her arms, folded them in front of her chest before changing her mind and allowing them to hang loosely at her side. Joel suspected she was making a conscious effort to try and conceal the effects of some summer afternoon boozing.

'So am I. I'm actually a little surprised I recognised you. I don't mean to sound rude or anything, but you don't exactly come across as the sporty type.'

'That's because I'm not,' said Joel, 'which is also probably why I look like a . . . what was it you said again?'

'Like a Victorian child that's suffering from consumption.'

'Right, yes. That. Or like I'm about to be sick.'

Joel had a bad habit of bringing up sick early on in conversations and, every time he did, he was reminded there was never an easy way out of it. It wasn't exactly a topic that encouraged people to chime in with their own experiences – 'Oh, yeah, I was sick once, too,' – and it was never sexy to imagine someone hunched over a toilet bowl. Nina, however, took Joel's mood-killing commentary like a champ.

'Please don't,' she said, smiling and showing off two sets of tastefully off-white and shockingly straight teeth. You could tell she'd had braces as a teenager and those years of sacrifice had paid off in dividends now she'd entered her twenties.

Joel replied with a laugh – not his uninhibited high-pitched one but a more baritone 'huh-huh' – and glanced at Nina just long enough to get a good look at her eyes. And when he did, he couldn't help but get lost in them. They were two deep pools of hazelnut ganache, rich and ready to coat the back of a spoon, but it was the hint of caramel running through them that grabbed him by the scruff of his neck. Those golden wisps reminded Joel of the crema you get on top of an espresso – a drink he dreamed of one day sipping at a Florentine café while wearing an elegantly tailored suit. He'd read in an online listicle once that a lot of places in Italy charged you extra to sit down and that was why most Italians would take their coffee standing up. Well, that, and it just looked really, really cool.

'Are you all right?' asked Nina.

'Yeah, sorry,' said Joel. 'I hit my head earlier, so I'm still feeling a little out of it. To be honest, I do just kind of zone out and forget to listen to what people are saying sometimes. I was actually thinking about coffee.'

'Coffee?'

'Yeah. And whether you would like to grab one. With me? Not now, of course. But if you're free later this week maybe?'

'Wow.'

'What?'

'Nothing,' laughed Nina. 'I guess I wasn't expecting a pick-up line about how you don't really listen to people.'

She had a nice laugh. It was husky and musical like the low wheeze of an accordion. Joel instantly felt at ease hearing it rumble from her chest. He imagined her sitting on the sofa next to him, her hand resting gently under his as he turned to her and laughed. His daydream was interrupted by the vision of Beth squeezing onto the sofa between them, her bike helmet dented and her face caked in blood.

'Yeah, not my best work in retrospect,' gulped Joel. He flexed his hand, trying to shake off the feelings of guilt and self-loathing needling their way around his central nervous system.

'That's okay,' said Nina, giving Joel a pat on the shoulder which turned his body into a butterfly house, 'but I don't think a coffee in this heat would be a good idea.'

'Ah,' said Joel, trying to put on a brave face.

'I'd love to grab a drink-drink, though,' she added. 'How does Wednesday work?'

'Wednesday would be great,' replied Joel, a second too quickly.

'Brilliant. You've got my number, so tell me when and where works best for you and we can have a chat. Hopefully when you're less . . . distracted.'

'Sounds good. I'll do that. Probably not tonight. Maybe tomorrow? To make it seem like I'm cool and aloof?'

'You do that,' said Nina. And with that, she left him where he was standing and returned to Aisha and her crisps. Joel knew this was his cue to leave, and so he did. He waved as nonchalantly as he could towards Nina and Aisha before turning around to leave, his head still throbbing slightly and a smile stitched on his face.

Days left to fall in love: 19

No Worries If Not

Joel had a natural talent – if you could even call such a thing a talent – for email etiquette, which made sense given its importance in his job. Sometimes, during the excruciating stretch of time between 4.30 p.m. and 5 p.m. when every minute seemed to flow like treacle, he found himself wondering how public relations had worked before the advent of the internet. Did PRs simply go out there and knock on every journalist's door, eager to pitch their clients' innovative and exciting ventures? Probably not. Joel suspected most PR back then had been conducted over elaborate lunches in swanky French restaurants. He couldn't help but pine for a bygone era of more sophisticated and recherché wheeling and dealing, a world that couldn't be further removed from the endless stream of emails that filled his workday.

Joel had only ever taken one journalist out for lunch, a finance editor at *The Sunday Times* he'd had an amicable email correspondence with for about five years, and had found it an incredibly seductive experience. Sinking two martinis at 1.30 p.m. was always a welcome treat, but it was especially welcome when you were drinking them on the company card.

The plan had been to work in PR for a couple of months before he landed his dream job, but years had slipped by without him noticing. Now, all he could do was hope and pray his skillset wouldn't become totally irrelevant once whatever form of communication was inevitably going to take over from email took the throne. He didn't want his grandchildren to remember their grandfather as the millennial version of a carrier pigeon.

Joel had honed his keyboard candour to a rather fine art, and he took an embarrassing amount of pride in his ability to disarm even the prickliest of correspondents with a well-timed quip or self-deprecating remark. Need high-res images? *Sure, no problem, mate – I'll get those to you in a flash.* Want an exclusive quote for the Sunday edition of the paper by the end of play? *Consider it done.* He got a kick out of being useful. An online quiz told him 'acts of service' were his love language.

He might have been a people-pleaser at heart but Joel didn't have any solid idea about what he actually wanted to do with his life. Or what that 'dream job' he'd hoped of landing would even be. Sure, there were lots of things he liked – some of which he even loved. But there wasn't much of a clear career path for a person whose greatest passions in life were finding nice editions of books in charity shops and eating pistachio gelato. He'd flirted with the idea of opening up a bookshop that doubled as an ice cream parlour, but it was telling he'd conjured up the notion with Alice when they'd been halfway through a bag of cocaine. Other great ideas they'd had that night included kissing (terrible – like getting off with your sister) and co-writing a grime song on Joel's iPhone they promised each other they'd never tell another soul on Earth about.

When Joel was confident no one in the office could see his screen, he opened up several internet tabs, each one containing a job description that sounded slightly too aspirational. He needed an achievable dream – one he could realise within a couple of years of graft before he eventually turned forty and started cracking on with his first, and inevitably most violent, mid-life crisis.

Truth be told, the job market wasn't something Joel was particularly enthused about exploring. Hearing the struggles some of his friends were going through in their search for employment made him thankful he had a reasonable amount of job security. As much job security as you could have when your boss was a sociopath.

One day in April, Sabine had thrown a house party to celebrate her thirty-eighth birthday. She'd invited everyone at work, via a mass email, apart from her personal assistant, Jess. She signed the email off with a caustic:

Lots of love,
Sabs
PS Let's keep Jess in the dark

Worried he'd be reprimanded if he didn't attend, Joel went along to the party with a bottle of Moët in hand. Everyone from the office was there, partly because they were afraid Sabine would fire them if they weren't. They spent most of the night cowering in the corners of her large kitchen, drinking and talking.

As Joel leaned against the sturdy kitchen island, his gaze met with Debbie from Accounts and she leaned in conspiratorially. Debbie had so much contour on her face it looked like she was about to take the stage as Fantine in *Les Misérables*. In a hushed tone, she let slip that Sabine had forced Jess to write the invitation, making her exclude herself from the guest list and email it to all of her colleagues. Joel shook his head in not-quite disbelief, simultaneously repulsed and utterly unsurprised.

'That's a new low,' said Joel, 'even for her.'

'She's a cunt,' slurred Michael the intern, who was standing nearby, nursing a cup of warm champagne. Joel took a large gulp. He didn't disagree.

Joel was never sure what mood to expect from Sabine. Some days, she'd let all the staff go home early so they could enjoy the sunshine. Others, she'd humiliate an employee in front of the entire office, getting them to stand up with their hands on their head while she berated them for a misplaced comma. Working for Sabine wasn't fun. Or enjoyable. But at least it wasn't boring, thought Joel. Was that what Stockholm syndrome was? Before he could google it, he was interrupted by a cough that seemed to stream itself through his ears and directly into his brain.

The cough belonged to Michael, who spluttered gently as they asked Joel whether he'd like his bottle refilled. Michael and Joel regularly took turns refilling each other's water bottles. It had become a strangely satisfying ritual, a little pas de deux performed around the office water cooler. Joel had never been so hydrated in his entire life. Although he didn't have a huge amount in common with them, Joel found Michael to be a refreshing presence in the stifling monotony of his nine-to-five routine. It was Michael's first real job, and they still possessed an earnestness that had long since evaporated from Joel's own attitude towards work. In a way, Joel envied them.

'No thanks, I've still got a bit left,' said Joel, jiggling his bottle until it sloshed to reassure Michael he wasn't just saying it so they would leave him alone.

'Not a worry,' chirped Michael, who started making tracks to leave the room and head to the cooler before their eyes caught the jobs page Joel had left marinating on his screen. Joel swiftly changed tabs but he knew from the look in Michael's eyes that they'd seen exactly what Joel was doing. It felt like the time his mum had caught him googling 'Kate Winslet sex scene'. His face had turned a similar shade of red back then, too.

'It's not what you think,' he'd pleaded to his mum before she left the room and tag-teamed in his father to give him 'the talk'. 'The talk' consisted of his father mumbling a few incoherent sentences about condoms and 'being safe' before telling him to 'just use the fucking incognito window next time'.

Joel was about to say something to Michael, maybe a lie that he was doing research, when Michael zipped their lips and gave him a wink.

Status Update

It had been a quiet day in the office. So quiet that Joel had had time to rearrange his desk, fix the wobble in his chair, stop the coffee machine from making that awful whirring sound and print out a frankly worrying number of media kits, burning through two cartridges of ink in the process – all before lunch. Sabine's absence meant she was either nursing a vicious hangover or her boyfriend, Richàrd, had succeeded in giving her an orgasm that morning. Joel didn't want to delve into the details of either scenario; from experience, he knew both would render Sabine incapable of functioning for at least a few hours.

The only thing that prevented him from falling asleep at his desk, and kept him awake on his journey home, was the thought of his upcoming date with Nina. They'd agreed to meet at a wine bar the next night – a neutral venue Joel had suggested because he knew it was somewhere they could actually hear each other speak. He had a habit of mumbling, and the last thing he wanted was for his first proper conversation with Nina to be a game of charades. He'd already met her in person, and that gave him some comfort, at least. He was glad they wouldn't have to go through the stilted rigmarole of pretending not to recognise each other when, in reality, they had already scrutinised each other's dating profiles so thoroughly Joel was pretty sure he could sketch out a star map of her freckles from memory.

A pang of guilt poked his lower intestines as he searched for Nina's Instagram profile. Sam had assured him this was standard practice in the world of online dating, but Joel couldn't shake the gnawing feeling he was trespassing on Nina's privacy. His mind conjured images of her catching him in the act, swiftly reaching for her phone to dial the authorities and unleashing a Twitter thread warning every woman in London to steer clear of him at all costs. As if that wasn't dire enough, he also feared the possibility of stumbling across a photo of Nina as a teenager, with braces and a bad haircut, and getting thrown onto a government watch list. He shivered involuntarily and hurriedly scrolled through a dozen Nina Harrises, hoping to locate her profile before he lost his bottle.

'It just feels weird knowing what she looked like as a sixteen-year-old,' said Joel. 'You're on loudspeaker, by the way,' he added as he chopped up a few stacked rashers of bacon into mini dominoes for the amatriciana he made, and ate, about three times a month.

'You live alone,' Sam barked down the line. 'Why would I care whether I'm on loudspeaker or not?'

'I don't know. I thought it would be polite to tell you.'

'Right. Okay. Well, for your own sake can you please stop looking at photos of sixteen-year-old girls on the internet? I told you to look her up and try to find some of the stuff she's into – not find out exactly what type of bikini she wore on her holiday to Zante in 2010.'

'It was 2012.'

'What?'

'She went to Zante in 2012. It was Corfu in 2010.'

'Fucking hell, Joel. You're meant to be working out which films you can talk about or what music you're both into, not getting yourself put on a register.'

'And how am I supposed to do that when she's private on literally every social media platform?'

Sam breathed a sigh of relief. 'So you haven't actually been scrolling through her 2012 bikini photos?'

'No,' laughed Joel. 'Of course not. All I've been able to do so far is zoom in up-close on her profile photo.'

'And?'

'And, yeah, it looks like a tiny version of her.'

Joel hadn't been sure what size digital footprint he would uncover but he'd thought he'd be able to find out . . . something. Unfortunately, Nina seemed to take her data protection a lot more seriously than he did. Her LinkedIn was the only profile available to the public so, using one of those incognito windows his dad had introduced him to, Joel looked at Nina's work history and tried to gauge what it could tell him about who she was as a person. Her current job as an assistant at a gallery let him know she was into art.

'It'd hardly take Poirot to fucking work that out, though, would it?' said Sam.

She had also been an assistant editor of her university's alternative culture magazine, and had once had an article on the male gaze published in *VICE*. He read that article three times front to back and immediately felt guilty about having noticed how well Nina's jumpsuit had clung to her body.

Days left to fall in love: 16

What Dreams May Come

'Tell me about this dream you keep having, Joel.'

Joel had been having semi-regular therapy sessions with Doctor Shah since Beth died. He wasn't sure if inheriting your dead girlfriend's therapist was a particularly healthy thing to do but he'd done it anyway, and Doctor Shah hadn't had any complaints about taking his money.

'It's nothing,' he shrugged. He'd forgotten he had this session booked in until his Google Calendar reminded him, churlishly, of its existence an hour before it was supposed to start. Joel preferred having a couple of days to prepare and get in the right headspace for a deep and meaningful conversation (Doctor Shah put the kibosh on him calling them 'DMCs'), but he figured having therapy before a date wasn't the worst idea in the world. Doctor Shah might even be able to give him some tips on interesting conversation-starters. Hell, maybe 'I've come here straight from therapy' was good enough.

'Nothing's nothing, Joel,' said Doctor Shah. She spoke slowly yet sharply, enunciating the tail end of every word as if she were speaking in serif.

'Okay,' said Joel. He turned his eyes to the ceiling and stared at the delicate petals bursting from the centre of a ceiling rose. He found it easier to speak when he didn't have to worry about looking into Doctor Shah's achingly sincere eyes.

'It's always the same,' he said, shuffling his shoulder blades deeper into the lounge chair and closing his eyes in zen-like fashion. 'I'm at a train station – it's not a specific station, just a vague generic dreamy one – and I'm just standing there, on the platform, reading a book. Let's say it's *Wuthering Heights*. Because it is *Wuthering Heights*. And let's say I'm enjoying it. Because it's a good book, and why wouldn't I? So I'm there, nose deep in the pages, getting all down and dirty with Heathcliff and company, waiting for my train, and then I see *her* on the platform opposite me.

'She's like this ray of sunlight sent down from heaven, cutting a spotlight through the grey of the world, and she's got this look of beautiful determination on her face. She hasn't seen me yet because her head is down and she's walking to her favourite spot on the platform – the place where she knows she'll be able to slide into the train and get a seat. Don't ask me how I know it's her favourite spot: I just do. So she stops at her spot and what does she pull out of her backpack but a copy of *Wuthering Heights*. Same edition as mine. Maybe a bit more worn and dog-eared. More read. Now, at this point, I'm transfixed, right? I can't believe what I'm seeing. Because what are the chances? I know it's not, like, a niche book or anything, but still.

Nearly Departed

Coincidences like that don't just happen. And then she looks up.

'Her eyes meet with mine across the train tracks and we share this . . . moment. It's not a long moment but it almost feels like time has stopped as she looks across at me and I look across at her and we have this quasi-religious feeling of belonging. And then it's gone. Because her train has arrived and the reality kicks in that she's travelling in the completely opposite direction to me. I think about running across the tracks and doing something spontaneous or stupid but I don't. Because I know I've got a train to catch, too. That's when I get this feeling in my gut — in my dream gut — that me and this woman are, like, soul mates. We're connected by some invisible lasso but our lives are destined to keep on moving further and further away from each other. It's bad timing, right?

'And I'm just standing there wishing I could have been on the same platform as her waiting for that same train. More than anything, I wish our trains were heading in the same direction — even if it was only for a few stops — so I could spend more time with her and get close enough to ask her what her name is.'

'And then what happens?'

'Then I wake up. And the next night, I do it all over again.'

First Dates

Their first date had been at a pub equidistant from their respective flats. It was an unseasonably cold April, two layers and a coat kind of weather, and the first year they'd spent living in London after university. Joel thought about that night every day, rewinding the way Beth had looked at him and smiled over and over again in his head, marvelling at how a single evening could have such a tremendous impact on the rest of his life. It was a proper butterfly effect moment for him – a decision to go out for drinks with a stranger on a school night that punched an impact silhouette in the rest of his life. He remembered the way his knees had trembled when she'd approached his table at the pub.

'It's Joel, right?'

He remembered almost spilling his pint when he'd stood up, too quickly, to give her an awkward hug. He remembered worrying about whether his breath smelled too much like the peppermint gum he'd just chewed. He remembered hoping he looked enough like his photos. He remembered she was 5' 5" and had eyes that disappeared into happy creases when she smiled. He'd made it his mission that night to make her eyes disappear as much as possible.

Joel wasn't really a man known for his self-control but he'd made a concerted effort not to give up all of his best anecdotes in The Spread Eagle because, even after just an hour of conversation, he'd had a hunch he'd be getting a second date. And he hadn't been wrong.

Four nights later, he'd met up with Beth again. Joel had texted her to make sure she'd got home safely after their three pints and they'd springboarded from there into sending a rally of messages back and forth. Joel would overthink every sentence she sent him, agonising over whether the orangutan emoji was saying 'let's fuck' or 'let's just be friends'. Turns out, it was neither. Beth was simply a big fan of orangutans.

Their third date involved sharing a bottle of wine at a cosy-yet-achingly-cool bar in Peckham, where everyone wore small knitted beanies while Larry Levan played over the sound system. Joel and Beth took turns asking each other what their dream Glastonbury line-ups would be.

Beth's dream Glastonbury line-up: 'Florence + the Machine, Fleetwood Mac, PJ Harvey and maybe The Chemical Brothers?'
Joel's dream Glastonbury line-up: 'Hanson, George Michael, Taylor Swift and, yeah, probably The Chemical Brothers, too.'

Beth loved how he wasn't ashamed of what he liked. Even if it was mostly shit.

When she'd asked him if he had any guilty pleasures,

he'd said: 'You should never be guilty about something you get pleasure from,' quickly followed by, 'unless we're talking about a serial killer like Ted Bundy who got pleasure from doing some objectively fucked-up shit. That's something you definitely *should* feel incredibly guilty about.' Her eyes disappeared, he smiled, and they knew they'd be spending the night with each other after they'd split the bill.

They'd climbed the stairs to Joel's flat together – he led, she followed, and that suited her fine seeing as it was his flat they were going to. Their steps synchronised after they reached the first floor and they continued to thump, thump on the faux marble of his apartment stairwell in silent unison until they made it to the fourth. Joel suppressed the urge to mention how they'd 'synced up' their strides because it stirred some unwelcome memories of the time all four of his flatmates had had their periods sync up during his second year of university. It had been carnage. And a memory he, exercising caution, deemed best left untouched. What he said instead, however, had been much, much worse.

'Ah, my humble abode!'

He'd hated himself the moment those words had left his mouth and even more when his arm, seemingly acting of its own free will, made a grand, sweeping gesture in front of flat 56. His face burned scarlet and not even Beth's laugh of acknowledgement – a polite exhale of breath through her nostrils – could soften the blow. She hadn't run away, though, and he could only take that as a good sign. Or, at least, not a bad one.

When he'd reached into his pockets for his keys, he'd realised he'd made another error of judgement. The keys weren't in the inside pocket of this coat (just left of his heart, his favourite place to keep them) but were lying at the bottom of his backpack, hidden under layers of workplace detritus he'd have to remove before he could pull firmly on the tab of his Tesco Clubcard and fish them out.

'I'm sorry about this,' he said, fumbling through half-used notebooks and loose pellets of chewing gum before carefully putting his laptop under one arm as he continued his search.

'It's fine,' said Beth. And what he couldn't know was that it was. He was cute, she decided. Flustered, sure. But the way he was holding his laptop reminded her of the chintzy clutch she'd taken to her sixth-form end-of-year dance. He looked vulnerable and awkward, like a lamb that'd just been told it was going to the slaughter – destined to become a plate of greying chops on a dinner table somewhere in the Midlands. He was, as it happens, very much her type. 'Has anyone ever told you you smell like a fireplace?' she said, burying her snub nose into the crease of his neck and breathing him in. Joel had been called many things in his life, but being compared to a fireplace was a first. In time, he would come to treasure Beth's left-field observations, her knack for slipping a non-sequitur into even the most serious conversations. But then, he simply closed his eyes and smiled.

★

Joel knew if he bathed in that memory for too long, he'd never want to leave. He could spend hours thinking about the laughs they'd shared on the many dates that had come after the night they'd first slept together. Unlike Joel's, Beth's laugh was low and bassy and so blatantly unsexy it came back around full circle to sexy again. He could listen to it echoing off the tiles of his brain until his fingertips wrinkled like raisins but Joel knew he'd have to wake up to the reality that that bath had run cold long ago. If he lost himself in those memories, he'd never make it out of the flat. That wasn't usually a problem but tonight – for the first time in a long time – Joel actually had somewhere to be.

There was someone out there who was possibly excited, and maybe even potentially nervous, to see him. Joel pictured himself getting cattle-prodded in the small of his back by a rancher with calloused hands and snapped to attention like the boy scout he'd never been. He wasn't sure how he landed on the cattle prod as his go-to visualisation technique; he'd never seen or used one in person. But, for some reason, imagining a sharp electric shock shooting up his spine was one of the few ways he was able to snap back to reality from a daydream or reverie. He'd been doing it for as long as he could remember. Doctor Shah had sighed an extremely deep sigh the first time he'd told her about his cattle prod.

With Beth pushed to the back of his mind, Joel diverted his attention to worrying about what to wear to meet Nina. They weren't going anywhere fancy, so he wanted to make sure he didn't look like he was trying too hard.

On the flip side, he didn't want to show up wearing his trainers with the Africa-shaped splodge of passata on the toe. Surely, he thought, his wardrobe contained some middle ground between the two.

He eventually decided on wearing what he called his 'uniform' – a pair of black cords, a white heavy cotton T-shirt he'd bought from Uniqlo and a dark navy worker's jacket. It was simple, familiar and an accurate representation of what Joel wore roughly eighty per cent of the time. Perfect for casual drinks with someone you thought looked fit in photos, he thought.

Joel flicked his wrist in a car-starting motion and checked the time. Six-forty. That meant he had plenty of time to kill before he hopped on the overground at half past seven. The beer he had put in the fridge earlier for this exact moment would be batting somewhere around the single Celsius figures by now and having a drink before a date was, in Joel's somewhat limited dating experience, always a good idea. It worked like a secret elixir, loosening him up, stretching out the muscles of his patter and making him at least thirty per cent more charming than he was sober.

The road outside his window was flooded with cars and bicycles tearing along to try and beat the traffic. He wondered whether he should start considering first date options slightly more inventive than 'drink?' but he knew in his bones he was not someone who could have a successful first date without the aid of any social lubricant.

The beauty of a pub or a bar was that, even if the company wasn't ideal, you could always count on getting a little drunk. And getting a little drunk was always better than getting nowhere. Alcohol helped to sand down the edges of Joel's personality and stopped his anxiety from getting the better of him. His stories became funnier, too – he was able to embellish all the right beats of his anecdotes and weave together a narrative most people found to be amusing. When he was sober, he would often miss out all the good bits, focusing instead on the unimportant, granular details of a tale and losing his audience's interest halfway through.

Joel let the lager slip into his stomach and warm him up from the inside. Was it ironic an ice-cold drink could make him feel hot and brave? Probably. But he had never properly understood what irony was. The only thing he was sure about was that Alanis Morissette had an even weaker grasp on the concept than he did. Joel embraced that Morissettian brand of misplaced confidence when he used words like 'liminal' or 'post-modern'. Sure, he had a vague idea of what made a space liminal or a play post-modern, but given the enthusiasm with which he used them in conversation, you'd think he was an expert.

He'd avoid using either of those words in front of Nina, just in case she turned out to be a theatre postgrad or the sort of person who read critical theory for kicks and wouldn't let him get away with it. Best to avoid looking like a berk straight away, thought Joel, hopping onto the overground and turning up the volume on the latest episode of *This American Life*.

Good Company, Good Wine, Good Welcome

Units of alcohol consumed: 2.3

They both smiled politely, pausing their conversation out of what felt like courtesy — but could just as easily have been a desire for privacy — when the waiter came and placed a plate of Serrano ham on their table. The meat left a lacquer of grease on Joel's fingers as he popped a taffeta slice of it into his mouth.

'We've got an exhibition on at the moment which is all based around the theme of utopia,' explained Nina, as Joel refilled her stubby wine glass before topping up his own. She was wearing a diaphonous merlot-coloured shirt that flared at the sleeves and suited her down to the ground.

'Oh, so it's like perfect world kind of stuff? What *Atlas Shrugged* is supposed to be for fascists.'

'I take it you aren't a fascist, then?' Nina looked at him sternly before the corners of her mouth inched up to give the game away.

'No,' replied Joel, 'but I have got an uncle who voted for Brexit if that counts?'

'You know what they say about the sins of the father . . . and the father's brother.'

'Mother's brother.'

'In that case, you're kosher,' she grinned, 'but did you know utopia actually means "no place" or "nowhere" in Greek?'

Joel shook his head. The wine bar was bustling with the cinq à sept crowd, young professionals and beautiful people, all of them looking to unwind and celebrate having conquered hump day. The atmosphere was relaxed and just the right side of pretentious, thought Joel, immediately hating himself, as the soft tenor of Gene Ammons' sax and the sound of drink-clinking laughter filled the air. There was a group of friends gathered around the table next to Nina's elbow, cackling and chatting animatedly, while a couple on a date sat on the other side, stealing glances at each other over their £12 glasses of wine.

'Okay, well it does,' continued Nina. 'I think it's Greek. But it could also be Latin. Anyway, the point is all these utopian views of the world are projections of a reality or a world that doesn't — and can never — exist. Do you follow?'

'I follow,' said Joel, enjoying the formality of Nina's train of thought. He took a sip of wine. It was cloudy and had a vague hum of straw, reminding him of the petting zoo his parents took him to every summer.

'I guess I don't really know what the point of a utopia is. Like, why are we so focused on imagining how wonderful the world could be when that's something so far out of the realms of possibility?'

Joel nodded.

'But I guess it's also what people want right now,' continued Nina, her voice raised in volume as she tried to feel her way towards the end of the point she was making. 'An escape from the overwhelming bleakness of life.'

Units of alcohol consumed: 6.9

A beat. He could see in her eyes she was trying to process whether or not he was joking but, considering they'd only known each other for a grand total of two hours, she wasn't quite able to gauge how sincere he was being.

'You seriously can't ride a bike?'

'I seriously can't ride a bike.'

Nina crossed her arms and leaned back against the Ercol-style stacking chair she was sitting on. What was it with restaurants in Hackney and reclaiming school furniture?

'So, what: you just never learned how?'

'No, no, no. My dad taught me when I was a kid, with training wheels and everything,' said Joel, swirling the amber-coloured liquid in his glass around in a bid to look sophisticated. 'But I was, like, five or something? I haven't ridden a bike since then.'

'You do know it's like riding a bike?'

'How do you mean?'

'As in, you can't just forget how to do it.'

'I thought that was elephants?'

Nina groaned in protest, then laughed.

★

Units of alcohol consumed: 9.2

'And I guess that's why I've always preferred animals to humans.'

Nina shifted her hips to inch herself closer to the table and looked out at Joel with what he'd been told were her mother's eyes. The wine was starting to make him sentimental. He didn't know whether she was this much of an open book with everyone she dated, but he got the feeling Nina was genuinely confiding in him, inviting him into a secret world of thoughts few others had ever accessed.

As she told him about the volunteer work she did at the Battersea Dogs & Cats Home, and how desperately she wanted to find her greater purpose in life, Joel found himself caught up in the cadence of her words. It was as if each sentence she spoke had been crafted with the precision of a surgeon, every comma and en-dash carefully placed to guide him through her thoughts. He wondered if she'd been a champion debater at school and couldn't help but think she could have a career in politics, if she wanted it. But just as his gaze was about to melt into her lovely brown eyes, he felt a violent lurch of panic – it was his turn to speak.

'I don't think that's strange at all,' he said, quickly, hoping it was the right thing to say. The cutlery placed on the table next to them made the pleasant rap of metal on wood. 'We're all just trying to pretend we've got our lives together. Aren't we?'

'I suppose so,' said Nina. He gave an internal sigh of relief – good save. She took a bite of heavily buttered bread and seemed to be digesting his words as she chewed. 'But what about the people who aren't pretending? Surely there's got to be someone out there who has got their life completely sorted out. I mean, they're probably living off Daddy's money without a real job. But that still counts, doesn't it?'

Joel knew at least three people whose lives were pretty much perfect. Two were currently holidaying in Corsica and having incredible suntanned sex, while the third had recently paid off the mortgage on a two-bed in Hampstead thanks to their recurring role on a popular BBC crime drama. He didn't say that to Nina, though. It wasn't the right moment to agree that, yes, the world was unfair and it always had been and always would be. Instead, he said:

'I don't think anyone anywhere can be truly, one hundred per cent happy with every facet of their life. It comes back to that concept of utopia, right? "No place". Even those people who live in a mansion with a perfect set of teeth' – at Joel's mention of the word 'teeth', Nina's tongue did a small but noticeable lap around her own set – 'must have days where nothing goes right. Days when the toilet won't flush or you put your T-shirt on the wrong way and you don't even notice until you're at the supermarket and, halfway through fondling the tomatoes, you realise you've got to spend the rest of the shop with a shirt that has a Nike logo on the back left that makes everyone around you think you're the village idiot.'

'I'm going to go out on a limb and guess you're speaking from personal experience here,' said Nina.

Joel nodded his head.

'Sainsbury's. 14 November 2016. A dark day.'

They laughed. Not the polite laughs reserved for casual acquaintances or Zoom calls, but the kind of laughter that erupted from deep within and rose up to the surface like a geyser. It was laughter that felt like a shared secret, one that bound them together in that moment, uniting them in a way only uncut pleasure can.

Units of alcohol consumed: 11.5

Nina excused herself to go to the toilet and left Joel with a slug of wine left in his glass and a great deal to think about. As he worked his jaw around a crust of sourdough, he contemplated texting Alice and letting her know how things were going so far. He mulled that idea over for about twenty seconds before setting it aside in the 'let's not' pile. He didn't want to be one of those people who reported on their date like a sports journalist, broadcasting every pass, hit and miss to his entire friendship circle.

Joel pulled out his phone and checked the time. 10.36 p.m. Not bad, he thought. They'd been talking so much they'd already got through two bottles and had moved on to a couple of glasses of 'why the hell not?' wine. Joel had known he was attracted to Nina from the second he saw her – she was both objectively good-looking and objectively out of his league. Yet, even then, he hadn't expected to laugh half as much as he had so far. Which felt a little unfair to her. Was not expecting attractive people to be funny a form of prejudice?

Nearly Departed

'Women don't want to marry Leonardo DiCaprio, Joel. They want to fuck Leonardo DiCaprio. Women want to marry Peter Kay.'

That was something Beth had told Joel on one of their earlier dates and, as he tried to shake the mental image of Peter Kay floating on a door with Kate Winslet, his eyes roamed around the room and landed on a candlelit table in the corner occupied by a solo diner. Seeing anyone eating or drinking alone always filled Joel with mixed feelings. A blend of envy and pity poured out of him in a ratio of seventy to thirty.

As he was trying to work out where sitting alone in a wine bar on a Wednesday night sat on his scale of sad to aspirational, Joel noticed something that set his teeth on edge. He recognised the woman in the corner. Like, *really* recognised her. It was too dark to properly see what she looked like from where he was sitting but the way she sat upright in her chair, crossing her arms in front of her like a good cadet, was innately familiar.

He knew Nina would be coming back from the bathroom at any second but something in his gut told him he had to keep staring at the woman seated at that table. He craned his head and squinted to get a better look but was relieved when he realised it was only Beth.

He was relieved, of course, until he remembered Beth was dead. Her ashes had been scattered at Brighton Beach over two and a half years ago. It had been a windy day and her remains had ended up embedded in sandcastles and peppered onto a portion of an elderly couple's scampi and chips. Beth was dead. Yet there she was: sitting at a table across the room, staring right at him. Joel's heart began to gallop. His head whirred as he tried to work out whether Nina had possibly spiked him.

Had he left his drink unmonitored at any point in the evening? Was Nina the sort of person who wanted, let alone needed, to spike their date? Did getting spiked mean you started seeing visions of your dead ex-girlfriend? All these possibilities were crowding his mind, each one eager to make its case, when three things happened. Nina returned from the bathroom. Beth gave a little wave. And Joel fainted.

Fucked It

'Are you okay, sir?'

The waiter who had brought Nina and Joel their jamón was now kneeling next to Joel on the floor, forcing a glass of water into his hand. Nina was crouching, too, and held a damp napkin against his forehead. For a moment, Joel felt entirely at peace. And it wasn't until he remembered why it was he'd fainted in the first place that he started to shuffle back up to standing.

'Ah, yeah, I'm . . . yeah,' was all he was able to spit out as he clambered onto the chair he'd fallen off moments before and started looking around for Beth. 'What am I like, eh?' he said to Nina, attempting nonchalance but failing spectacularly, patting her hand in a way that felt more like an awkward consolation prize while he periscoped his head from left to right.

'I don't actually know,' said Nina, moving her hand out of his reach. 'We've literally only met – what – twice and both of those times you've managed to fall over. Are you sure you're okay?'

'Uh-huh,' said Joel. He couldn't see Beth anywhere.

Maybe she'd left the wine bar. Maybe she was halfway down Dalston Lane by now, strolling with purpose. Maybe she was floating somewhere above the ceiling. Or maybe he was imagining things.

Doctor Shah had told him visions like this weren't uncommon — they were a manifestation of grief or something like that — but she'd also told him he shouldn't read too much into them. She'd said, 'It's just your mind playing a trick on you. It's showing you what you want to see. Like how travellers who walk the Mojave are prone to seeing imaginary lakes.' Her voice, which was as angular and clinical as her Marylebone office, contrasted with the roundness of her moon-shaped face and her even rounder eyes.

The logical half of Joel's brain knew there was no way Beth had actually been in the same room as him; she was just an imaginary lake trying to make him feel guilty for going on a date with someone who wasn't her. But still. He was spooked. And the room felt different somehow, as if an electric current was running through it, leaving a static crackle in the air. Joel could have sworn the smell of Beth's perfume was lingering in the air, too.

'Maybe I should take you to hospital,' said Nina. Although the offer sounded sincere, the way she checked her watch while she said it told Joel all he needed to know.

'No, no, don't worry about me,' he said. He knew he'd fucked up the evening and didn't want to waste any more of Nina's time. 'I'll be right as rain. I've just felt . . . off the last couple of days, I guess.'

'Sure,' said Nina, 'that's totally understandable.'

'I also thought my girlfriend was sitting at the table in the corner.' Joel gestured towards the table where Beth had, to all intents and purposes, appeared to be sitting about five minutes prior. 'I don't think that helped.'

Nina winced.

'Your girlfriend?'

'Sorry. Shit. My *ex*-girlfriend.'

'Ah,' said Nina. 'Look, if you are feeling okay, and you don't want any help going to hospital or anything, then I should probably get back home. It's a Wednesday, you know, and . . .'

Nina paused before she finished her sentence, her hands grasping at the air like she was playing cat's cradle. Joel didn't know whether he should wait for her to finish making her invisible string figures or come in with his own objection, your honour. He decided on the former and kept schtum until she decided on what it was she wanted to get off her chest.

'Okay. I don't really know how to put this without sounding like a bitch,' said Nina. 'I had a nice time tonight and you seem like a good guy. But – and I don't want you to take this the wrong way – it seems like you've got some serious shit going on, Joel. And I don't think I'm ready to take whatever that is onboard.' Her kind caramel eyes looked straight into his.

'You don't sound like a bitch at all,' he told her, putting his hands up in a prayer-like motion to indicate he didn't have any hard feelings. His feelings were soft and malleable and smelled a bit like Play-Doh. 'I think maybe I thought I was ready for this. Whatever this is. But now I've had time to think about it, I don't think I am.'

'I think you think too much, Joel,' laughed Nina, slipping her smooth arms under his and giving him a friendly squeeze.

'I think so too,' he said, laughing. As they began to walk out of the bar, an exasperated waitress came and reminded them they hadn't settled the bill. 'I'll get it,' offered Joel. 'It's the least I can do after forcing you to be my nurse for the evening.'

'Thank you,' said Nina. Joel reached into the inside pocket of his jacket, fumbled around to get his card out of his wallet, and waved her off into the warm navy night.

Take Me Home Tonight

Faced with the choice of a twenty-minute bus or a forty-five-minute walk, Joel made the executive decision to make his way home on foot. The air would be good for his head, he figured, and he could use the silence of the night to try to make sense of what had just happened.

He double-checked what his route home was before tucking his phone snugly into his pocket and taking two left turns followed by a right. He'd go without any music or podcasts tonight. He'd free up his ears to the sound of the city happening around him. The vehicular hums and occasional clanks of the capital might even help him concentrate on what was going on inside his head. That was what you were supposed to do after you'd bumped into someone you'd presumed was dead, wasn't it?

Walking purposefully along the pavement, he tried to picture the last thing he'd seen Beth wear. She'd always woken up earlier than him, having the insane and enviable ability to get up before the sound of her alarm, so the last thing he must have seen her in was whatever she'd worn to bed the night before. Depending on the season, Beth would either be wearing the two-piece pyjama set her mum had bought her for the previous Christmas or one of the oversized football shirts she'd kidnapped from Joel. The first time Joel had seen Beth wear the vintage West Ham top he'd won in a tragically dramatic eBay auction, his fate had been sealed.

He knew it was a cringe-worthy cliché but when he'd seen Beth draped in that claret and blue shirt – and nothing but that shirt – he'd been overcome by a sensation unlike any he had experienced before or since. It was a primal urge, a visceral hunger that seemed to tap into something deep within his DNA, something that must have been hardwired into the male psyche since time immemorial. Joel couldn't help but wonder if that feeling of undiluted lust was the driving force behind the explosive growth of the human population, a chemical impulse that defied all rational thought.

'What do you think?' Beth had asked, her hand on her hip in mock Kate Moss fashion. But Joel could not think. The way the Dagenham Motors logo rested gently on her chest and the way her smooth, milky thighs leaked out of the bottom of the jersey, spilling into the ease of her calves had emptied his brain of all thoughts and replaced them with pure feeling. He was hopelessly in love.

Now, as he passed the neon glow of kebab shops and off-licences selling cheap vodka to students, he wondered where he'd put that shirt.

Nearly Departed

Joel contemplated texting Nina but he'd already sent her a message telling her he was, again, extremely sorry about what had happened and '*it'd be great!*' if she could let him know when she got home safe. Chasing that with another text would only make him seem even more desperate than he was. On the other hand, he was starting to think she'd never want to see him again anyway. He wasn't simply below average height, and violently short-sighted without his glasses on, but it turned out he was also prone to having visions of his dead ex-girlfriend. He wasn't exactly what you'd call a catch.

A trio of teenagers, two drenched in glitter and the third completely topless, jogged across the street to catch a bus. They made it in time. Just. The blue plastic bag of cans they were carrying between them was still swinging in a pendulum when they leaped on and brushed their Oyster cards on the bus's canary yellow card reader. Their night was just getting started. A Wednesday, no less. Yet Joel's had already come to a fairly sombre close.

Watching that group laugh and run and dive headfirst into the hope of the next few hours – a night where their bodies would rebound off countless strangers, exchanging sweat and saliva and phone numbers in the darkness – made Joel feel old. He wasn't even thirty yet but he already felt weary within his own body. Heavy in the coat of his skin. Hangovers now lasted at least three days. He couldn't kneel down without his joints cracking like bubble wrap. The thought of ever having to take off his shirt in public made him feel physically ill. He wasn't in terrible nick but his body had grown softer and furrier in recent years. Dark hairs had started sprouting on the backs of his arms and shoulders and were now slowly snaking their way across the upper part of his back. He used to get Beth to pluck them out using a pair of tweezers. That's love, he thought.

Joel reached up his shirt and pulled out one of those hairs using his thumb and index finger, giving a sharp yank that left him with two black curls in his palm which he blew away into a nearby bush. Thinking about the journey those strands of his DNA would travel, and realising he'd never know where they ended up, made him feel small. Inconsequential. A mere cog in the machinery of the universe. Some people said there was freedom to be found through not knowing. Ignorance is bliss, and all that. But Joel couldn't help but feel a creeping sense of powerlessness in the face of the unknown.

Trying to work out whether it really had been Beth he'd seen, or simply someone who looked like her seemed futile – deep down he already knew the answer was a solid 'neither'. Beth was dead, therefore it couldn't have been her sitting there. And, as far as Joel was aware, she didn't have a twin who had the exact same haircut, eye colour, mouth shape, nose piercing, and skin tag on her neck as she did. So it couldn't have been someone who simply looked like her either. The only rational explanations were (1) that Joel was seeing things or (2) going mad. He wasn't entirely confident about which of those was correct.

Madness and hallucinations, after all, weren't necessarily intertwined. You could see things without being mad and, equally, you could be utterly mad without ever having seen a single spectre or spirit. Joel's experience could probably be chalked up to a simple case of sensory deception. A trick of the light. Then again, wasn't that precisely the rationale a madman would cling to?

As Joel opened the door to his flat and stared into the thick black of a hallway he knew every inch of, his phone flashed with a message.

Nina: Home safe now. Thanks again for getting the drinks (and ham). Very kind. Hope you made it back in one piece.

'Just about,' typed Joel before hitting Send and switching his phone off for the night. Home, he thought. What did that feel like again?

Search Engine Optimisation

Joel's love life had hit such a low point that he barely blinked when the sound of the foxes shagging outside his window jolted him awake. Before, their unholy shrieks would have been enough to make him hurl a shoe at the glass in fury. Now? He just lay there, gripped by an emotion far more disconcerting than anger: envy. Their cries were jarring, yes, but who was he to kink-shame? Even the foxes, it seemed, had figured out something he hadn't. Joel thought the critters had been trying to kill each other the first time he'd heard them knocking boots in the bushes, much like the first time his ears had been assaulted by the sound of his parents having sex. At fifteen, Joel should have known better, but it had still taken him a good thirty seconds of listening to the soundtrack of his parents fucking in their bungalow for his brain to clock what was going on. When he'd realised what, and who, he was hearing, he'd muffled his eardrums with the nearest pillow available and forced his eyes shut until the morning.

At breakfast the next day, he'd glared at his parents with a quiet fury. An anger that, looking back now, seemed embarrassingly misplaced. While he'd stewed and seethed, they'd gone about their morning routine, whistling the theme tune to *Thunderbirds* as they emptied the dishwasher and put the squeaky-clean crockery back in the cupboard where it lived. Joel had picked absently at his Weetabix until each biscuit had soaked up all of the milk in the bowl and transformed into an oblong of grey mush. It was one of the few times Joel could recall waking up without an appetite.

He took out his phone and started to type out a message to Alice. He bashed out *We need to talk . . .* and began to recount the whole sorry tale of Wednesday evening before swiftly deleting everything he'd written and starting over again. He didn't want to make her worry but he also wanted to make sure she knew he was in quite a tender headspace.

Joel: Hey! Hope you're well??? Feels like forever since I've seen you. Let's grab a coffee this weekend or something. Would be great to catch up. Much to discuss!

Alice wasn't much of an emoji person so he threw in one of the dancing women emojis at the end to give the sincerity of his message a tinge of irony. He didn't want to come across as too needy, but he'd barely slept in the three days since his imaginary brush with Beth. He'd been up all night, every night, tossing and turning and interrogating his own version of events with the fervour of a barrister in full flow.

He couldn't actually have seen Beth. Could he? That

wasn't possible. Was it? He thought about talking to Sam about it but he knew Alice was the person he really needed to speak to. She'd seen him wear spray-on skinny jeans. He knew he could rely on Alice and her slightly asymmetrical fringe to talk some sense into him.

She took about five minutes to reply.

Alice: Yes. Much. I actually had something I wanted to tell you. Also, I've got some new flatmates! Mice! And lots of them. I'm free Saturday if you're around?

Joel responded to the message with a time and a place before leaning back into his sofa. He tried looking up some information about ghosts on the internet but couldn't find anything concrete to corroborate what he'd experienced. There were heaps of anecdotes from people about their harrowing experiences moving into ancient buildings and hearing screams during the night, but nothing about seeing your deceased ex in a bar that only served biodynamic wine.

It was only when he was closing the tenth tab he'd opened up on some tangential aspect of the occult that he noticed a listing for the '14 Best Mediums & Fortune Tellers In London'. He clicked and watched the little blue circle at the top of the tab whirl around and around before it spilled its guts all over the screen.

Maybe there was an expert he could speak to about what he'd been going through – get some insight from someone in touch with a higher plane of reality. His eyes scoured the page for an east London postcode. There were tarot readings at bookshops, tarot readings at breweries, secret tarot clubs and even a pair of psychic sisters operating out of Selfridges. Nothing called out to him, though, and he was about to close the tab when he saw a listing for a clairvoyant and psychic based in west London. The address wasn't far from Sam's place in Hammersmith, as well as his own office, and Joel mulled over the idea of taking Sam along with him as muscle.

Reading through the services Karishma offered was like finding out there was an entire city underneath the streets he'd never even known about. Not only did she have what she described as 'competitive rates' but she also provided clairvoyance services over the telephone, Monday to Friday, and in one-to-one sessions at her shop in Shepherd's Bush on Saturdays. A thirty-minute crystal ball reading cost £40; a thirty-minute palm reading cost £40; an hour's telephone reading was £90. Joel wasn't sure how his mind could be read over the phone but he did think Karishma was missing a trick by not offering a video-call option. Maybe he'd bring that up in conversation if he ever actually mustered the courage or funds to pay her a visit.

According to Karishma's website, her crystal ball was able to show you 'colours, images and people' alongside a glimpse into the 'past, present and future'. For a man who loved nothing more than knowing what the plan was, the idea of having his entire future mapped out for him like a meeting agenda piqued Joel's interest — even if his scepticism about fortune tellers bordered on contempt. Still, some of Karishma's testimonials were pretty enticing.

'*Very positive, genuine and spot on,*' wrote Roger from Chiswick.

'*Her prediction came true. She told me the house would be sold in December and it was. She also told me that my ex-partner would come back and he came back. Thanks, Karishma,*' wrote Megan from Bayswater.

'*Straightforward and straight-talking. I always smile when I come out from Karishma as I know that all her predictions will come true,*' wrote Janice from Croydon.

The more Joel researched, the more he came to realise what Karishma was offering was an alternative form of therapy. Its primary selling point? Answers. It was easy to see the appeal.

He whipped out his phone and bashed out a follow-up message to Alice.

Joel: What are ur thoughts on mystics?

Alice

When Joel had told Alice he'd seen Beth, she'd laughed. She'd assumed it was a dark bit he was trying out but the look of hurt that crawled across his face told him all she needed to know. 'You're sure you saw her?' she'd asked, searching his eyes again for a sign he was taking the piss. They didn't show so much as a glimmer of insincerity.

'I'm sure,' he said. 'But even if I wasn't, there's got to be a reason that I thought I saw her, right?'

'I guess,' Alice replied. 'Have you spoken to any medical professionals about this? Like your therapist?'

That's when Joel told her he wanted to visit a clairvoyant who could provide him with some 'actual answers'. In spite of her open-mindedness to the woo-woo, Alice was wary about people who claimed to be in contact with the dead. Especially when it seemed like the only time they ever used that power was in exchange for large cash sums. She considered warning Joel but knew that, at the very least, being a good friend meant hearing him out first.

As Alice stood in line, waiting for their coffees to be

magicked up from the back of a black van, she thought about the complexities of grief. It wasn't easy to know what to do with yourself when someone you loved died, but it was even harder to know what to do when faced with the death of someone you didn't. The death of a tenuous connection like that – of a friend's sibling or a colleague you never spoke to honestly and openly aside from one time at the office Christmas party – was difficult to navigate.

Everyone thinks about the day their parents are going to die. Alice was certain about that. She'd imagined exactly what would happen at her dad's funeral on a number of occasions. She knew the music that would play, the poem she would read, the way her mum would start to wear black, and only black, after a lifetime of wearing the gaudiest colours and patterns imaginable. Alice guessed that was how the human brain prepared itself for getting grief-fucked: by running through all these scenarios ahead of time, sometimes years or decades before the event actually occurred, so you were already somewhat prepared for how you were going to feel when you were eventually (and inevitably) orphaned. The death of someone you weren't as close to was a lot harder to prepare for.

Alice had liked Beth. She'd got along with her whenever they'd met and the two had been more than capable of holding a conversation and even, at a push, spending a whole day together without any of Joel's input. But Alice hadn't loved Beth. She hadn't, hand on heart, even known her all that well. And that had made her death difficult. She'd been heartbroken, obviously. Anyone dying that young was a tragedy. The fact it had been the woman Joel had dedicated the previous few years of his life to loving had made it even more tragic. She'd known it had torn his world apart and the thought of Joel, someone she cared for deeply, being toppled like that had made her upset. But she hadn't lost any sleep over it. Was that a terrible thing to admit to?

She'd told Joel she was sorry as soon as she'd found out, and had done everything the *Griefcast* podcast had told her to do. She'd cried for hours on the day — it was a cruel thing to have happened, after all — and had been so distressed she couldn't even face cooking dinner. Alice's boyfriend, James, had ordered in pizza and the sensation of eating not-quite-crisp-enough pepperoni was still inextricably linked in her mind with Beth's death. By eleven o'clock that night, however, she had run out of tears. A feeling of change buzzed in her body, and made the air feel dull and foggy, but she'd still been able to stick to her skincare routine before she went to bed. She hadn't had any trouble dozing off to the sound of James pointedly turning the pages of a tome he was reading about World War II.

The coffees appeared on the van's countertop and Alice picked them up and shuddered as she shook off the memories of that day. Shepherd's Bush Market wasn't a bad place to kill time. Alice's eyes and ears were bombarded by the blaring sights and technicolour sounds as she snaked her way through the textile stores with Joel and scalded her tongue on her too-hot coffee. Joel didn't flinch when he drank his, but grunted as if to acknowledge: yes, this is hot. Alice stopped to take a look at a fishmonger's stall, soaking in the sharp smell of salt and guts that singed her nostrils and made her eyes water, before moving on to the next attraction.

As Joel continued to recite the Wikipedia entry for 'reincarnation' at her, her mind reeled in and out of focus like a fishing line, taking some information in and leaving other bits entirely ignored. She finished her coffee with a satisfying gurgle that startled the woman standing next to her, then hoovered up the last dregs sloshing at the bottom and threw the cup into the nearest recycling bin. Alice wasn't sure how much of the rubbish thrown into those bins was actually recycled but, even if it did all end up in the same rubbish heap in the ocean somewhere, it was better than not giving it a go, right?

Maybe that was an optimist's point of view. Maybe Alice would become more cynical once she got older and had more of her life to look back at and be disappointed by. For the time being, though, she was still young and had hopes she'd actually live up to her ambitions. She had people who worked under her at the office; people who, she assumed, went home and complained to their partners about how much work she gave them to do. She didn't think she was a bad line manager by any means, but one of the fallouts of being someone's superior in a workplace was the people beneath you in the pecking order were bound to resent you a little. You could be friendly with them but you couldn't be their friend. Christ, thought Alice, even my internal monologue is starting to sound like an employee handbook.

Alice trundled past the busiest of the falafel shops and the smell of amba and hot oil, kissing in the warm summer air, made her stomach growl. Maybe Joel would fancy going out for dinner or something later. She couldn't remember the last time they'd been out for a meal together. Maybe after a few glasses of wine she'd have the courage to tell him what was on her mind.

They sat down at a free bench and watched as the entire world seemed to rush by, shopping bags and mobile phones swinging wildly. Alice could feel the hot prickle of stares on her bare legs. She repressed the impulse of wishing she'd shaved them for the occasion.

It was at the point at which Joel began explaining the seven realms of the spirit world to her, in excruciatingly specific detail, that Alice decided she'd had enough.

'You know who you've got to go and see, don't you?' she barked decisively.

Joel's heart sank. He knew where this was going.

'Don't say it.'

'Come on, Joel. You know she'd be good at this—'

'Don't say it.'

'—sort of thing. If you really want to get to the bottom of this, she'll be—'

'I'm warning you.'

'—the best person to ask. I know you guys haven't always—'

'Please.'

'—seen eye to eye but we both—'

'Alice.'

'—know I'm right. Don't we?'

Joel's mind raced. The last thing he wanted was to involve anyone else in this mess, but Alice had a point. She was the only one who could help him now. He looked over the rims of his glasses. Alice's hair was shorn in a Joan of Arc-like fashion, allowing him to see the tips of her ears poking through her mousy hair. She stood up, slowly, raising her eyebrows at Joel in a way that suggested he should do the same.

'All I'm saying,' continued Alice, shepherding Joel gently towards the high street, 'is that if I were you – which, of course, I am rather thankfully not – I'd think about getting on the next train to Surrey.'

The image of the pair leaving the bench together touched a chord with the owner of the falafel stand. He turned his head to watch them go and sighed sadly to himself as they disappeared around the corner. It was two-thirty. An hour later, Joel was at London Bridge station, staring at a day-old copy of the *Metro* and waiting for the four o'clock train.

June

'Joel! Dar-ling! How are you?'

As June embraced Joel, wrapping him up in her turquoise pashmina, his nose was assaulted by the overwhelming aroma of patchouli oil. It was earthy, sweet and slightly spicy. The first time Joel had met June, it had been a totally alien smell to him; something new for his nostrils to pore over and investigate. Now, it was as familiar as the taste of his own breath. It reminded him of getting spat out onto the road outside Redhill station and the brisk twenty-minute walk to the front door of the Lewis residence. The pebble-dashed house had a large garden with two malfunctioning water features and a lopsided bird bath. Inside was a handful of rooms whose photo-plastered walls would make most homes feel nude in comparison.

'I'm good, thanks,' answered Joel unconvincingly. 'How are you doing?'

Graham Lewis pulled himself up from the sofa, ungluing his eyes from Sky News to give Joel's hand a firm shake. He held it in a vice-like squeeze for about three seconds too long, clearly trying to impress upon Joel that he was still the alpha male around these parts.

'I've been expecting you,' said June.

'I know,' said Joel, wrestling his hand free from Graham's grip. 'We texted earlier.'

'Yes, yes. But even before you texted. I *knew*.' She waved her hand towards the geode amethyst squatting in the corner of the room. Graham and Joel exchanged a short glance that reeked of solidarity.

'Tea?' asked Graham, puncturing the silence. 'We've got lapsang souchong, rooibos, and builder's.'

Joel said thank you but no and June, who had been buzzing about the living room like a worker bee, suddenly stopped and rested her hands on Joel's shoulders. They locked eyes; Joel, strained, looked back out of politeness while June's unrelenting gaze pierced and stung like iodine on an open wound.

There was so much of Beth in her. The gappy front teeth. The fox-coloured hair. She even struggled with her Rs in the same way, occasionally letting a W slip into a 'red' or a 'really'. June wasn't perfect. She openly dismissed her bipolar disorder as 'a Celtic temper' and privately struggled with an eating disorder Beth had blamed on Trinny and Susannah. Yet spending time with her felt like getting a glimpse at the future her daughter had been robbed of. It was painful. Intoxicating. Like staring directly at the sun.

He knew he ought to spend more time with June and Graham – they were good people, kind people – but every moment with them was a heart-rending reminder of how much he missed Beth. Being in their home was like walking through a museum of her life.

Her go-to teacup, the one with the chintzy rose pattern and chip on the rim, still hung untouched on the mug tree in the kitchen. The forest-themed jigsaw puzzle she'd started on a grey afternoon one February still sprawled, unfinished, on the dining-room table. Countless portions of spaghetti bolognese (no carrot, just how she liked it) dammed up the freezer so badly the door wouldn't shut without a slam. Although they'd made grand plans to turn her room into a study, Graham and June had never been able to work up the courage to throw out any of Beth's possessions. To an outsider looking in, it was as if they were waiting for her to return any day now.

June touched Joel gently on the hand. 'It won't last forever,' she said. He tried to smile but gave up on the endeavour halfway through.

'And I know why you're here,' she added.

'You do?'

'I do.'

Before he could think of a coherent response, Joel's eyes fastened on the photo of Beth on the mantelpiece. It had been taken at her graduation. She was wearing a bright green silk shirt under her cap and gown, clutching a PVC pipe with a red ribbon tied around it to give it the appearance of a paper certificate.

June's eyes followed Joel's.

'She's why you're back,' said June, softly.

June's face was bright and beautiful, she had a smile

that could stop traffic, but a sadness had seeped into the cracks of her voice. A stranger wouldn't have been able to pick up on it but anyone who'd known June before the accident could hear the change in register: a hush of hurt coated every word she spoke, each syllable aching with the knowledge that Beth was no longer around to hear it.

'Let's go to the healing room,' said June, clasping her hands together in front of her chest.

Joel followed June as they made their way through the garage. The interior was carless and bare. The only objects taking up space in the darkness were a box of Graham's golfing trophies, two broken mini-fridges and a still-warm lawnmower scrawled with italics of wet grass. On the other side of the room was a screen door which separated the healing room from the rest of the garage. A large om symbol had been printed out and sellotaped onto the upper third of the door. As June swung it open, Joel was hit in the face by a blast of smoky incense. Following the smell of jasmine and resin, he walked towards a thick velvet curtain which felt inordinately heavy as he pushed his fingers into the parting and ducked into a room that looked much larger on the inside than he'd expected.

Golden Feldspar

The walls were covered in natal charts and every square inch of the shelves was taken up with a myriad of trinkets ranging from a half-dressed troll doll to what looked to be the skull of a dog. There were two chairs in the room, both of which were plush and seemed to be made from the same material as the curtain, and a football-sized crystal ball on the table in between them.

June was a fully fledged member of the London College of Psychic Studies, having studied the Tarot according to the teachings of renowned clairvoyants and tarot readers. She regularly attended courses and workshops at the London School of Astrology to further grow and develop her spiritual path. She worked the antique market circuit and could be found every other month at the Alternative Bring 'n' Buy in Tufnell Park – her stall sat between Purple Poison Jewellery and a steamed sweetcorn cart. Joel knew all of this because it was written on the pamphlet June handed him when he entered the room.

'Take a seat,' she said, ushering him towards the chair on the other side of the table. Joel did as he was told and immediately sank deep into the chair. It was lower than he'd expected and much comfier, too. He considered asking June where she'd got the chairs from but stopped himself at the last moment. This didn't seem like a place to have conversations about interior design, and he was painfully aware every pointless question he asked would prolong the amount of time he spent in the Lewis garage.

'This one is lapis lazuli,' she said, palming a smooth blue stone across the table into Joel's hand. 'It resonates with both the throat and the heart chakra, aiding communication and the ability to speak from the heart. Lapis is extremely calming and can help reduce stress – I think it'll be good for you. It's a very healing and protective stone, Joel.'

Joel nodded.

'It also helps open the third eye.'

Joel nodded again. He could feel his throat chakra tighten.

June had always been 'spiritually sensitive', which along with 'kind' is how Beth had accurately described her mother to Joel before he met her for the first time. Yet, since her daughter's death, June had burrowed herself deeper into the rabbit hole of the occult.

If it helped, it helped. But Joel couldn't shake the feeling June's born-again fervour for mysticism was a coping mechanism. Moreover, as the son of a doctor, who had grown up hearing his mother incessantly complain about her patients not taking the right prescriptions, he couldn't abide by June's decision to stop taking her lithium cold turkey in favour of herbal remedies. He knew it was natural to try to make sense of grief, to try to understand. He'd asked himself the same 'whys' a million times: Why now? Why her? Why me? But if there weren't any answers to be found, what was the point of searching for meaning? It was only his recent ghosting that had made Joel wonder if maybe, just maybe, there was something bigger at work in the universe.

'How have things been?' he asked.

'Oh, fine,' she said, smudging her crystals with a sage stick. 'I've been *fine*. Work has been *fine*. The weather has been *fine*. That's what you're supposed to say, isn't it?'

He said it was.

'And how have you been?'

Joel pushed his tongue against his bottom teeth, feeling out the rough ridges of hardened plaque. 'Oh, you know,' he said. 'Just fine.'

June smiled. She squeezed his hand, so tightly he could feel her rings leaving an impression on his skin, and he squeezed back.

'Are you really?' she asked.

'Am I really what?'

'Fine.'

'Fine?'

'Yes, fine.'

'No,' he sighed. 'Not really.'

'Not really?'

'No.'

'Why?'

'People are always telling me that they miss her,' Joel said.

'That's because they do.'

'I know. It just seems unfair, I guess. Unfair that they get to miss her and talk about all these memories they have of her when they didn't even know her like I did. Like I do. It feels like those memories should be mine.'

June fixed him with a serious glance. He could tell she was picking out the right words to say.

'It's natural to feel frustrated about and even envious of the time others had with Beth, but you can't have a monopoly on pain.'

'I never liked Monopoly, I was more of a Ludo man,' said Joel, forcing out a laugh and trying to move the conversation back into safer territory. Trying, as always, to bury his sincerity beneath some kind of joke. June didn't bite.

'You know, I think this is the longest we've spoken about Beth since her death. I can see the lapis lazuli is already starting to work its magic.'

Joel tried to keep smiling, but couldn't. The house was crowded with too many memories of Beth – of nights spent curled up together like packing peanuts in the tiny bed she'd had since childhood. He could still recall their idle conversations about the future, when they'd fill whatever wall space there was left with photos of their own inevitably red-haired children. Beth had been the best thing about him, and he was tired of pretending things were okay without her.

Nearly Departed

'It looks like you'll need this, too,' added June as she passed him another smooth stone. As he accepted it, wordlessly, he was struck by its glacier-blue hue. Unlike the lapis lazuli, which had soothed him with its deep indigo, this stone was more delicate, resembling a small robin's egg. He couldn't help but shiver as he ran his index finger and thumb over its smooth surface, feeling the chill of the stone settling in between his shoulder blades.

'Angelite,' said June.

Joel asked what it did.

'It enhances telepathic communication,' she answered casually. 'Some say it enables out-of-body journeys to take place while still letting you maintain contact with everyday reality.'

'Have you ever,' said Joel, 'had, like, an out-of-body journey?'

'Oh, you know me, Joel. I'm always flitting back and forth between the realms!'

June smiled. Joel smiled.

'What about telepathic conversations? Have you ever had one of those?'

'Oh, many, many.'

June smiled. Joel smiled.

'What about telepathic conversations . . . with someone that's dead?'

June was silent. She tilted her head to the side and her smile faded from her face, as effortlessly as a wisp of smoke rising from an incense stick.

'Now, why would you go and ask that?'

'Because,' said Joel, 'I've sort of been having them. With Beth.'

June's eyes widened. He couldn't tell if she was excited or furious or both.

'If what you're telling me is true, Joel – then we simply must investigate this further. I never knew you were so in touch with your spirituality,' she said, a wild mania surging in her eyes. Joel started to question whether he'd made a grave mistake in visiting.

'Let's do a quick reading and see what the cards have to say,' she added hastily, before Joel had a chance to protest.

She vaulted from her chair and wrenched out a dusty deck of tarot cards from the small box wedged under the feet of the semi-nude troll doll. She fanned the cards out onto the table, face down, and smooshed them around in a clockwise motion before pulling them back into her hand with a beautiful bit of legerdemain. Her thin fingers moved in precise, rapid movements. She kept her eyes locked with Joel's the entire time, and since he didn't know where else to look, he smiled back, nervously.

She shuffled the deck with practised ease, then abruptly stopped, set the cards down next to the crystal ball and cracked her knuckles, deftly popping each finger from index to pinky.

'It's time,' she said.

'Right,' said Joel.

Silence. Joel stared at June. June stared at the deck of cards. The deck of cards stared down at the paisley tablecloth. Just as Joel was about to mumble something for the sake of it, June peeled off the card at the top of the deck and placed it face up on the table. Joel looked down. June looked down. The Ten of Swords looked back up at them, blinking in the dim, comforting light that seeped through the fabric of a shawl-wrapped lamp.

The card bore an art nouveau illustration of a man splayed face down on the ground with ten long swords plunged into his back. A red cape was draped around his legs, and the sky brooded in ominous black. The only saving grace as far as Joel could see was that the man was turned away from the viewer, giving Joel a barber's view of the back of his head and shielding him from the full impact of the brutal tableau.

'That doesn't look good,' he said, attempting to inject a bit of levity into the prediction of a future that looked, to all intents and purposes, to contain a rather gratuitous amount of violence.

'Get out of my house,' said June, softly.

'What?'

'I said: get out of my house.'

She spat the words out with venom this time.

Joel put up his hands, confused, his palms facing outwards. 'June,' he said, 'I'm so sorry but I don't really understand what's going on. I never meant to cause any offence, I . . .'

'You know what?' barked June. 'For a moment, I actually thought you'd come here so we could spend some quality time together, but it turns out all you wanted to do was barge into my home, bringing this dark energy – this terrible omen – with you and dredging up all these painful, horrible memories.'

'That was never my intention,' stuttered Joel. 'I just thought that you might be able to help with—'

'Help?! Help?!'

June stormed across the room; she was a thundercloud, erupting over every surface. She knocked over a side table with a swift kick and sent a rainbow of semi-precious stones skittering across the floor.

'The only "help" I need is help getting you out of my house,' she shrieked before throwing in an ear-piercing: 'Graham!'

Like a dog hearing its name bellowed across the park, Graham obediently came bounding into the room. June was in hysterics. Graham looked apologetic. All Joel could think about was the untouched vial of lithium in the downstairs bathroom.

'I think it's best you go now, Son,' he said, resting his hand on Joel's shoulder. 'It hasn't been a good week.'

Joel turned to leave the room.

'And take this with you!' cried June. 'You're a cursed man, Joel Foster!'

As he turned to see what she meant, with a swift and forceful motion she hurled an object through the air which collided sharply with his head. He winced in pain as he reached down to retrieve the source of the attack – an amber stone, glinting in the light. As he pocketed it, he closed the door behind him as gently as he could, leaving June to wail about 'portent' and 'pain' behind him.

Nearly Departed

It took a while for Joel to identify the stone as he sat on the train home, feeling the familiar groan of the wheels beneath his feet, but judging by its honeyed colour and the light gold stretch marks spread across its belly, he concluded it was golden feldspar. Google said:

This is a stone of optimism, it helps you to live in the present and have a positive outlook. Aids in moving forward from the past. It is a reiki stone that stimulates healing.

With the past sitting heavy in his stomach, as if he had swallowed years of his life whole that afternoon, Joel nodded to himself and turned back towards the window.

'X' Marks The Spot

Sometimes a meal isn't about the food. Sometimes it doesn't matter that the sourdough is so fresh its crust crackles under your teeth like the sound of boots in fresh snow or that every bite of its chewy crumb hits your tongue with a ringing lactic tang. Sometimes it means very little if the pasta is cooked perfectly al dente and comes coiled around a mineral whisper of *cime di rapa*. Sometimes you don't even care that the samphire adds a nice oceanic touch to an otherwise one-note ragù.

Sometimes restaurants are background noise – the scenery for a school play, painted by an eager teacher, that's only there to add texture to the occasion. Yes, a painstaking number of hours have been spent making sure the manger looks suitably rustic (and that the freshly made ravioli have been perfectly crimped) but you're not there to marvel at the work of Mrs Pierce and her paintbrushes. You're there to watch your child do their best at pretending to be a wise king or shepherd. The brioche doughnuts, though generously filled with lemon curd and meringue, are ancillary to the reason you've booked a table. They're not the fucking point.

Nearly Departed

Sometimes you look up at an old friend after three courses of laughing, and a carafe of white wine, and realise you were both so lost in conversation and the pleasure of each other's company that you've already forgotten what anything you've eaten even tasted like. Sometimes that's exactly what you need. And that's exactly what Joel needed that night to feel like he was somewhat sane again.

As Joel and Alice exited the restaurant, they promised – as they always did – to 'do this more often' and 'not leave it as long next time'. Both of them knew, though, they wouldn't do it more often and would leave it just as long next time – not because they didn't want to see each other more, but because life, as it tends to do, got in the way. Spare evenings were hard to find and, in between work and holidays and sporadic visits to see their respective families, it wasn't easy for them to sync up their schedules.

Regardless, the time Joel and Alice spent together meant a lot to them. He felt comfort in having someone in his life he could be glib with one minute and completely earnest the next. Alice was someone who understood Joel when he asked her questions like: 'If you could only eat foods that start with the same letter for the rest of your life, which letter would you choose?' So, when Alice told him he should try and give it another go with Nina, he knew she was probably right. Maybe it was because she was a woman. Because she knew how these things worked. Maybe it was because she wanted him to forget about seeing dead people and concentrate on making a connection with someone who was actually alive.

Joel thought about what he should say to Nina but his mind was blank. He'd already apologised for his actions – both on the day he'd fainted, and via a string of increasingly manic text messages in the days afterwards. While he'd made it clear he was sorry about what had happened, what he hadn't done was let her know *why* it had happened. He hadn't let himself be vulnerable and open with her about his situation. And by obscuring part of the whole picture from her, Joel had ensured she'd only ended up with a second-hand account of the story. His thumb was smudging the lens and blocking her from observing, debatably, the most crucial aspect of the situation: the corner of the photo where the body of his girlfriend lay cold and dead. Without that bit of key information, he was just a man who wasn't over his ex-girlfriend. Well, not just that. He was a man who wasn't over his ex who also happened to faint on a worryingly regular basis.

'Don't overthink it,' was something Joel's dad had told him more times than he could count. Like his son, Rob Foster was a short man with a stocky build. He wasn't fat, but solid. Dense. Sturdy. Welsh. He had a low centre of gravity, which had come in handy during his many decades of playing rugby, but was rarely useful since he'd been forced to stop at the age of sixty-seven. Rugby union was his greatest passion, and he'd run out on the field every Saturday until a slipped disc following a collapsed maul put an end to his rucking days. Joel had

Nearly Departed

never got into rugby and only knew what a few of the words in that sentence meant. Joel's mum, Helen, wasn't a big fan either, and had been unable to hide her relief when the local GP told Rob he'd never play again. Much to Helen's chagrin, Rob still spent every weekend at the rugby club, supporting his team. And drinking. Mainly drinking, to be honest.

At times, Helen had wondered aloud to Joel whether Rob was doing it to spite her, but they both knew deep down he wasn't. The rugby club was simply somewhere Rob felt like he belonged and, as much as Helen might resent the amount of money he spent on lager every week, she couldn't deny that having an active social life was good for him. He needed somewhere he could escape to every now and then. Somewhere he wasn't weighed down by the expectations of work and family. At the Rhiwbina Recreation Club, he was simply a man who'd used to be a half-decent flanker and could finish a pint in three gulps.

Taking a leaf out of Rob Foster's book, Joel hit the brakes on this thought process and sent Nina the first thing that came to mind.

> **Joel:** My ex is dead. She died almost three years ago. I'm sorry I didn't tell you before, but that's why I freaked out when I thought she was at the bar. Because she can't have actually been at the bar. Because she's dead. Just thought you should know.

For the first time in what felt like forever, Joel had sent a text without re-writing it half a dozen times. He hoped the authenticity of it would strike a chord with Nina. He hoped she wouldn't think he was using bereavement as an excuse for bad behaviour and that he, like most men, was trash. Three little dots appeared, disappeared and reappeared on his screen in the space of about five seconds. He imagined Nina was standing at a bus stop like he was – typing, deleting and re-typing her message until she was happy with it. The three dots taunted Joel one final time, Cerberus gnashing its teeth, then vanished, leaving him alone with his thoughts.

The only thing the ellipsis confirmed was that his emotional state was very much up for grabs and, as it turned out, entirely dependent on what Nina wrote back. He was convinced his phone was looking at him funny, mocking him for resting so much of his mental well-being on whatever Nina could cram into a 160-character limit. Joel hadn't even realised how much he cared about what Nina thought of him until that instant.

It was funny how a crush could sneak up on you like that – he hadn't known Nina existed until a couple of weeks ago. But now? Now he couldn't concentrate on anything apart from the way she smelled or the way little crow's feet formed next to her eyes whenever she concentrated. She had a beautiful, expressive face prone to crinkling like tracing paper.

Joel wouldn't be surprised if she was terrible at acting. She seemed to wear her emotions on the outside at all times – they practically jangled from her wrists like bangles – so it must have been difficult for her to conceal her feelings. He'd never fully grasped the meaning of

Nearly Departed

'crestfallen' until he saw the look on her face when he casually mentioned he'd seen Beth. But even when staring at the dictionary definition of 'sad and disappointed' in her lovely face, he hadn't had the courage to tell her the truth. He hadn't wanted her to pity him or look at him differently, and because of that, he'd ended up hurting her instead. Why he hadn't realised all that sooner, he didn't know. Maybe his breakneck tarot session with June had finally helped him gain some clarity. Maybe he was still high from all the incense.

Just as he was starting to give up hope, two things happened. They felt like they happened at the exact same time to Joel but, as when a one-hundred-metre runner dips ahead of another for a photo finish, it was inevitable one of the events happened ever so slightly before the other. Those two things were: one, the bright red 26 bus finally reared into view and, two, Joel's phone vibrated to let him know Nina had replied to his text. He gave a silent prayer of thanks and shifted up the stairs of the bus to his favourite seat at the front. It was the only seat in the house he could occupy and be reasonably confident he wouldn't feel like he was going to throw up. Once he'd sat down and safely and securely gripped his tote bag between his feet, he checked his phone.

> **Nina:** I'm so sorry to hear that, Joel. And I really appreciate you telling me. If you ever want to talk, I'm always around. Just maybe no fainting next time. Okay? X

That little 'X' went straight into his chest, branding his heart like a smiley burn from a BIC lighter. Was there a more emotional letter in the English language? What other single character could be the difference between being over the moon and utterly heartbroken? And who the fuck had decided an 'X' stood for a kiss anyway? Was it because saying 'X' out loud sounded like the dry, awkward kisses you'd have to give your mum's friend whenever she came round for a cup of tea?

The next thing Joel had to worry about (there was always a next thing to worry about) was what he'd text back. He knew an 'X' was on the cards. His psyche had wrung all the water from the flannel of that topic by now. But he wasn't sure if he should go right in there with a time and date to meet up. Alice had told him that was something women found attractive – not fucking about with a *I've got a fairly open calendar W/C 14 August, if that works?* and going for a confident *Thursday. The Prince Arthur. 7 p.m.?* instead.

Was that a good idea when he'd only just managed to convince Nina he wasn't still pining after his ex? Joel wasn't sure. He took a moment to think, giving his legs a quick squeeze to make sure his bag was still between them, and looked back on what he and Nina had spoken about on their date before they'd been rudely interrupted by Joel's potential insanity.

They'd talked about the climate crisis. They'd talked about what they did for work. They'd talked about the aimlessness they'd felt after leaving university. They'd talked about their families. Joel had learned Nina had a younger brother, Isaac, who she adored, and Nina had learned Joel had an older brother, Billy, who he wished he knew better.

'Billy and Joel?' she'd said. 'Really?'

'I know,' Joel groaned, 'but it's not what you think. My parents don't even listen to music, so it's not like they did it on purpose. And his full name is William anyway. Which is, y'know, a lot less Billy Joel-y.'

She asked him why they weren't close and Joel hadn't got a boilerplate answer he could give her. He didn't have an answer because he didn't know the answer. He guessed it was because they were very different people. Billy was sporty like their dad. He would skip to the back of the paper for the transfer rumours, while Joel would race to see how many stars his favourite film critic had given the latest Scorsese.

'I guess it's because we're very different people,' he told Nina. Which was true. But Joel knew one of the main reasons he'd lost touch with Billy over the last seven or so years was because he was scared of losing him. Or, more accurately, he was scared of losing a version of him that no longer existed. He didn't want to ruin the memories he had of them getting muddy in the garden or save new, unfamiliar images over those on the memory card of the early childhood they'd spent perennially half-naked and happy. He didn't want to accept they were now simply two men who had nothing but genetics in common.

Joel had thought that was all a bit heavy for a first date, so he'd served the conversation over to Nina's side of the family and she'd paddled it back with a story about the time her dad had picked up the wrong suit from the dry cleaners for her graduation.

'You can literally see him squirming in every photo because it didn't fit properly – it barely came down to his forearms,' laughed Nina, tears streaming down her face, 'and it wasn't until we came home and my brother asked him when he'd found the time to buy a black Moss Bros suit that we all realised what had happened.'

He'd laughed a lot that evening. His mum had always told him laughter was the most important thing when it came to finding someone to spend the rest of your life with. 'Just remember to fall in love and laugh a lot,' she'd said. 'There's nothing else.' Joel wasn't sure if she knew she'd stolen that wisdom from The Chemical Brothers – did his mum even know who The Chemical Brothers were? – but it still rang true. His parents were always laughing with, and at, each other and they'd been married for over thirty years now. They were obviously doing something right.

Joel pulled out his phone and flipped it around like a Zippo, partway satisfying a desire to whip out a six-shooter pistol he'd had since he was a cowboy-obsessed six-year-old.

Joel: Thanks for being so understanding. Honestly. I'd love to have the chance to properly apologise in person, too. How about we go to the National Gallery next Saturday and you can pretend like you're working even though it's the weekend? J x

Nearly Departed

Joel hit the send button with his right hand as he circled his left around the nearest pole and pushed the cherry red button with a sweet clunk and ding. The 26 pulled up to Joel's stop and he threw himself down the stairs and out of the door in one harum-scarum motion, taking care not to pelt anyone with his tote bag as he exited out of the bus's gaping side-stomach.

Nina: Sounds like a real busman's holiday. Count me in! N x

The sky, which had turned a threatening grey over the course of Joel's journey home, began to weep. Joel looked up and let several fat drops of rain land squarely on his face. He closed his eyes and, for the first time in a long time, felt his mind relax. All the acidic anxiety he'd been carrying in his shoulders melted away, leaving him lightheaded with excitement.

A little bit sodden but full of anticipation for the week ahead, Joel walked into his building and bounded up the stairs, the contents of his tote bag bouncing off his thigh with every two-step leap. He didn't care that he'd be out of breath by the time he got to his front door. In fact, he almost relished that feeling of exhaustion. He had so much nervous energy to use up he even thought about doing some push-ups when he got back in. Which was ridiculous. And something he'd never actually do. He slotted his key into the keyhole and turned it until the mechanism conceded and escorted him inside.

He walked into the hallway, kicked off his shoes, and

bounded into the living room for a well-earned sit. Joel's nostrils flared. The air was thick with a scent his nose hadn't encountered in a while. It was sweet, subtly floral and intimately familiar. It was the smell of waking up in the middle of the night and feeling at peace with the gentle tossing and turning of the person next to you. It was lazy Sunday mornings spent reciprocating oral sex and reading the weekly restaurant reviews out loud in posh accents. It was feeling her arms wrap around your stomach like an inflatable rubber ring as you stirred something slowly on the hob. It was Beth.

'Hi, Joel,' said Beth, who was perched cat-like on the left arm of the sofa.

'Hi, Beth,' said Joel. The half-smile on her face, which trod a fine line between happy and sad, was the last thing he saw before he came crashing down to the floor.

Days left to fall in love: 12

PART TWO

Lazarus

Joel woke up several hours later. When he remembered why he'd spent the night face down on his seldom-hoovered carpet, he screwed his eyes shut and covered his ears with his hands. It was something he used to do whenever the Child Catcher came on screen during *Chitty Chitty Bang Bang*. Drowning out the world around him, turning the volume down on everything outside his head so he could think more clearly inside it, still gave him a sense of lo-fi comfort.

Beth wasn't actually there, sitting on his sofa flicking through his stack of half-read magazines. She was just a figment of his imagination. A manifestation of his grief. A phantom. A glitch in the matrix. His brain was simply giving him a friendly reminder of all the things he'd never said to her when she was alive, that's all. These things happened all the time, he thought – it was all part of the process of moving on. She was not a flesh-and-bones version of his deceased lover brought back from the dead.

Joel took a deep breath, swallowing once long and hard, and opened his eyelids to a pinhole. He'd once made a pinhole projector in primary school and used it to watch a solar eclipse. Eight-year-old Joel had been incredibly underwhelmed. This time, however, instead of seeing a slightly brighter sun through the medium of a cardboard box, he saw Beth sitting on the sofa, clear as day. His ex-girlfriend, Beth. His dead ex-girlfriend, Bethany Rose Lewis.

No one but her passport had called her Bethany when she was alive, not even her mum. She was Beth to everyone who loved and knew her. Death, however, had calcified her as a Bethany in Joel's mind. It's what the priest who'd said her last rites had called her and Joel had assumed that was the name she would be taking with her to the afterlife, too. That was how those things worked, right?

It had taken five months after her death for Joel to finally accept he'd never kiss Beth again. Yet here she was, looking thoughtfully at the framed posters in his living room. The bitch. She wore a loose-fitting white T-shirt tucked into a pair of Levi's 501s, with a sheer lilac blouse – the one she'd bought from a charity shop in Lewes for £5 – layered over the top. Her trainers were scuffed to shit. She looked perfect. But, more importantly, she looked alive.

'What are you staring at?' asked Beth.

He didn't know what to say. Did he tell her what he was actually thinking? That he thought he was having a psychotic episode and should probably ring his mum so she could come over and get him sectioned as soon as possible? That didn't seem like a good idea, so he said the only thing he could.

Nearly Departed

'You,' he said, unclenching his fists. His eyes were fully open now, soaking all of her in.

'*You*,' she said, mimicking the generically Welsh lilt of his accent in the way she always used to. 'Always one for the amateur dramatics, weren't you?' She was smiling now. He loved her smile. He also loved the way she gently mocked the way he sounded, his short As in the way he said 'bath' and 'France' instead of 'barth' and 'Frahnce'. Not that he ever let her know that. No, Joel's role whenever she parroted him was to pantomime offence and make accusations that her jibes were some form of deep-seated classism bubbling to the surface of her psyche. Those were the roles they'd played, and they'd performed them rather excellently for the four years they'd been together. Now, he wasn't sure what to make of her tone. He was angry. Confused. She was dead.

'Are you making fun of me?'

He was starting to pace back and forth across the room now. Joel had never paced before. The movement was new to him. It was something he'd only ever seen in films and yet here he was, pacing around his living room at 8 a.m. on a Sunday.

'Me?' said Beth, feigning surprise and making a small 'o' with her mouth.

'Yes, you,' said Joel, frustration rising up inside him. Were the dead even capable of making jokes? Was a sense of humour something you took to the grave with you?

'No,' she answered. Beth stared at him, letting her

emerald eyes focus on his to let him know she meant no harm. It was an old trick of hers – the ability to instantly make Joel feel peaceful, regardless of whatever mayhem was going on.

'It feels like you are,' he said, lulled into a sense of comfort by the soft grassy meadows of her eyes.

'I'm not.'

'How do I know you're telling the truth?'

'You're either haunted or insane, Joel. The choice is up to you. Besides, do you really think I'd come all the way back from the dead just so I could fuck with you?'

'Honestly? Yes, that seems like exactly the sort of thing you'd do.'

'Yeah, you're not wrong, to be fair.'

Beth laughed and unfurled herself from the sofa. When she was standing up straight, the tip of her nose came up to meet the tip of Joel's. This was something most people didn't realise because Beth had a tendency to slouch and Joel had the proportions of a much taller person. On video calls, most people assumed he was roughly average height because his torso gave off that vibe, and it was always a shock – in so much as a handful of spinal inches can be classified as a shock – when anyone met him in person. Beth took a step towards Joel and wrapped her arms around him.

That's when a thunderbolt of pain was hurled through his body.

After The Afterlife

Joel's head felt fuzzy, as if it held the static charge of an old television. His fingers, meanwhile, were like electric eels, wriggling into the arms of the sofa he'd sat on to stop himself from collapsing. Instinctively, he hauled his phone from his pocket and checked the time. Once his eyes had focused in on the digits, he checked his watch to corroborate his phone's account of what had gone down. 'Thirty-two past eight,' is what they sang in harmony. He'd been sitting down for about twenty minutes and the sharp peak of the dizziness had only just started to subside.

'You've been sitting there for about twenty minutes,' confirmed a disembodied voice, calling from the kitchen. That body-less voice was smartly given a pair of legs, a torso, arms and a head as Beth returned to the living room where Joel was gingerly shifting in his seat. Doing things 'gingerly' was what an old person did, thought Joel, afraid either the world was going to break apart or they would break before it ended. He wasn't in the best position to judge the elderly, though. He was, after all, the one currently seeing dead people.

'Do you want anything to drink? Water? Tea?'

'No,' he said. He felt his brain pulse and press against the inside of his skull. 'No, thank you.'

'Just as well,' chirruped Beth. 'I don't think I can actually make tea anymore. Everything I try to pick up or move doesn't budge. It's like trying to shift an ionic column. Or a building.'

'Why was an ionic column the first thing that came to your mind?'

'I don't know. They're just, like, especially solid, aren't they? Like Ozymandias and his trunkless legs of stone. Immovable.'

'Are you really quoting Shelley at me right now?'

Beth said she wasn't sure why she felt so inclined to poetry, but she did know that trying to grab hold of one of Joel's novelty mugs while he'd been bent double in pain had felt like trying to shift an Atlas stone. Experiencing true powerlessness like that had moved something inside her. An ironic choice of words, she noted, considering it didn't seem like she could move anything at all.

Joel was slouched on the sofa – sofa, couch, settee; he wasn't fussy about what he called it – idly wondering if that made him unusually adaptable or just deeply uncommitted. Sometimes he'd swap from one name to another in the same sentence. Language was shifting all the time. Words came and went, and even spelling and grammar changed their outfits according to whatever people considered to be common parlance or whatever

Nearly Departed

new slang was allowed to be written and published by broadsheet journalists.

And if words could alter their meaning, like a pop star swapping into something more sequinned between songs, then couldn't the rest of reality be just as changeable? Joel wasn't sure if he was on to something or if he was genuinely losing his mind. He kept picturing the words 'dead' and 'alive' flashing alternately in his mind. It felt like a visual effect that would require an epilepsy warning at the start of a film and reminded Joel of when Liam Brown from second set maths had shown him a way of writing the word 'true' so it also looked like the word 'false'. Joel debated looking Liam up on Facebook to see what he was up to now. He'd do it later, he thought. Best to deal with the whole dead girlfriend brought back to life thing first.

'So, this is really happening right now?' he asked.

'Yes,' said Beth, gesturing from her real-looking thighs to her real-looking head, 'this is really happening right now.'

Joel nodded. If his brain were a laptop, it'd be making a high-pitched whirring noise, and blowing hot air out of every available port. He looked at Beth and drank in as much of her as he could. While he had gained three deep stress-induced forehead wrinkles and several kilos over the last few years, Beth looked as fresh as the day she and her bike had been slammed into non-existence. She looked solid. Joel had expected her to look spectral, to glide ethereally rather than echoing the usual movements of her previously sentient self, but Beth moved as endearingly gracelessly as ever. He tried to squint at the poster on the wall behind her but he couldn't see a damn thing through her.

'But . . . why?' he stuttered once he'd accepted Beth wasn't transparent in the slightest.

'I don't know,' she said. She told him how she'd been dead one minute and then alive – 'Okay, nearly alive' – the next. She'd been following him for the past couple of days, keeping her distance so as not to startle him. And yes, as far as she was aware, no one else was able to see her. Just him.

It was obvious this speech was something she'd been practising for a while, and once she'd got all of that exposition out of the way, Beth let out a deep breath. Joel hoped he had been a receptive enough audience. He reached out to push a few strands of hair away from her eyes but Beth pulled back before his fingers could brush the loose waves that fell around her heart-shaped face, framing her features in a halo of coppery light.

'You don't want to do that,' she said, holding up her hands in a 'Whoa, Nelly!' gesture Joel had only ever seen used by cowboys in fifties westerns.

'Why?' asked Joel. He had dreamed of holding Beth again for so long, of tracing his fingers along the soft butteriness of her thighs, that the thought of being so close to her but unable to touch her was pure torture.

'Because every time you touch me, you'll get sparked out like last time.'

'How do you know that?'

'Because I can feel it inside me,' said Beth, who took a moment to move from the arm of the sofa to sit on the seat parallel to Joel. 'It's hard to properly explain it but there are a lot of things I just know now. It's not something I've been sat down and taught by a higher power or anything like that. It's more like a software update, if that makes sense?'

Joel nodded. He understood the words Beth had said but he didn't – and couldn't – comprehend the feeling behind them. Seeing as he hadn't yet crossed over into the realm of the dead, he figured he would never properly understand where she was coming from until he died himself. So, in that case, what was the point in trying?

'What was death like?' he asked, rubbing the nap of his favourite cushion back and forth in a businesslike fashion, changing its shade from dark mauve to light mauve and back again. He found the stroking motion therapeutic, he used to rub a mole on his mother's arm in a similar rhythm when he was younger, and made a mental note to invest in a cat.

'You really want to know?'

'Yes,' said Joel, and the confidence of his answer surprised him.

Death had juddered Joel's life so violently – muddling it in a cocktail shaker with such gusto that when it had come out the other side it had been frothy and unrecognisable – that he'd never considered embracing it before. At least, not consciously. There had been times, back in the early days of grief, when every bridge and oncoming train would whisper something delicious at the back of his neck. They'd promise him an end to the stress and the pain and the worry. A sweet and easy way out.

Joel was too angry at death, though, to ever consider giving suicide a serious go. It had taken away the person he had loved the most and he wasn't going to give it the satisfaction of having him, too. In spite of all the anger he kept bottled inside, Joel was still intrigued about what it would be like to die. He'd read countless accounts of people who'd come back to life after being pronounced dead for five minutes, and all of them had profoundly uninteresting things to say about the experience. Maybe Beth was back so she could let Joel know what it was actually like – assuage his fears and let him know joining her in the afterlife wouldn't be so bad after all.

'Do you want to go for a walk?' asked Beth.

'Sure,' said Joel. 'Anywhere you had in mind?'

Big Light

The Heath squelched beneath his boots. Last night's rain had been a long time coming; the arid ground had opened up its mouth as wide as it could and drank greedily from the sky until it could take no more. Joel was thankful for his sensible choice of footwear and wondered, looking at Beth's trainers, if ghosts could get muddy.

We can't, said Beth, foregoing speech and funnelling her answer right into his brain. It was an uncanny experience – like trying on bone conduction headphones for the first time – and it made him jump. A nearby family wheeled their children away from the strange, fidgety man.

I didn't know you could read minds, he thought.

Only when I want to, funnelled Beth.

In that case, thought Joel, can you not? It's freaking me out.

'Sure,' she said. 'Is this better for you?'

'Much,' he said, as he marched up and over a mound. 'I'd rather people think I'm talking to myself than have you going through the drawers of my inner thoughts every thirty seconds.'

'Oh, I'll still be going through those drawers, don't you worry,' laughed Beth. 'But I'll try and be a bit more subtle about it.'

'Thanks,' said Joel, trying to make his gratitude sound genuine when it was swaddled in a delicate layer of pain. He'd assumed having his girlfriend brought back to life would involve a spot of shagging and a lot of reminiscing over the good times they'd had together but, so far, all they'd done was chat about death. He supposed that was his fault for asking in the first place, but it was starting to feel like getting visited by the ghost of Christmas past without any of the festive bells and whistles.

The sun hadn't hinted at making an appearance and Joel was relieved by this bit of pathetic fallacy. At least the set designers had got the memo. Hampstead Heath didn't look right in the sunshine. It was too cheerful and there were far too many loved-up couples setting down picnic blankets and eating expensive olives. On dreary days like this, the Heath came into its own – it brooded and scowled and went on seemingly forever in every direction you looked. It was a fitting place to go for a weekend walk with a ghost.

'It was quick,' said Beth, standing by Joel as he looked out over the figure of Henry Moore's *Two Piece Reclining Figure No.5*, which erupted like a bog creature from its plinth in the mud surrounding Kenwood House. At first glance, the sculpture appeared to be nothing but two amorphous chunks of stone, but the longer Joel stared at it, the more human it seemed to become, as if it were alive and sighing before his eyes.

'How quick?'

'Very quick. Like blowing out the last candle in a pitch-black room.'

'Poetic. And did it hurt?'

'No.'

'No?'

'No.'

The sculpture was supposedly of someone split in two. Or what was left of a someone. Joel saw frustration in every tautly flexed muscle that rose from its plinth in a conflicted state of movement and stasis. 'Moore's metal creature is constantly yearning, craving to be alive yet eternally and tragically cut short in its incompleteness' was the kind of thing Joel would write in a GCSE paper on the topic.

'And it wasn't like I couldn't see after that candle was extinguished, either,' continued Beth, her voice barely above a whisper, 'it was just that all I could see after that was darkness. I could still see, you know – my eyes still worked. But there was nothing *to see*. If that makes sense? It was as if I was surrounded by four walls of shadow that were always out of reach, no matter how far I stretched my arms. It wasn't like a darkness I'd ever experienced before. It felt thicker. Deeper. It felt personal.'

The vertically orientated torso-looking half of the sculpture and horizontally orientated arse-looking part reminded Joel of a pantomime horse. The unreality of the sculpture made him skip past wondering *what* Henry Moore was trying to say with his art to *why* he was trying to say it in the first place. What was the point?

'And then what happened?' asked Joel.

'Someone turned on the big light,' said Beth.

Joel peeled his eyes off the sculpture and took a long, hard look at Beth. Back when they'd been together, and both alive, Joel had sometimes felt as if he was only half of a person when he wasn't with her. He was more like the person he wanted to be when they were together. He was more charming. More intelligent. More Joel. She completed him in so many ways. And, after she'd died, he felt like a severed torso dragging itself from room to room. A part that would never be whole again.

'It's just a sculpture, Joel,' said Beth. She turned stiffly and strutted away at a pace most Olympic race walkers would be envious of. It took him a solid ten seconds to realise he was meant to be following her.

Grave Encounters

The cemetery was an excellent excuse to say lots of old names out loud. Agnes. Fanny. Horace. Gwyneth. Edmund. Joel and Beth had visited Highgate together on a handful of occasions, relishing the opportunity to stroll beside each other and murmur the most peculiar names at a volume only they could discern. The first time they'd gone to Highgate had been as part of a month-long mission to visit all of the 'Magnificent Seven' cemeteries in London. It was a cute date idea which had morphed into something they'd committed to perhaps a little too seriously.

As well as offering a chance for them to speak about the prospect of death openly and honestly with each other – it's amazing what comes up when there aren't any screens or steaming plates of food to lead the conversation – traipsing around the city's graveyards had been a nice way for Beth and Joel to see parts of London they wouldn't otherwise have visited. Sometimes, in the case of Nunhead Cemetery, for the better. Other times, as with West Norwood Cemetery, for the worse. Highgate was positioned somewhere in the top half of the cemetery rankings. Joel thought the way it was split into two separate cemeteries was a neat touch. Beth thought the toll you had to pay to walk among the dead was considerably less neat.

According to the brochure Joel had grabbed at the entrance, there were approximately 170,000 people buried in over 53,000 graves across the west and east cemeteries. If his maths was correct – which it rarely was – that meant there were about 117,000 bodies buried there without a grave. Either that, or numerous bodies had been forced to share graves. Joel wasn't sure which of these, if either, was true, but the image of thousands of coffins stacked on top of one another like sardine tins on a supermarket shelf made him shiver.

Being wedged under your parents and their parents and their parents' parents was no way to spend eternity, he thought. According to the brochure, grave space in the cemetery could only be purchased for an 'imminent funeral'.

'It is not possible to purchase grave space in advance unless you are over eighty years of age or terminally ill,' said the brochure in a rather stately manner. Joel read that sentence out to Beth.

'Speaking as someone from "beyond the grave", that sounds pretty fair,' she replied, with a hint of amusement in her voice. 'Did you ever have any grand plans to get me buried here?'

'I did think about it,' admitted Joel, 'but June was extremely insistent we cremate you and then chuck a gravestone in Kensal Green Cemetery next to your nan.

She didn't want your energy trapped underground.' Joel's arms moved towards his middle in an attempt to mime a feeling of entrapment. To every guest in the cemetery curious about the man babbling away to himself, it simply looked like he had a particularly bad stomach ache.

'She felt it would be better if your particles were allowed to spread as far and wide as possible,' he added, stretching his arms out theatrically at the word 'wide'. It was a gesture that made a Leica-toting tourist snapping photos of a nearby headstone flinch.

'That sounds about right,' said Beth. While the chance to rub elbows with Douglas Adams and George Eliot was enticing, Beth figured her physical body would have felt claustrophobic cooped up down there anyway. Much better for your bones to be burned to dust, she thought.

They continued to amble around the cemetery, millipeding their way around the queue of teenagers waiting to take selfies with Karl Marx's head and taking in their surroundings. Joel continued to nervously consult his emotional support brochure, searching for some interesting titbit of information, and told Beth about a £40 grave-search service the cemetery offered.

'What's included in a grave search?' asked Beth.

Joel brought the brochure close to his face so the letters on the page went from inky and vague to sharp as cut glass. Beth had always said he reminded her of Penfold from *Danger Mouse* whenever he tried to read her something out loud. 'It says here the package includes a search of the register, a copy of the entry in the burial register, digital photographs of the grave, a copy of the original cemetery map showing the location of the grave, a map showing the location in the context of the cemetery as a whole, and an appointment for you and up to three others to be accompanied to the grave.'

'Does it mention at all whether you need to know the person whose grave it is you're looking for?'

Joel furrowed his brow and returned his nose to the brochure for a second consultation.

'No,' he said, 'it doesn't mention anything about that.'

'So you can just, like, give them the name of a random person who's buried here and they'll give you the full shebang?'

Joel looked down for a third and final time, mainly for comedic effect but also — in part — to make sure he wasn't actually missing out on any crucial morsel of information the brochure could use to defend its honour.

'Yep, looks like it,' he said, beaming, after he found nothing to contradict Beth's assumption. He swung his head back up from the brochure and shimmied his glasses up his nose.

Looking at the way the light danced in his swimming-pool-blue eyes, Beth couldn't help but break out into a gappy smile. She remembered the first night he'd touched her, and how wet she'd been. She remembered biting his earlobe so hard, pinching its soft flesh between her incisors, that they'd had to stop to make sure it wasn't bleeding. She remembered everything.

And although she didn't know why she was able to interact with Joel again, or what had brought her back to him, she couldn't ignore how much she'd loved the man when she was alive. Or how violently she wanted to forget how much she had loved him now that she wasn't. Beth wanted nothing more than to be able to reach out and touch him: to lay a hand on his cheek and feel the warmth of his face beneath her hand. But she couldn't. It wasn't like the way it was impossible for her to physically pick up a coffee cup or place a sheet over her head to spook strangers. What was holding her back from embracing him and kissing him and trying to finish off the job she'd started on his earlobes all those years ago was the uncertainty of how much damage she might inflict on him every time she touched him.

A dangerous energy coursed beneath her skin, a prickling current desperately seeking a target. When she'd hugged Joel in the flat, she'd known it was a mistake. The guilt weighed on her before she'd even acted, as if she were committing a sin hardwired into her, but she hadn't thought it would cause any real harm. The twenty minutes he'd sat there holding his head in his hands had been agonising. She knew she hadn't killed him — Beth was an expert on what dead people looked like, and that much was obvious. But she wasn't sure about the lasting damage of what she'd done. Had she short-circuited him and given him the equivalent of, say, ten concussions? Would he end up raddled by dementia at the age of forty, all because she'd wanted a hug? Beth had no way of knowing. So she vowed to resist physical contact with Joel and focus on whatever it was she'd been brought back to do. Because she knew she had to do *something*, right?

She couldn't explain it properly to Joel – also, she didn't want him thinking he was Jimmy fucking Stewart – but there must be some reason she could think and feel and walk and talk again. She just didn't know what it was. Or what she was. Was she a ghost? A phantom? Or was she a sack of leftover energy – a sort-of mass of sort-of somethingness that just so happened to look exactly like how she had back when she was alive? Maybe it would have been easier if she'd been brought back as a floating orb or something equally vague, she thought. At least that way Joel wouldn't keep making puppy-dog eyes at her every two minutes.

With every passing second, her exhaustion deepened, and the only thing she knew for certain was she didn't want to be in the land of the living for much longer. Breaking that to Joel, of course, wouldn't be easy. She could tell he'd already become accustomed to having her around again. He was far too comfortable spending his Sunday with someone who was, by every metric, as dead as a doornail.

Just as she was in the process of working out how she was going to politely tell Joel something that would ruin his life all over again, Beth realised he'd stopped staring at her with his big blue eyes. He had shifted his attention to his phone.

Nearly Departed

'Who's that?' she asked.

'Who's who?' he said, putting his phone back into his pocket a little too quickly.

'Who's the "who" who messaged you just now? God, I sound like an owl, don't I?'

Beth narrowed her eyes, trying to look jokey about it and loading her voice with forced merriment.

She knew she shouldn't, but she couldn't stop herself from sneakily funnelling into his thoughts. Apparently he was under the impression she was trying to friend-zone him – and, in classic Joel fashion, was wondering if he was the first person to ever be friend-zoned by a resurrected corpse.

'Is it Alice?' she continued, deciding to keep her mind-reading to herself for now. 'I always thought you guys had chemistry . . .'

'It's not Alice,' said Joel, perhaps a little too quickly once again.

Shit, he thought, as Beth listened in. Now Beth will think it *was* Alice who'd texted him. She'd think he'd had a thing for her for years and had only been dating Beth in the first place because Alice's boyfriend, James, had always been in the picture. Which wasn't true in the slightest. Or, even if it was, wasn't a truth he was actively cognisant of.

Beth decided to put him out of his misery. Don't worry, Joel, she funnelled. I know it's not Alice. I can hop into your head whenever I like, remember? So, who's Nina?

'I don't know,' said Joel. 'At least not really. Not yet.

And please, for God's sake, don't just jump into my head like that. It's not fair.'

'Okay,' she said. 'I'm sorry. From here on in, I promise to stay completely out of your head and only listen to what you're comfortable telling me. All right?'

'Thanks,' he said, 'I appreciate it.'

'But seeing as we're making promises,' she said, with a knowing smile, 'do you remember what you promised me all those years ago?'

Joel sighed. 'I do.'

Days left to fall in love: 11

Puttanesca

Once they were back in his flat, Joel recounted the two brief-but-memorable encounters he'd had with Nina, punctuating his reportage with a sigh that came deep from the dingy basement of his diaphragm.

'It sounds like you're pretty serious about her,' said Beth.

'We're not at that stage yet,' said Joel, 'but I do think I'm pretty serious about potentially getting pretty serious about her.'

His heart thumped erratically, as if it were a stubborn baby kicking against the confines of its mother's womb, every time he thought of Nina. Her name pressed the shape of itself up against his aorta, its four letters gently pulsing inside his chest. It was your classic puppy-love crush. But Joel was no stranger to heartbreak, and he couldn't help but wonder if he was setting himself up for another fall. They'd only met twice, after all. Was he actually as smitten with her as he thought, or was he simply grasping at the idea of love? And where did Beth fit into all this? Because if Nina's name was leaving baby-sized footprints on his heart, then Beth was stomping on it with size twelve Timberlands.

Although he'd been walking around with Beth as though everything was fine, as though not a day had passed since the woman he'd once loved had been reduced to a mangled corpse on the tarmac, the demands of Joel's normal life were scratching at the door.

The sun was sinking low in the sky, casting long shadows across the city streets, and the thought of a nine-hour workday weighed heavily on his mind. It was a surreal experience, trying to act like his world hadn't been flipped by Beth's resurrection. It was enough to make him want to scream into the void, but instead, he buried his emotions deep down and knitted his brow. He would carry on as if nothing had changed.

Joel entered his flat and flicked on the lights using the first knuckle of his index finger. Had he not already laid the groundwork of faking an illness earlier in the day, he would have been firmly in the grip of the Sunday scaries.

Joel: Hey Sabine, sorry to message on a Sunday but I'm not feeling so hot right now. Think I've caught a bug or something?? I'll try my best to make it in tomorrow but I thought you should know.

She hadn't responded yet but Joel was hopeful his tall tale would be enough to buy another day of catching Beth up on his life. While he waited for his phone to buzz with Sabine's verdict, he started his daily dinner-making routine.

'What do you fancy?' he asked, turning to Beth while he used a wooden spoon as a makeshift microphone.

Nearly Departed

'I don't fancy anything,' she said. 'I'm dead, remember? I'm past the point of fancying anything anymore.'

The way she said 'anything' seemed pointed but Joel wouldn't let that dampen his mood. He'd put on his 'Eating' playlist and he felt like pretending, even if it was only for thirty minutes, that he was a normal man cooking a normal dinner for his normal girlfriend.

He missed the aching normality of his life with Beth. Cooking for her had been one of his favourite things to do. Even if he'd had a shitty day at work, the ability to come home and lose himself for an hour or two in slicing and simmering was enough to pull him out of a slump. He found cooking therapeutic, and providing Beth with a bit of corporeal joy as a result of that therapy made it an even more worthwhile pursuit in his eyes.

Nothing had given Joel a greater pleasure than placing a heaped plate of pasta in front of Beth, resting a hand on the back of her neck, and fiddling with the television remote to find something suitably forgettable to watch while they ate. Maybe that was the hunter inside him rearing his neanderthal head. Maybe it was just his way of showing love. Joel wasn't into any macho alpha Joe Rogan bullshit but he enjoyed the feeling of providing sustenance to Beth, of feeling like he was capable of giving her something tangible (dinner) as well the intangibles (love, affection, etc.). Cooking Beth a meal that made her reach out for seconds was almost as satisfying to him as giving her an orgasm that left her gasping for breath.

'But if you were alive, what would you want to eat right now?'

He watched Beth chew over that question for a minute as he wrapped his apron strings around his stomach, then picked up a dishcloth from the counter and hung it over the loop of his apron for quick and easy clean-hands access. He knew seeing him take the ritual of cooking seriously never failed to turn her on. One time, following two negronis and a caponata, she'd insisted on calling Joel 'chef' during sex. 'Yes, chef,' she'd moaned as Joel filled her mouth with his penis, and they'd both collapsed into a heap of naked laughter.

Beth said, 'Puttanesca.'

Joel said, 'Perfect.'

While Beth hopped onto the counter, kicking her heels gently against the cabinets, Joel started getting all of his ducks in a row. Sorting out the chopping, dicing and general assembly of each ingredient he'd be using before he started cooking was a habit Joel had picked up when working as a kitchen porter at his local pub. Beth watched as he finely chopped a bunch of parsley, white-knuckling the greens in his left hand while his right controlled the knife. He glanced up to find her watching him with affection as he gently removed the lid of every tin he intended to transform into dinner.

He'd almost gone for a whole pack of spaghetti – the measure he and Beth would sometimes get through if they'd had a particularly long day – but he remembered, at the last moment, that Beth didn't have a stomach anymore. Half a pack would do.

With the pasta boiling away, Joel dropped four anchovies into a screaming hot frying pan along with finely chopped garlic and a heaped teaspoon of chilli flakes. The mixture sizzled furiously as he stirred, breaking down the whiskery anchovy spines with a wooden spoon. After a minute, he poured in a tin of plum tomatoes, mashing them into a rich sauce with the back of his now crimson-stained spoon before throwing in two tablespoons of capers and olives. He liked salt.

Right on cue, Joel's phone made a noise and after cleaning his hands using his crotch-level tea towel like an NFL quarterback, he pulled his phone out to see what it wanted from him.

Sabine: Oh God. Sorry to hear that! There's definitely something going around. Don't come in tomorrow if you're not up to it.

Mission accomplished, thought Joel. He let the tomatoes cook down for a couple of minutes before he looked up at Beth who was still sitting on the counter, transfixed, and added a ladle of starchy pasta water to the sauce. He didn't know the exact science behind adding pasta water to a sauce but he knew it made it thicker and glossier like the coat of a well-fed Irish setter.

He drained the pasta through a colander, its metal feet teetering dangerously on the sink's edge, then transported the tangle of spaghetti into the saucepan, moving it around to coat each noodle in a good lick of hot red sauce. His stomach rumbled as the aroma of garlic filled the small kitchen, a reminder of how long it had been since he'd last eaten.

He plated up a generous serving, added an extra sprinkle of parsley for colour, and 'Voilà,' he said. 'Dinner is served!' But as he turned to take that Matterhorn of carbohydrates into the living room, he realised Beth had vanished.

Around The World

Alice was one of the smartest people Joel knew. Even at university, she'd been at the top of her class and no one – including Alice herself – was surprised when she came out with a first. Joel wasn't sure whether it was in spite of, or because of, Alice's intelligence that she had a mean competitive streak. Perhaps growing up as an only child without any healthy sibling rivalry had left her starved of competition.

Whether it was a high-stakes pub quiz or a casual game of Perudo at the dinner table, Alice played to win. She'd even compete to win in activities that weren't inherently winnable, like conversations or karaoke, and sulked when things didn't go her way. Joel, on the other hand, wasn't fussed about winning. More often than not, he would lose whatever game he was playing because he simply didn't care as much as the other people involved.

Joel's dad, like any proud Welshman, had had visions of his son becoming a professional rugby player. Nothing would have made him happier than watching his boy bellow out 'Bread of Heaven' at the Millennium Stadium. But those dreams had crumbled before Joel had even hit double digits. His tag rugby coach had howled commands until his face turned crimson, demanding push-ups and piety from his nine-year-old minions, but Joel had met each order with a nonchalant 'Why bother?' Team sports just weren't for him.

Being with Alice, however, brought out a more competitive side to Joel. Their personalities collided in a way that made any match-up between them surprisingly entertaining to watch. Something about the way Alice became even more riled than usual due to Joel's relative lack of combativeness always ended up making him more into whatever they were playing.

'I don't know why I even bothered with uni,' said Alice, after she launched a dart cleanly into the treble-six segment of the board, 'I should have become a professional darts player.'

'I don't think professional darts players play Around the World,' said Joel, pulling each dart out of the board by its plastic flight like carrots from the ground. He shuffled back behind the white line on the floor, worn faint by years of tread, and lined up his next throw.

With his right arm cocked in a playing-the-maracas stance, Joel gripped the dart between his thumb and forefinger as if it were a hefty joint. Before he sent it off on its journey, he rocked his arm back and forth, stabbing at the air to gain some momentum and feel for the movement. Neither Alice nor Joel were particularly good at darts and, because of their similarly low skill level, every game they played ended up ridiculously close. The two often missed the board entirely but, somehow, every match came down to the wire.

Joel's dart lurched towards its intended target, the segment filed under the number seven, before dipping at the last second and landing in the dark and mysterious black of the board. 'This might be a long game,' he said to Alice, and asked her if she wanted another pint. 'Go on,' she said. And with that green light, he pushed his way through to the bar.

He was surprised at how busy the pub was for a Monday night. Located right opposite Alice's flat, it was an average boozer that resembled just about every other average boozer in the city. It had a decent range of beer on the taps, it had hot food, and it had a pool table and dartboard. If the pub hadn't been located literally a couple of yards from James and Alice's front door, Joel was fairly confident they'd never have stepped foot inside.

Lately, though, the pub had started becoming a lot busier. A lot cooler. They had a Korean small-plates pop-up there every Saturday and Sunday, and rumour had it members of a currently charting indie band used the pub as their local. Joel would much rather they left it alone. He hated how much of a sheep he felt in crowded places. Not simply because the feeling of getting herded towards an IPA tap made him feel physically uncomfortable, but because it was in busy rooms like these that he was able to notice how much of a slave to the latest trends he was.

Even during his short walk to the bar, Joel spied at least four other men wearing navy chore jackets that were nearly identical to his. Two others were wearing replicas of the small red beanie he also owned but was saving for the cooler months of the year. Was he surprised? No. But he still couldn't help feeling mildly ridiculous ordering a pint of Guinness and a pint of lager next to two men dressed exactly the same as him. It was like the three of them were on a stag do and the theme was 'men in their late twenties who work in marketing'. Joel felt sheepish as he wheeled those pints, one wearing a subpar shamrock on its head, back to the dartboard where Alice was waiting patiently, thumbing through her phone.

'Cheers,' said Alice, taking her lager and raising her glass towards him.

'Cheers,' said Joel, as he met her glass halfway with a satisfying dink.

'To Beth?' asked Alice.

Joel paused his pint. Alice hadn't been all that close to Beth and he knew she wasn't convinced he'd actually seen her the other day. This was, however, her way of extending an olive branch to him – of reaching out and letting him know she knew what was on his mind.

He nodded. 'To Beth.'

Toast made, the two of them got back to the business of making slow but steady progress around the dartboard. Thankfully, no one else was waiting to play; Joel and Alice could take as much time as they pleased to finish up. 'As much time as they pleased' turned out to be an hour and a half. Alice won the game eventually, striking the board plum at eleven as last orders were called, but Joel didn't mind too much. He might have lost the game but he'd won an evening of friendship – a statement so cloyingly cheesy he promised himself he would never let Alice know he'd ever thought it in the first place. Drunk on beer and a lack of dinner, he excused himself to use the bathroom for the sixth time that night.

Whenever Joel used a public toilet, he worried about the prospect of the person at the urinal next to him trying to start up a conversation. He had nightmares about burly men turning towards him with their burly eyes and asking, burlily, if he'd 'had a good night?' How was he supposed to respond to that? Was there literally anything to say other than a reticent: 'Yeah, good, mate. You?' All Joel wanted to do was stare at his penis in peace while it did what it needed to do. The last thing he wanted to do when he was pissing on a strawberry-scented urinal cake was have a chat with a stranger.

The lights overhead flickered as he doused his face with successive handfuls of cold water from the tap. Unlike the imaginary cattle prod, this was a more physical activity Joel used to wake himself up and get his mind back on track. He made sure to run cold water over his wrists, too, remembering something he'd read in a waiting-room copy of *New Scientist* about it being the most efficient way to cool down.

Staring at his reflection in the mirror, he deliberated whether he should bring up his toilet-related anxiety with Doctor Shah during their next session. He'd already brought up a lot of the problems he had with his physical appearance. Surveying the face they'd been staring at for twenty-eight years, Joel's eyes jotted down every issue they had with how he looked. For the sake of parity, they started with themselves. His eyes were so blue that no one would take them seriously. They were the eyes of a child, the eyes of 'pretty please, Mummy', and looked out of place on a full-grown man. Wedged between those too-blue orbs, his nose sloped lazily to the left-hand side of his face. It wasn't without a certain Roman charm but it was too crooked to be considered symmetrical and nowhere near crooked enough to be considered rugged. His top lip, printed just below his nose, was far too thin and looked like it'd lost out at every mealtime to its fatter, bottom-lip brother. His teeth were straight but stained from years of coffee. His hair, albeit thinning around the temples, was not a major cause for concern just yet.

Joel dried his hands on the backs of his jeans and strode back into the mass of people nursing their last pint of the night. The matey twang of Oasis had taken over the speakers and a group of suited men and women had started a small singalong while racking up lines in a secluded nook of the pub. They didn't sound half bad. Most of them could hold a tune and Joel briefly thanked the British school system for forcing hymns on its youth. Little could the men who'd written those songs have predicted that endless rounds of 'Shine Jesus Shine' would perfectly prepare the children of the nation for ketty music festivals and late-night karaoke sessions.

Alice had told him to meet her outside because she wanted to tell him something 'important', and that's where he found her, leaning against the wall of the pub. Before Joel could ask Alice what was on her mind and how she

Nearly Departed

was planning to get home – a joke he made every time they visited this pub – his thinking was interrupted.

'Fancy seeing you here,' said a voice that beamed in from somewhere to the right of Joel's head. It was a familiar voice. A woman's voice. Low and husky, like cigarettes and honey.

Joel's lips, loosened by the four pints of Guinness he'd got through, parted in disbelief as he looked up and saw Nina standing by a table outside. One hand rested on her hip, and she held a dewy gin and tonic in the other. It was a calculatedly relaxed posture – one she'd obviously thought about long and hard in an attempt to convince Joel she hadn't thought about it at all. And it worked. 'Fucking hell,' he mumbled, unable to mask his admiration.

Alice sprang up and introduced herself to Nina, their conversation quick and easy. Joel couldn't help but marvel at how effortlessly women could make friends, forming bonds in a cluster of seconds. Joel had lost count of the number of times Beth had returned from the women's toilet at a club with a brand-new best friend she'd then spent the entire night dancing with before promptly forgetting about forever. Men were less good at being friendly. Meeting someone new usually involved a Mexican standoff of handshakes with neither party keen to be too friendly until they were certain the other was all right, actually.

Although Joel had faith that male friendships were somehow more resilient than female friendships, able to endure years of silence before being picked up right where they'd left off, he still felt self-conscious whenever he reached out to Sam and asked if he wanted to 'have dinner or something'. Mainly because Joel felt like it was always him who was doing the reaching out. Sam seemed content to pass memes and texts back and forth for eternity; that appeared to be enough connection for him to keep the fire of their friendship burning, while Joel craved more face-to-face time. When they did meet up, though, it was like nothing had changed. Sure, there would be a couple of awkward minutes at the start as they found their footing, but once they got back into the rhythm of conversation, everything flowed as if no time had passed.

'So, how have you been?' asked Joel when his lips got over the shock of seeing Nina in a public space. In all honesty, he shouldn't have been surprised. He knew she lived nearby and didn't exactly hate pints. But he'd never imagined their paths would cross like this. Especially not when he was down to his least-attractive pair of underwear – the sort that made you pray no one, under any circumstances, would ever see them – and sporting a haircut that hadn't been tended to in the best part of a month. That general feeling of oh-I-wasn't-expecting-this, combined with the whiplash of having seen and interacted with a very dead Beth over the previous couple of days, left Joel rattled. As a man who liked to plan, Joel had not pencilled talking to Nina tonight into his agenda.

'I'm good, thanks,' said Nina. 'I've been out for post-work drinks. This is Dan,' she said, gesturing to the man standing next to her, 'who might make the leap from colleague to acquaintance tonight, if he's lucky.'

Dan laughed politely. Joel laughed less politely. And as

Nearly Departed

Dan mumbled something or other back at Nina at a volume neither Joel nor Alice could properly decipher, Joel couldn't help but notice how much Dan looked and acted like a Dan. He was wearing the exact clothes you'd expect a Dan to wear, plaid shirt and whatnot, and had such a Dan-ish haircut it was almost distracting. Joel was chewing on the stark difference between a Danish and a Dan-ish haircut when Dan decided to turn up the volume.

'I've actually got to head home now,' he said. 'Work tomorrow and all that, you know. It was great to meet you guys!'

As Dan gave Nina a hug and walked off cradling his phone like a treasure map, Joel felt a pang of guilt for judging Dan too quickly. He'd been rash in writing him off as a bit of a wet wipe but the way Dan had said, 'It was great to meet you' had rung through Joel like a church bell. Because he'd meant it. He'd actually fucking meant it. Dan had said it was great to meet Joel and Alice because he genuinely did, deep down in his heart, think it was great to meet new people. Joel wasn't exactly a nihilist but he lacked the Labrador sincerity Dan seemed to possess so naturally.

'Nice guy,' said Joel, who was instantly stunned at how much he meant what he said. Maybe this sincerity stuff was rubbing off on him, after all. Nina took a puff of her rollie and blew it into the night. It mingled in the air with the smell of spilled beer and aftershave.

'Right, okay,' said Alice, 'Joel lives quite nearby. Don't you, Joel?'

Joel nodded, still too distracted by Dan's charm to verbalise a response.

'Maybe he could walk you home?'

As Alice's mouth made the pleasant 'o' of 'home', she nudged Joel forward towards Nina.

'Yes,' said Joel, finally bringing his brain back up to pace, 'I live quite nearby and maybe I could walk you home.'

'Maybe you could,' smiled Nina. 'It'd be good to catch up.'

Alice bid them both a good night and they watched as she crossed the street and went straight into her building, bounding up the stairs with the grace of a drunken antelope.

'You can totally walk home alone, if you want,' said Joel. 'Alice can be a little . . . pushy, at times.'

'She seems great,' said Nina. 'And besides,' she added, as she walked down the road and looked back at Joel, 'I could use the company.'

Days left to fall in love: 10

A Skulk Of Foxes

It was 11 p.m. and the moon was round and full. It had swelled to such a size in the dark summer sky it seemed almost in danger of bursting and dripping molten silver onto the stars below. Two foxes skittered by at speed, startling Joel for a second before he realised what they were. Maybe they were the same foxes that wouldn't stop having sex outside his window. Lucky foxes, in that case.

'Do you remember the first time you saw a fox?' asked Nina.

He did. It had happened when he was thirteen, walking home after dinner at Calum Price's house. They'd all sat down at the table, said a half-hearted prayer about being thankful to Jesus, and eaten spaghetti bolognese while watching *Strictly Come Dancing*. Circling the bowl with a rhombus of garlic bread to catch the last tomatoey dregs of bolognese was Joel's favourite part of the meal. He liked going round to Calum's house because Calum had an Xbox and his mother, Pat, would give him a hug when he arrived. She smelled like Parma Violets.

Thirteen-year-old Joel had stopped dead in his tracks when he saw that fox staring at him in the middle of the road. He knew what it was, obviously. He'd seen plenty of photos and videos of foxes, and had watched Disney's *Robin Hood* enough times growing up to have had some fairly dubious dreams involving the fox version of Maid Marian, but he'd never seen one in person until that night. Its eyes reflected the light from a streetlamp, shining out at him like two glass marbles.

'That sounds pretty magical,' said Nina.

'It sort of was,' agreed Joel. 'What about you?'

'I think it was when I went camping with my dad for the first time. I must have been around the same age you were when you saw yours – funny that, isn't it? Anyway, I remember waking up early in the morning, before anyone else was up, and unzipping my tent to let in some air. You know how tents get all stuffy even when it's freezing outside?'

Joel nodded.

'So I unzipped the . . . zip and poked my head out to have a look at what the campsite was like in the morning. It was dead quiet. I must have been, like, the only person awake in the entire place. It felt as if everyone in the whole world had upped sticks and disappeared in the night. And then, just as I was thinking about what I'd do as the last person on Earth, I heard this strange rustling sound coming from the side of the tent. It was like a metallic scratching.' Nina attempted to recreate the sound she'd heard for Joel. It sat somewhere between a cat's miaow and a pig's squeal. She even scrunched up her hands like she was a small woodland creature when she did it. It was extraordinarily endearing.

'I pushed my shoulders and arms out through the gap in the tent to see what was making the noise,' she continued, putting a relatively undesirable image of a baby being birthed into Joel's head, 'and there was this baby fox – I think they're called pups . . .'

'Pups,' repeated Joel. 'That's cute.'

'Yeah.' Nina smiled. 'And he was burrowing his little face into this empty bean tin like he hadn't eaten in days. Poor thing must have been starving.'

'So what happened then? Did you get up and feed it?'

'No,' said Nina, and her smile drifted away. 'He tilted his snout up to see me halfway out of the tent and then he shot off into the distance. I must have spooked him or something.'

'I wouldn't take it personally,' said Joel. 'He'd probably never seen a half-human, half-tent before.'

Nina gave him a furtive glance – can anything else be furtive apart from a glance? – and let a small exhale out of her nose to acknowledge his joke. Although these gestures were intended to let Joel know Nina was still present in the moment, he could tell her thoughts had gone somewhere else.

She might have been walking next to him on the pavement, right foot loyally following left, but he knew her mind was back in that field. He imagined her feeling the brown, scratchy grass sanding her palms as she watched the pup's tail sink into the treeline.

Nina murmured something.

'What?' said Joel.

'Huh?' said Nina, pulling herself back in from her memory like reeling in a kite.

'I think you said something about winking and stars?'

'Oh,' she said, looking sheepish. 'The only things that wink are people and stars. It's something my dad says quite a lot. I didn't realise I'd said it out loud. Sorry about that.'

'No, don't be. It's nice,' said Joel. 'Very poetic.'

'He'd get like that sometimes. Poetic. Especially after Mum died.'

Joel made a sound like he'd been socked in the stomach.

'I'm sorry that happened,' he said, and reached out to give Nina's hand a 'I know there's nothing I can say or do to make this better but I'm here if you want to say fuck really loud or scream or something' squeeze. He'd received enough of those squeezes over the last three years to be a relative expert at giving them.

'It's okay,' she said, giving him a polite 'thanks for that I appreciate it' squeeze in response, before letting his arm swing back down like a pendulum.

'That camping trip was the first holiday me and Dad went on together after Mum died,' she added. 'We spent the weekend talking about everything and nothing and skirting around the fact she was missing from this picture we were trying to paint of a happy family. Dad taught me all the constellations that weekend, as a distraction I think. That's when he first said that thing about stars and people winking.'

Joel gently touched her arm. 'If you do ever want to talk about it, I'd be more than happy to listen,' he said.

Nina's head bobbed in assent. It was the type of soft bob you'd do listening to a catchy pop song on the radio.

'The same goes for you,' said Nina.

Joel's head bobbed back. It was less the type of soft bob you'd do listening to a catchy pop song on the radio and more the desperate bob of a drinky bird toy.

The air was warm and pleasant and Joel enjoyed the way the headwind buffeted his face and gently tugged at Nina's curls. They walked in contented silence next to each other, not holding hands but close enough to one another that they could if they wanted to, for about five minutes.

'It was cancer, by the way,' said Nina, breaking the silence.

'Fuck,' said Joel.

'I know,' said Nina.

Their surroundings shifted violently from road to road in the way that only London scenery could, pretty mews alternating nonchalantly with council estates with no distinct separation or warning of what would appear next. It was odd to exist in a city that was so rich and yet so poor. And it was odd to sit somewhere in the middle of those two extremes, feeling both guilty and thankful about what you had.

'Cement truck,' said Joel, as they passed a billboard advertising a new app designed to make your workplace more efficient. 'She was dead before she hit the ground.'

'Fuck,' said Nina.

'I know,' said Joel.

They made the executive decision to shift the conversation away from death for the final leg of the journey. They talked about the television shows they loved to hate-watch and the books they weren't reading enough of. They talked about how they found it difficult keeping in touch with all of their friends and worried they'd end up only ever having a revolving door of colleagues to communicate with for the rest of their lives. They talked about how loud the section of the Victoria line between King's Cross and Highbury and Islington was. They talked and talked until they realised they'd already passed Nina's front door.

Looping back around to drop her off, Joel couldn't help but glow on the inside. He felt comfortable talking to Nina; it was like drinking a glass of cold water after a long run, and he was excited to be able to do it again at the weekend.

'Still on for Saturday? National Gallery?' he asked, trying his best to disguise the anxiety lacquering his throat.

'Of course,' she said, giving him a smile that turned the brightness of his vision up several notches. 'I'll see you there. Get home safe.'

Nina shut the door behind her, leaving Joel alone to marinate in the day's events. He walked back to the

Nearly Departed

road, eyes fixed on the sky, watching the clouds shift and morph like memories. Professional footballers celebrated goals by gazing up at the heavens, and Joel felt a sudden urge to thank his lucky stars in a similar fashion. Or, at the very least, get a good look at their shiny little faces. He basked in the afterglow of human contact, the lingering warmth of Nina's presence still prickling his skin. No need for headphones to fill the silence; his thoughts were loud enough.

He strutted with the assurance and swagger of a Shakespearean theatre actor for about 200 metres before he was forced to break character and double-check the maps app on his phone. Once he'd made sure he was pointing in the right direction, he stuffed his phone deep into the left-hand pocket of his jacket and prepared his feet for the rest of their journey.

'She's pretty,' said a familiar voice behind him. And Joel stopped dead in his tracks.

Back (Again)

'You can't keep ignoring me, Joel.'

He kept ignoring her. He glared at the pages of his book, an act of defiance he'd been pursuing since he'd woken up, even though the words had stopped going in hours ago. He'd been sitting in his armchair and staring, statue-like, at the same sentence for so long it had lost all meaning entirely.

There would be wild mustard on the hills.

That sentence was no longer a string of decipherable words he could hear inside his head: it was simply a thing to be gazed upon. An object to be picked up and picked at. A relatively short assembly of curves and lines – some soft and round like the shape of the letter 'o', others sharp and harsh like 'w' – that filled up his vision until his eyeballs ached. Still, he wouldn't look up. He didn't want to give Beth the satisfaction. He couldn't believe she'd made him go through the process of losing her all over again. That wasn't fucking fair.

'I know you think it's not fair,' said Beth, 'but I'm the one who's dead. You can go about drinking in pubs and talking to people. I'm stuck doing . . . this. Talking to you. You're all I've got. So please speak to me, Joel. I'm going to be awfully bored otherwise.'

'If I'm all you've got, then why did you leave me again?' said Joel, still hiding his face behind Joan Didion.

'I don't know,' said Beth. She sat down on the floor and crossed her legs, primary school-style.

'What do you mean you "don't know"?' he demanded.

She stretched out her arms towards the ceiling. 'I mean: I don't know. In the same way I don't actually understand how planes or the internet work, I don't know anything about the physics of being a ghost.'

They paused their conversation as a frantic ambulance tore along the road outside and filled the room with its high-pitched whine.

'So, you didn't do it on purpose?'

'No, I didn't.'

'But how can I believe you?'

'The same way you can believe anyone. I promise you I do not have any control over when I come or go. Scout's honour. I tried to explain that to you last night but you wouldn't listen.'

'I was upset,' barked Joel. He raised his head above the parapet of *The Year of Magical Thinking* and showed Beth his most serious 'I'm actually very upset with you' expression. It landed somewhere between a pout and a grimace. Joel wasn't a man suited to anger. Seeing a scowl on his face was like seeing a chimp in jeans – it just didn't fit.

'I know you were,' said Beth, who took advantage of the chink in Joel's emotional armour to uncross her legs and perch herself on the table. 'But I want you to know I never intended to hurt you.'

She was still wearing the same clothes she'd worn the first time she'd come back. Joel figured that must be one of the rules about ghosts. Maybe it was dictated by the same logic behind having cartoon characters wear identical outfits all the time. Did bringing Beth back in the same outfit help her animator (whoever that may be) save time by not having to cel-shade her a new set of clothes each and every time she made an appearance in the real world?

Joel wanted to stay angry at Beth but he wasn't physically capable of it. She was so beautiful it hurt. He laid his book cover-side down on the coffee table and unfolded his arms. He might not have control over how long Beth was going to be around for, but he could control what he did in the time they had together. To spend it angry at her for not being alive suddenly seemed futile. Maybe that was the point of all this – maybe Beth had returned as a walking, talking metaphor for life and how to live it. Or, then again, maybe he should get a fucking grip.

'I'm sorry for being an idiot,' he said. 'I just . . . I thought I'd lost you again.'

'It's okay,' Beth replied. 'You're allowed to feel that way, but I won't lie to you. You are going to lose me again, Joel. I can't stay here forever.'

'But what's the rush? Couldn't we have a few more years together? Crank out a couple of ghost babies?'

'I'm already late.'

'Late for what?'

Nearly Departed

'For the rest of my afterlife.'

He paced across the room and leaned out of the open window, resting his elbows on the sill and gazing into the sunny street. People bustled up and down the pavement. His eyes lingered on a teenage couple who raised their clasped hands over a postbox, refusing to let go of each other for even a moment, before vanishing around the corner.

'What's so great about being dead anyway?' Joel asked, squinting as he turned back to the room.

'It's peaceful.'

'And living isn't?'

She fixed him with a look of silent pity. He stared back.

'I'm not supposed to be here,' she said, finally.

She moved across the carpet in a small half-moon pattern and spoke with open palms. Her posture reminded Joel of the preachers who skulked around Speakers' Corner. She could say any old rubbish and it would come across as a convincing stance to take.

'I haven't got any agency over what's happening, but I know I don't want to be stuck here watching life from the sidelines.' She sighed, taking a deep breath that rattled in her chest. The sound caught Joel off guard. He had tried to remember what her sigh was like on multiple occasions over the past year. But he hadn't succeeded. It was one of those little things, like the PIN to her debit card and the name of her childhood best friend, he'd forgotten long ago.

She said, 'It's like I'm caught in a current dragging me along next to you. Or like I'm a frisbee and I can only get so far before I do a complete 180 and come gliding back to you.'

'Boomerang,' said Joel.

'What?'

'You're thinking of a boomerang, not a frisbee. Frisbees don't come back.'

'Oh, whatever,' said Beth, throwing her hands up in defeat.

Joel stood up so he could look her square in the eyes. He wondered if she could tell he was more than halfway to forgiving her.

'You packed a lot of metaphors into that little speech, Beth. I'm worried you're starting to sound like me.'

'Oh, that's nothing new,' she laughed. 'I think we merged into the same person around our three-year anniversary. Do you remember when we—'

'—both asked for the bill at the same time and did that obnoxious but unavoidable little signature gesture in the air? Yeah, I remember that. And I remember how we thought it meant we'd reached a new psychic level in our relationship.'

'Remember how bemused the waiter was that we made such a big deal about it?'

'Yeah,' said Joel. 'I guess the joke's on him now.'

After their laughter died down, Joel drew in a breath. He wanted to bury his hands in her hair, inhaling the faintly chemical yet floral scent of her shampoo as he pressed a tender kiss on her crown. As he watched Beth's smile light up her face, something inside him stirred – an animal yearning that pressed up against the glass of his ribcage, like it was trying to escape, or at least get a little closer to her. He knew he should look somewhere else, maybe get up to make a cup of tea so he could have something to do with his hands.

Beth could feel Joel's eyes boring into her body. It was a feeling she used to crave – that feeling of want and need and desire. She'd hungered for his touch, for the rush of power that coursed through her body when she took him inside her. She'd wanted to feel his beard sandpaper her neck as she aimed a calculated gasp into his ear, sending a shiver of pleasure crawling up his spine. But now all she could think about was how all that potential energy was getting wasted. Her corpse was hardly an appropriate vessel for Joel's love and she desperately needed to help him redirect that energy to somewhere where it could be more useful. Or someone. Someone it was better suited to. Someone whose heart was still beating. She knew this would probably be the ideal moment for her to show her hand, but she couldn't quite muster up the courage to let him know the truth. He looked too happy.

'So, how's Nina?' she asked.

The tractor beam pulling Joel's eyes into Beth's was switched off at the plug. He turned away quickly, embarrassed, as his face turned red. What could you possibly tell your dead ex-girlfriend about the woman you'd currently got the hots for?

Would you tell her you wished said woman was a professional podcaster so you had a non-creepy means of listening to her voice whenever you wanted? Would you tell her you'd like to potentially see said woman naked at some point and the chances weren't zero that that might eventually happen? Would you tell her you were going on a date with said woman to the National Gallery? Would it be weird to ask for some pointers? Was that a position anyone had ever been in before?

If he did ask Beth for help, Joel was certain he would become the first person in the history of human existence to get dating advice from their dead ex-girlfriend – he would be the Neil Armstrong of awkward conversations. Then again, maybe Beth already knew all about his frayed thoughts and feelings. She had, after all, come back with an obnoxious level of omniscience after she'd shuffled off her mortal coil.

'She's good,' is what Joel eventually decided on.

'Just good?'

'Yeah, just good,' he said, before adding in a flurry of staccato sentences, 'I'm actually seeing her soon. This Saturday. At the National Gallery. We're going together. It's a date.'

Joel rubbed his bearded chin, as if he were petting a small dog.

'That sounds lovely,' Beth said, beaming. 'I'm very proud of you. It's healthy, you know – getting yourself back out there. But there is one teeny, tiny problem with your plan.'

Joel looked up at her. His eyes were startled and wild.

'What's that?'

'You don't know a fucking thing about art.'

Turn Off Your Phones

The days leading up to Joel and Nina's gallery date raced by: the mornings and evenings bled into one another at the frenzied tempo of a noughties music video. Somehow, Beth's second coming had given Joel a boost of energy. A double espresso to the soul. He moved with more agency, with more verve, with more life whirring behind his eyes. He brewed cups of tea with grace and poise. He unloaded the dishwasher like a man possessed. He'd stopped being so insular and started looking outwards with a fresher perspective on life. He started watching the fucking sunset.

There are pros and cons to hanging out with a ghost, though. On the plus side, you never have to worry about your ghost needing the toilet or feeling tired or getting hungry – a ghost requires less maintenance than a colony of Sea-Monkeys in that respect. The cons, however, are a little more complicated. People look at you funny when you stare passionately into dead space and mumble things like 'Sorry, what was that?' and 'Christ, this is weird'. Waiters judge you when you ask to have two seats by the window all to yourself. Booksellers, inquisitive souls that they are, wonder who you're trying to impress when you pick up and put down a dozen hardbacks in a minute, announcing to seemingly no one that you've read them all. And, yes, it's more expensive booking two tickets to the movies but at least it means your ghost isn't forced to stand in the aisle.

The cinema enveloped them in its cool, cave-like darkness. It was quiet. Serene, even. A silence hung comfortably in the air before the surreptitious scrunches of popcorn and whispers were drowned out by an orchestra of screeching tyres and gunshots. The film was the fourth entry in a popular franchise neither Beth nor Joel were familiar with, but they had wanted to take refuge from the muggy weather outside and it had been the first screening available. The promise of air conditioning and an escape from reality for two hours was what Joel needed. Split-second shots of flexed biceps and CGI helicopters flashed over the screen.

'What's going on?' asked Beth.

'I have no idea,' muttered Joel.

In the seat in front, a woman with a shock of short, spiky blonde hair flicked her eyes, curiously. Who's he talking to?

Two of the CGI helicopters collided head-on and imploded in a mash of twisted metal. Joel resisted the urge to check his phone. Shards of glass hurtled towards his face in a way he could only presume was designed to thrill those who had paid extra to see the film in 3D.

'Are you actually enjoying this?' hissed Beth.

'Shut up,' said Joel.

Nearly Departed

'Who? Me?' said the blonde, swivelling around. Her jaw went stiff.

'No, sorry. Not you. Her,' said Joel, tilting his head to the empty seat on his left.

'Me?' cried Beth.

'Yes,' said Joel. He turned from Beth to the blonde in front. There was a confused pause.

'Yes what?' said the blonde.

'No, nothing,' said Joel as a man emerged from the helicopter wreckage, miraculously unscathed except for his sleeves, which looked to have taken the brunt of the damage. The torn fabric unveiled a pair of arms glistening with sweat.

'You've got to remember that I'm dead,' said Beth.

Joel flinched. She looked at him as though she was seeing him with a fresh pair of eyes. 'You're going to end up sectioned if you keep arguing with yourself in public.'

'Yes, I probably am.'

'Is everything okay?' asked the blonde. Her eyebrows were knitted in confusion.

'I don't know,' said Joel. He mumbled a quick apology to the kinks in her platinum hair before picking up his bag and hunching his way down the aisle and out of the cinema.

Days left to fall in love: 8

Short Back And Sides

It didn't take Joel long to figure out one of the few places he could talk to himself for a couple of hours, with no questions asked, was the pub. When he'd worked in the kitchen at his local, there'd been a regular who used to sit and drink exactly four pints of Stella by himself every single Sunday. They used to call him 'Clockwork'. And 'that old cunt'. Joel had always felt sorry for Clockwork, dressed as he had been in a three-piece tweed suit regardless of the weather, and he'd felt sad whenever he'd caught Clockwork mumbling to himself in the corner. But now? Now he was finally starting to understand where Clockwork had been coming from. More people were haunted than you'd think.

Tuesday greeted Joel with a hangover that was worse than it had any right to be, hammering his temples and gluing his parched mouth shut. The man on the news said it was the hottest day of the summer. Joel flashed his sun-strained eyes around the room, feeling the thick, stuffy air envelop him. Seeking respite from the heat and his pounding head, he dragged himself out of bed and went for a walk along the path tracing the Regent's Canal. It seemed like everyone in the city had had the same idea; ducks paddled lazily and sun-kissed bodies lounged along the water's edge. They were halfway to Islington when Beth managed to convince Joel to stop outside the mesmerising red and white stripes of a barber's pole, saying a haircut would give him a confidence boost before his date with Nina.

The barber's thick, hairy forearms were attached to thick, hairy hands which wielded a pair of scissors leopard-spotted with rust. Every minute, Joel would crane his neck to stare at Beth with panicked eyes and the barber, grappling Joel's head in one of his meaty paws, would twist it back to centre like it was a wind-up toy. This went on for the entire duration of the haircut. Joel was convinced the bastard burned him with his hairdryer on purpose.

The barber then dusted Joel's head like it was a priceless artefact, sending plumes of talcum powder into the air, as Beth read an ancient copy of *FHM* over someone's shoulder. Joel knew what happened next. He would be shown the back of his head in a greasy hand mirror and he would have to pretend he liked what he saw even though the only thought running through his head would be: yes, that is the back of my head.

As Joel put his glasses on and twisted his head to get a better look at what he was about to part with £15 for, he felt his heart sink. The mirror didn't show him an image of an immaculately groomed man but a man who had the naked and vulnerable look of a freshly shorn sheep. A cold breeze whistled above his ears and his eyes made notes of moles he'd never even known he had. He was distraught. He'd been scalped. So, of course, he said the only thing you could say in a situation like that.

'Yeah, no, it's perfect – cheers, mate.'

Beth looked in silence at Joel, who brushed small clumps of hair off his shoulders and looked back at her with a forced smile. She raised her eyebrows and then gave him a double thumbs up. He gave her a sarcastic thumb back and the barber, who was counting out coins at a lethargic pace Joel knew was intended to make him tell him to 'keep the change', looked momentarily regretful about burning this obviously absent-minded man.

Shopping raised similar problems. At first, Joel was put off by everyone's constant staring, but by and by he got used to the attention. People must think I'm a maniac, he thought, looking at the queue of people waiting for him to finish consulting Beth on the 'ideal silhouette' as he clumsily rifled through a pile of trousers. Still, at least he wasn't alone. Anything was better than being alone again.

He shot a glare at a helpful-looking young man, his bright red name tag revealing he was Nathan. He wanted to explain himself to Nathan. He wanted to tell Nathan he was talking to his girlfriend, whose calming voice made everything she said feel like a cool breeze through an open window. And it was a shame, he thought, that he was the only person who could enjoy the gentle rustle of her company. He used to adore being seen with Beth in public – it made him feel like a vital part of some greater tapestry or story, affirming his reason for existing to the outside world.

Two teenagers were talking about Joel, loudly, behind his back. He could feel their eyes drilling holes into the patch of sweat between his shoulder blades. His face burned with embarrassment.

'Who does he keep talking to?' whispered one.

'Fuck knows,' muttered the other.

Straightening up and casually patting his wallet to make sure it was where he thought it was, Joel made a shameful beeline to the changing room.

'What do you think?' said Joel, tugging at a pair of navy trousers that pooled in a puddle at his feet. He plunged both of his hands into his pockets before taking them out and dipping the right one back in. With his dominant hand still buried deep in his pocket, Joel executed a 360-degree turn as if he was a ready meal in a microwave, trying to inspect himself from every possible angle.

'How do they look?' he asked Beth, who sat beside him on a stack of discarded clothes.

A sound interrupted him – a shrill voice that sounded worn down and hollowed out by the trials of working in retail.

'We're not allowed to come into the dressing rooms, sir.'

The voice had come from behind the thin grey curtain hanging in front of the cubicle, a semi-porous partition which separated Joel's half-naked body from the rest of the room. It wasn't the first time the voice had interjected. Roughly five minutes earlier, the same hollow voice had asked Joel if he was 'all okay in there, sir?' after he'd got a bit too enthusiastic about the quality of their linen shirts.

'I wasn't talking to you!' shouted Joel.

'Of course not, sir,' said the voice.

Hot Desking

How long had Joel been standing there, staring into the eyes of a red-faced giant whose bulging neck veins resembled a spaghetti junction? Had it been thirty seconds? A minute? Five minutes?

'You're a straight shooter, Foster,' barked Peter Barette, finally breaking the silence and patting Joel firmly on the back with his shovel-sized hand. Joel was half afraid Peter was going to kill him – or worse, that he wouldn't kill him and Sabine would have to finish the job – after he'd been brutally honest to the man about his hokum business plan. Peter was one of the agency's high-priority clients: a Canadian trust fund baby who wanted to break into the UK market with his innovative idea of selling a mint-flavoured sparkling beverage that tasted like a cross between San Pellegrino and Listerine. He had an awful lot of money and not an awful lot of sense. Joel had been given strict instructions by Sabine not to ever, under any circumstances, tell this man the truth.

'It's refreshing to meet a guy who isn't just trying to pump my tyres,' added Peter, pummelling Joel's back as if he'd caught him choking on a bit of bread roll. 'I'll make sure to be in touch with you directly from here on in.'

Sabine wore a sour expression on her face as she directed Peter out of the glass box they called a meeting room while Beth gave Joel a wry smile.

Having run out of adequate excuses to keep air quote working from home air quote, Joel had dragged his bones to Hammersmith and brought Beth along for the ride. The office was located in a large glass building called 68 Brook Green, which everyone called '68'. It was all windows, no walls, and of course, full of absolute wankers.

Much to his surprise, things went relatively smoothly at 68. The only hiccup in Joel's 'bring your ghost to work' policy happened when Michael tried to plant themselves on Beth's lap during lunch. Joel, seizing the moment milliseconds before Michael's impending lap invasion, made a noise like he'd stubbed his toe on something painfully solid in the middle of the night. Realising he'd shrieked at the person he managed with little to no context, Joel managed to bleat out a strained: 'Don't sit there please!', his voice reaching a comical falsetto at the 'ease'.

'Why not?' asked Michael. They looked confused. They were confused. Joel had been nothing but generous with his time since Michael had joined the company and they'd formed a fast friendship. One night, when they'd both been forced to work late to get one hundred rote spreadsheets finished, Michael and Joel had come up with their definitive best-to-worst ranking of the nine main films in the *Star Wars* franchise (V, IV, VIII, VI, VII, III, IX, I, II).

'I just can't have anyone sit in that chair right now,' said Joel.

Joel looked down at the chair and saw Beth. Michael looked down at the chair and saw a chair. Beth looked back at Michael from the chair and saw someone who was trying to weigh up their options, crunching the numbers on the social capital they'd earned with Joel and desperately trying to work out whether or not he was joking. Beth decided to make things easy for sweet, sweet Michael by getting up and moving to an empty chair in the corner of the room. Joel watched her as she did it, almost in slow motion, taking care not to make any sudden movements in case it interfered with her journey.

Michael watched Joel's eyes swivel, slowly and dramatically, from the empty chair next to him all the way to another empty chair in the corner of the room. If this was a joke, it wasn't a particularly funny one.

'Okay,' Joel said, 'you can sit in the chair now.'

'Thanks, Joel,' said Michael. And, as Michael sat down and the pneumatic cylinder of the chair gave a gentle sigh, they laid a reassuring hand on Joel's arm. 'I really appreciate you letting me use this chair,' they added. It wasn't a big gesture. It was, in the grand scheme of things, a small one. But it was heavy with compassion and care.

'That's okay,' said Joel, returning the hand-on-arm gesture in a clumsier but no less heartfelt fashion, 'I really want you to sit there.'

Time Is Of The Essence

Whenever they got back to the flat, Beth and Joel would spend hours talking, listening to music and sometimes even combining the two activities by talking about the music they were listening to. Their conversations would skirt around whatever cultural smog was fogging up the news and focus, instead, on vaguer issues relating to art and more general concepts of human nature. Like, for instance, whether or not the innate savageness of mankind William Golding wrote about in *Lord of the Flies* was a realistic take on what would happen if you threw a load of British children onto an island. Or tangential theories about how child actor Danuel Pipoly, who Joel thought had played the role of Piggy rather well in the 1990 film version of *Lord of the Flies*, had gone from a buzzed-about actor with a leading role in a major motion picture to playing the role of 'Kid #3' in 1995's *3 Ninjas Knuckle Up*. What had happened in those five years?

'I don't know,' shrugged Beth. 'Drugs?'

'Probably,' sighed Joel, immediately feeling sorry for

a man who would by now be deep into his forties and was likely doing completely fine.

Although she indulged Joel in these late-night ramble-chats, much more than she'd intended to going into this whole arrangement, Beth would make sure to end the night by giving Joel an art-themed pop quiz. It was a way for her to put an end to the chapter of each day. Years past the point of physically needing to sleep, she couldn't use the excuse of 'I've got to go to bed now' and, besides, it gave her a means of trying to maintain at least an air of professionalism now she was taking on the role of a quasi-guardian angel. If it hadn't been for the quiz-and-then-bed routine, Joel would have happily brewed another flagon of coffee and spent the entire night talking Beth's ear off about everything and nothing. And, although she'd roll her eyes and try to dampen his puppy-dog energy as much as possible, she knew she'd treasure every second of it.

Time had flown like a Concorde, though, and it wasn't long before they only had one night left to get in some last-minute revision before Joel's big date with Nina. They went over the floor plans of the gallery together, getting granular on the 'what's on now' section and creating a cohesive plan of attack. Beth didn't want Joel entering the lion's den of the National Gallery unprepared. Even to an experienced art history graduate with years of lectures and Dr James Fox documentaries seared into their brain, the National Gallery could be an overwhelming place. There was simply so much to see and digest you could easily walk around for hours without properly taking anything in.

The last thing Beth wanted was for Joel to embarrass himself in front of Nina. At least, she was pretty sure that was the last thing she wanted. It was hard to tell these days. After being numb for so long, the return of her emotions had unsettled her. It hadn't been an instant process but more of a slow burn, like the feeling of coming back in from the cold and having your toes tingle back to life with a million hot needles. She began to remember what it was like to be angry, sad and happy, all at once – a chaotic muddle that left her drained and questioning whether she wanted to keep going at all. But if she actually wanted out, wouldn't she have told Joel the truth by now?

'What do I say to this?' asked Joel. He was holding up his phone for Beth to read a message that had come through from Nina. Beth squinted and the words came to focus in her field of vision.

Nina: Hey stranger, just checking you're still on for the Nat Gal tomorrow? N x

'Are you kidding me?'
'What?' said Joel, bemused.
'That is quite literally the easiest text in the world to reply to. Jesus Christ, Joel. I don't need to do everything for you. Do I?'

Beth sighed. He'd become so used to having her around again that he'd stopped thinking for himself. She knew he had a track record of losing himself in relationships – of adopting the traits and mannerisms of a new friend or partner and forgetting his own in the process. Joel had told her that once his friendship with Sam had been cemented over a bottle of Stolichnaya during pre-drinks, he'd started absorbing a lot of Sam's slang into his own vocabulary. Films became 'far out', plates of pasta were 'killer'. Joel's mum had worried he'd fallen in with a crowd of sixties beatniks when he'd come home for Christmas and asked her to 'pass the cauliflower cheese, man'.

'Sorry. You're right. I've got this.'

Beth watched as Joel made his concentration face; brow furrowed, tongue peeping out between his lips. After a solid minute of tap-tap-tap-tap-tap, he hit the little green arrow and sent his words flying at breakneck speed towards their intended target.

Joel: I am indeed. I'll see you there! J x

Bull's eye.

One Small Step For Man

The National Gallery jutted out onto Trafalgar Square like a stiff bottom lip, standing all proud and true and stoic while a revolving door of buskers and street artists eked out a living by its entrance. Joel briefly considered making a point about the dichotomy between the works of art nestled safely inside the gallery and those transient chalk scrawls on the pavement outside, but Beth vetoed the idea immediately. It could far too easily be read as a classist comment, she explained. And although that definitely wasn't the point Joel was getting at, he conceded Beth was – as always – right in her judgement.

There was a ripple of wind as they stood at the bottom of the steps, side by side, waiting for Nina to arrive. Joel was early, as he usually was to any event or social engagement he was anxious about, and continued to nervously consult the twenty-four-hour clock on his phone every two minutes or so. The time they'd agreed to meet remained fifteen torturous minutes away. Every passing minute felt like an hour.

'Relax,' said Beth, resisting the urge to give Joel's hand a comforting squeeze. 'You're going to be fine.'

'I hope so,' he said, before giving his T-shirt a swift sniff check to make sure the smell of his aftershave still came through but wasn't too overpowering. He didn't want to fumigate Nina when they hugged but he did want her to peel herself away from his body with the impression he was one of those boys that smelled nice.

The way Joel smelled used to drive Beth wild. It wasn't just his aftershave but what he jokingly referred to as his 'natural caveman pheromones', which worked her into a frenzy. She'd nuzzle her nose into his chest whenever he got home from work so she could take it in: the faintly sour, lingering smell of sweat on another human body. A body you were intimately familiar with. She picked at her cuticles, trying not to breathe in his scent as they waited for Nina to arrive.

The sky was the same colour as the stone step beneath Joel's left boot, raised a level above the right which stayed grounded to give him the look of Washington crossing the Delaware, but the weather didn't exactly matter, did it? Their date was going to be conducted within the quiet walls of the gallery, where the internal temperature was kept consistent to prevent the paintings from melting during the summer months. Having once applied for a job at the National Gallery, Beth knew the tasks carried out by the staff who worked there ranged from regular checks on the condition of paintings to control of the light, temperature and humidity.

All of that persistent maintenance was the opposite approach you had to have when creating the ideal climate for a house plant. Much as you'd ply an American boy with corn-fed beef and whole milk if you wanted him to one day make the NFL, you wanted to make sure your living-room monstera was kept in a condition in which it could achieve the maximum growth possible. Close to sunlight, plenty of water, etc. In a gallery, the opposite was true – stasis was the be-all and end-all. If a day went by and nothing changed, that was considered a success. Growth, and the subtle swell of a picture frame, could spell disaster for all involved.

'I think she's coming,' hissed Beth. It wasn't until the words left her mouth that she realised how even just the thought of Joel holding hands with someone else made her stomach drop.

'What makes you say that?' said Joel. He squinted out across the square and couldn't see anyone walking towards him he recognised or anyone who looked vaguely Nina-shaped. There were lots of people who looked like people he knew, but only in the sense any stranger can resemble someone you know by having a face and a nose and all the other features shared by most human beings. He saw an awful lot of couples wearing hiking gear, decked out head to toe in expensive Gore-Tex. They looked comically out of place in the concrete wilderness of central London and he wondered where it was they were going to or from.

'Because I'm pretty sure that's her coming up behind you.'

Joel turned on a point and filled his eyes with the vision of Nina walking towards him. The tips of her chunky trainers took turns peeping out of the bottom

Nearly Departed

of her olive cargo pants as she got closer and closer. Her top, a baggy white T-shirt, looked so soft and durable he knew it must have been expensive. Their hug lasted the appropriate length of time for two people who weren't even friends yet, let alone lovers, and Joel only felt slightly awkward doing it in front of his dead ex-girlfriend.

'How've you been?' she asked.

'Great, thanks,' said Joel, 'and you, too.'

Beth did a full-body cringe, her face taking on an expression of mild agony as Nina's eyes narrowed and her ears attempted to Duolingo what Joel had just said.

'I mean, you look great. Sorry,' he added, panicking now, 'I'm a little nervous. And my mouth sometimes says things before my brain has a chance to catch up.'

'That's okay,' smiled Nina, 'I've already had a couple of vodka tonics to settle my nerves.'

'But it's midday,' said Joel, shocked.

'I know,' she said, slightly abashed, 'I was joking . . .'

'Oh, phew,' said Joel. 'I mean, not phew. Because who actually says phew? It would be, like, totally okay if you had had a few drinks beforehand. To settle the nerves.' He hid his mouth with his fingers. A nervous tic he'd picked up in primary school.

Nina offered a reassuring laugh, not that Joel particularly deserved one.

'Don't worry,' she said. 'We're on the same page.'

'All right, then,' he added, gesturing towards the entrance of the gallery in the least amateur-magician manner he could muster. 'Shall we?'

As the two of them walked up the stairs, taking one step at a time, Joel turned to give Beth a secret smile. She returned it with a sad half-smile that didn't exactly fill him with confidence but, still, he was glad she had his back.

The Sainsbury Wing

They'd survived the grand entrance and had made some pretty amusing small talk so far; feeling each other out with slight digs and sparring verbally like prize-fight boxers, exchanging jabs in the way only people on first or second or third dates do. The chemistry was there, all right. They weren't having to force conversation and seemed to be sharing an equal proportion of questions and answers so far. Even the time they spent not talking was good. They'd stand in front of a painting or a statue and be able to soak it in without feeling the need to make an unnecessary comment or pass any particular judgement. The silence they shared was a comfortable, duck-feathery one. Joel had even managed to calm his nerves to the point where he wasn't just holding it together – he was actually enjoying himself. He'd thought the combination of Beth and Nina would have been overwhelming but, much to his delight, it had been smooth sailing so far.

Joel made sure his attention was focused on Nina, listening to what she was saying at all times, while Beth acted as a helpful prompt. She was the reluctant Navi to his Link – a companion in his quest to woo Nina that would occasionally pipe up to provide him with pointers or useful titbits of information.

'The Sainsbury Wing might have been one of the more modern additions to the gallery but, if you look closely, you can see that the arches in the upper galleries are an obvious aesthetic ode to the scale and grandeur of a Florentine church. Fitting considering it's a wing used to house early Renaissance paintings,' whispered Beth, as the trio passed a stunning smattering of Raphaels.

'I love these, er, arches,' said Joel, drawing what looked to be the McDonald's logo in the air with his fingers.

'Me too,' said Nina, 'they're very church-y.'

'Yes,' agreed Joel, 'I was thinking the exact same thing.'

Everyone has their own preferred speed of consumption when it comes to art. Finding out how quickly someone is capable of shooting through a room full of priceless paintings can tell you a lot about the person and, more obviously, the style of art they're interested in. Joel noticed how Nina would always give each individual work the time of day, offering it a polite smile and a nod as you would with a stranger you'd made eye contact with in the street, but she definitely leaned away from the religious stuff. Joel gleaned from her distinct lack of interest in Michelangelo's *The Entombment* (she did one of those subtle closed-mouth yawns literally everyone has done and is therefore able to recognise, immediately undoing the intended subtleness of the action) that Nina probably wouldn't be caught dead chatting to a Jehovah's Witness in a shopping centre. She might have gone to the Christian Society socials at university for the free pizza though.

Joel wasn't exactly what you'd call religious but he was definitely open to the idea of something more than your eighty-odd years on planet Earth. He liked to believe that your soul, if there was such a thing, went somewhere afterwards. It'd be rude for him not to believe in some kind of heaven, seeing as he was currently being haunted by rather concrete proof of an afterlife.

'Did you know roughly one-third of the paintings in the National Gallery's collection of Western European art are of religious subjects,' said Beth, 'and that nearly all of those are Christian?'

'I didn't,' said Joel.

'Didn't what?' asked Nina, her head still turned away from Joel as she did a drive-by of a painting possibly by El Greco.

'Oh, nothing. I was just talking to myself.'

'You do that a lot.'

'I know.'

And they kept on walking. For a while nothing happened. Which was nice. They walked together in contented silence before Joel decided to ask Nina how she'd got into art in the first place. She said she'd had a good teacher at school.

'That's how most of these stories start, right? By having someone who believed in you.'

'I suppose,' said Joel.

'You don't sound sure.'

'I guess I'm not sure if I've ever been that passionate

about something before. Does admitting that make me sound like the world's most boring man?'

'No,' said Nina.

'Yes,' said Beth.

A still life of lemons in a wicker basket next to her head made Nina's brown eyes seem brighter than ever. Beth caught herself seething at the way Nina looked at the world with so much hope; envious of how full of fucking life she seemed.

'Don't get me wrong,' said Joel. 'I've always been passionate about people. I can't remember a day of my life where I haven't had a crush on at least one person. But I've never had, like, a calling.'

'Who've you got a crush on at the moment, then?' asked Nina.

'Right now it's the cashier with a nose ring who works at the Tesco Express near my flat . . .'

Beth rolled her eyes.

'. . . and you.'

Beth's heart plummeted to the pit of her stomach. She felt a wave of nausea as a smile flickered at the corners of Nina's mouth, making her already charming face even more infuriatingly charming.

The Rokeby Venus

It'd been roughly thirty minutes since Nina and Joel had stumbled upon a painting they both agreed was a 'two thumbs' masterpiece. The thumbs-up system was something Joel had patented when he was around thirteen-and-a-half years old. Too young to be drinking litre bottles of cider in the local park and too old to be seen earnestly playing there on the swings, Joel and his friends would spend a lot of their free time hanging out at the cinema. During the adverts before the film started, Joel had got into the habit of encouraging everyone in whatever group he was with to rate the trailers, silently, by giving them either a firm thumbs up or thumbs down depending on whether they wanted to watch the film or not. Joel jokingly suggested to Nina that they deployed the same thumbs-up system in the National Gallery. He was slightly taken aback by her enthusiasm.

'Sounds fun,' she said with a genuine smile on her face. And it was.

If either Nina or Joel thought an artwork was a bona fide masterpiece – in that the painting/sculpture/ornament excelled as both a technical and emotional triumph of the human imagination – they had to give it a thumbs up for all to see. If it was merely good, they'd give it a halfway thumbs up with their thumb running parallel to their knuckles. If they thought it was straight-up bad or otherwise hackneyed and overwrought, they'd give it a thumbs down, Caesar-style.

Getting one thumbs up was a real sign of approval, not to be given lightly, and there were many paintings they had each individually thought to be worthy of a thumbs up. Getting a thumbs up from both of them, though? That had proved to be far more difficult. The only pieces that had been awarded the fêted two thumbs so far were:

Jan van Eyck – *The Arnolfini Portrait*

Joseph Mallord William Turner – *The Fighting Temeraire*

Needless to say, they were both worried about the lack of diversity in the canon they'd created and had promised each other to be on the lookout for methods of removing some of the barriers to entry and implicit biases that might be affecting their judgement.

Nina and Joel endured another fifteen minutes of good but not captivating art, with Beth trailing behind them dutifully like the ghost she'd become, before they found another two thumbs masterpiece. It was in Room 30 that Joel was brought to a screeching halt by the sight of *The Rokeby Venus* – a painting by Diego Velázquez that Beth had had a postcard of Blu-Tacked to her wall when they first started dating. He turned to look at Beth, who'd been feeling left out for the last hour, and she looked back at him with glassy eyes.

Nearly Departed

This was a moment. They were having a moment. He closed his eyes for a few seconds and then opened them again.

Nina stood in front of Velázquez's canvas, tilting her head to the side like a puzzled boxer dog, and gave it an energetic thumbs up. She was about to move on to the next painting in the room when she noticed Joel was still transfixed.

There was something about the use of light – the way that Venus's shoulder blades scalloped together combined with the mirror's unsatisfactory reflection of Venus's visage – that spoke to him. He was already raising his thumb towards the ceiling, but it wasn't until this exact moment he'd actually 'got' the painting. Maybe it was to do with the scale of it. The small, A6 version Beth had displayed at eye height above her dresser hadn't done justice to the finer details of Velázquez's work. Then again, maybe it was all to do with the context. Seeing a painting he knew so well, one he intimately associated with the light streaming through Beth's blinds and their weekends spent sipping coffee under the duvet with a crossword, blown up to scale for everyone to see, made him feel a little violated.

'You like this one, huh?' asked Nina.

Joel and Beth nodded. 'I do,' they said, simultaneously.

'So do I,' said Nina, 'but I've always been perplexed by the fascination artists had with chubby little children.' She stood back and crossed her arms to get a better look at the painting.

'Putti,' said Joel. Nina and Beth did a double-take.

'All those chubby male cherubs you see in Renaissance art — they're called "putti", right?'

'Yep,' said Nina, who looked at him with burgeoning affection. He'd obviously done his homework, bless him, and it was even more obvious he was trying his best to make her like him. Beth gnawed at her bottom lip. She knew the look Nina had on her face; she knew it because it was the same look she'd once given Joel after he'd used a set of salt and pepper shakers and a bevy of knives and forks to give her an accurate re-enactment of all the sexual relationships that had transpired between the various members of Fleetwood Mac.

'One of my exes used to call me "putti" — it was like an affectionate pet name,' said Joel, powering on in the way he always did when he got a full head of steam, before lowering his voice conspiratorially: 'I think it was because I have a really smooth ass.'

Beth and Nina laughed in unison but the melody of Beth's was cut short when she noticed Nina was laughing a little *too* hard. Joel, on the other hand, noticed nothing; he was too distracted by the sensuous whisper of the 'That's good to know,' that Nina poured into his ear as she patted him gently on his left arse cheek and moved on to the next room.

Room 41

Room 41 was a minefield. Not only did the works of Cézanne and Monet and Renoir test Joel's ability to distinguish one French artist from another, but the room was a barrage of unrelenting beauty. A double-bill screening of *Snow Scene at Argenteuil* (two thumbs up) and *The Water-Lily Pond* (two thumbs up) forced Joel to come to the startling realisation that he was actually quite into Monet. And although Beth was still piping facts and trivia into his ear – 'the term "Impressionist" actually derives its name from Monet's *Impression, Sunrise*,' she whispered – Joel found he could get by just fine on feelings alone. It also turned out Beth wasn't the only person in the room capable of providing useful information about art.

'There's some evidence to suggest Monet could see colours on the ultraviolet spectrum,' said Nina, accepting a sip from Joel's matte black water bottle.

'You're telling me Monet could see like a bee?'

'Apparently. He had this cataract surgery that meant he had to have the entire lens of his left eye taken out. That gave him a condition called aphasia . . .'

'Aphakia,' said Beth, curtly.

'. . . and that meant he saw everything a little bit blue. If you look at his work before and after the surgery, his painting style – specifically his use of colours – changes pretty drastically.'

'Because he saw the world in a different way,' said Joel.

Nina said, 'exactly.'

'I can tell you're good at your job,' said Joel, genially, as he tucked his bottle away into the depths of his tote. It jangled gently against his keys and wallet before laying itself down to rest on its side.

'Why's that?' she asked. Nina had an excellent way of asking questions. She'd do it subtly and earnestly, without making Joel feel as if he was under investigation.

'Because it seems like you give a shit,' he said.

'I guess,' smiled Nina, 'but I don't think the ability to give a shit is all that relevant when it comes to being an assistant. Most of my job involves sorting out the meeting schedules of the gallery's director and making sure she doesn't accidentally piss off an important artist.'

Her eyes shone with stories Joel could only assume she'd signed numerous NDAs preventing her from ever telling. 'Well, it's that and making sure everyone's signed up to payroll,' she added.

'It's still important work, though,' said Joel, trying his best not to sound too much like he was conducting a job interview.

'If you say so,' said Nina. She pulled at his sleeve playfully and dragged him onto the next painting before he had a chance to ask her to endorse his communication skills on LinkedIn.

Beth stood with her arms crossed, perhaps slightly symbolically, in front of Henri Rousseau's *Surprised!* (two thumbs up). This was what she had wanted – wasn't it? Hadn't this been her grand plan all along? To help Joel forget all about her so he could move on with his life and she could go back to being properly dead? With every passing minute, she could feel whatever energy she had left seeping out of her. All she wanted was a bit of rest. A lifetime or two of eternal sleep. But if that was the case, then why did helping Joel move on hurt so fucking much? And why did it feel like she was being left out of something?

Because, of course, she *was* being left out of something. And Beth couldn't pretend she was enjoying it very much.

She didn't resent Joel for striving to make a connection with someone still living – and who had so much to live *for* – but that sour taste of rejection sent Beth back to the time in her life when her two best friends, D'anna and Barbara, had decided they didn't want to be friends anymore. Or rather, didn't want to be friends with her, specifically.

The three of them had been like the musketeers at school – inseparable all the way from Reception up until their Year 9 SATs. Something had changed, though, during the summer before Year 10. Beth had gone to Center Parcs with her family for a week and come back to find the tectonic plates beneath her feet had shifted a good couple of feet. On the surface, it might not have looked like any obvious damage had been done, but it had had a devastating effect on where Beth stood socially. Her internal compass had been set askew.

D'anna and Barbara had, almost overnight, gotten into designer clothing and boy bands and messaged each other about designer clothing and boy bands practically non-stop on their BlackBerry handsets. Beth, meanwhile, was more interested in getting her homework done so she didn't have a panic attack during Double Geography. Neither of them was actively nasty to Beth but they began slowly and surely to ice her out of their conversations. They'd roll their eyes at each other whenever Beth would ask questions about why they were discussing the weight of a reality TV contestant or whenever she said she couldn't afford to eat out more than once a week.

While the three of them had walked to school together in a dependable trio for years, taking up as much space as the pavement could offer, the situation morphed into one where Barbara and D'anna would walk together in a linked-arm twosome up ahead while Beth lagged a couple of steps behind. She'd stuck to it, at first. Fooled herself into thinking they simply wanted to be more conscientious of the people walking in the other direction, giving those strangers adequate space to move around the duo rather than forcing them onto the road. But as the weeks went by without D or B making anything more than tertiary eye contact with Beth, she got the picture.

Nearly Departed

She stopped trying to hang out with them during break and devoted all of her free time to her schoolwork instead. Which worked out. To an extent. She'd got better grades than both of them and gone to a university ranked higher than theirs by the *Times Higher Education*. But, unlike most of the friends she went on to make as an adult, she didn't have any 'home friends' to speak of. She'd put all of her eggs into D'anna and Barbara's baskets and they'd hurled them back in her face. So be it, she thought now. But as she watched Joel and Nina waltz up to the Sorolla she'd told him so much about, Beth couldn't help but feel a sick-making sense of déjà vu.

The Drunkard, Zarauz

The man at the forefront of the painting – depicted in loose, fluid brushstrokes – wore an expression that was lusty and alive. He was sitting in his chair, leaning precariously forward. Joel could practically hear him panting and smell his sweet and stale beer-soaked breath. This is a painting tinged with longing, he thought.

'This is a painting tinged with longing,' said Joel, pointing at the face of the man at the centre of the oil-on-canvas tavern.

Nina peered into the face Joel was gesturing at, struggling to understand. To her, it looked like a painting of some men who were all at various stages of being pissed. She could find a similar tapestry at any pub on a Friday night.

'What makes you say that?' she asked.

'The use of light. The way the figures are so close to one another yet seem so far away. The fourth wall breaking that makes it seem as if they wished they lived in our world and weren't stuck inside a canvas,' rattled off Beth like a machine gun.

'I don't know,' said Joel. He turned from Nina to

give Beth a loaded look before directing his eyes back to the painting. He stared into the watery eyes of the main drunk until his own started to water. 'I guess it's a feeling I can relate to,' he continued, not breaking contact with the drunk's lascivious gaze, 'I don't know a lot about a lot of things but I know what it's like to want. And I know what it's like to have and still want at the same time.'

Nina looked at Joel and noticed the water pooling delicately at the bottom of his eyelids. Beth noticed it, too. While she'd been busy dissecting the historical importance of *The Drunkard, Zarauz (El Borracho, Zarauz)* and its wider context within the gallery, she'd failed to consider whether or not Joel would be moved by this specific piece of art. Something about the muddy browns and greys of the painting seemed, much to all their surprise, to have touched Joel.

Beth was happy to see him so caught up in his emotions, open with his feelings in a way he seldom had been when she was alive, but she couldn't help but feel a pang of jealousy. He'd never had this visceral a reaction to a painting in all their years of going to galleries. The closest he'd ever come was the time he'd stood, silently, in front of a Rothko for fifteen minutes at the Centre Pompidou. She'd thought he would crack that afternoon and burst into overwhelmed tears as a sea of faces and tour guides passed by, but he'd been able to regain his composure and had moved nimbly from soaking up *Untitled (Black, Red over Black on Red)* to googling the best place in Paris to find a good sandwich.

Now, though, it looked like he was properly going to blub. Nina and Beth looked on in concern – four eyebrows furrowed to conceal a fear that they wouldn't know what to say or do if Joel did break down. Joel bit the inside of his lip to stop himself from sobbing and a metal tang of blood snaked its way around his mouth and down his throat like a plume of liquid smoke. He did this all in silence, of course, as Beth and Nina waited patiently for his next move.

'I've never been very good at expressing myself,' he said eventually. The two women jumped at hearing his voice – not because of what he'd said, but because his sentence punctured a silence that had seemed like it would never end. 'It's something I've spoken about with my therapist quite a lot,' he continued.

Nina tried to make eye contact with Joel but he kept on staring straight ahead. He found it easier to say what he was going to say when he was looking at Sorolla's drunk.

'And I guess there's something about this painting I don't feel like I've ever experienced before. Or, at least, something I never realised I've experienced before. There's a compassion to it, you know?' Joel turned to Nina, searching for an answer with his irises. She dipped her head slightly as if to say: 'Go on.'

'And I guess,' he looked towards the ornate ceiling before finally scrolling down to meet Nina's eyes, 'I guess I get the sense Sorolla isn't passing any judgement on these men or what they're doing. Because, hey, they've probably had much harder lives than he has. They've got real jobs. Hard jobs. Jobs that will one day maybe kill them. So, who is he to judge what they do in their spare time? But at the same time, I don't think he's condoning their behaviour either. It's as if he's simply given us all the facts written down – or painted down – and he's asking us or, like, anyone who's looking at the painting, to come to their own conclusion.'

'What conclusion have you come to?' asked Nina. She shuffled sideways and reduced the gap between their bodies. Joel could smell the top notes of bergamot and jasmine in her perfume knotting themselves together with the familiar scent of Sure deodorant. It wasn't an unpleasant combination.

'I've come to the conclusion we should probably get some lunch.'

'Same old Joel,' muttered Beth, as he fished out his phone to look up the nearest place to find a good sandwich. Once he'd tapped on the opening times of somewhere Eater described as 'worth a visit', the trio turned and tried to shuttle themselves towards the nearest exit as swiftly as possible.

Chinatown

'I've got a real thing for roast meat,' said Nina as she transported a mound of crispy lacquered pork from her plate to her mouth with a well-practised snip and flash of her chopsticks. Joel grunted in affirmation. His own mouth was filled with the rich and unctuous wobble of mapo tofu. Minced pork and bean curd was a combination Joel had been sceptical of at first, but he'd fallen head over heels for it after he'd lost his mapo virginity at the tender age of sixteen. The contrast between the softness of the tofu and the sharpness of the Sichuan peppercorns left his mouth buzzing with pain and pleasure. It was the closest a dish could get to giving you that deliciously sore tingling feeling you have after a good fuck.

Ordering mapo tofu had become Joel's go-to move whenever he went to Chinatown. Although the sandwich shop he'd wanted to visit had been inexplicably shut for the afternoon, he could tell from the moment they'd walked into the Cantonese canteen Nina had recommended 'most ardently' (à la Mr Darcy) that she was someone who was passionate about eating. He couldn't help but be charmed by the way the waiting staff smiled at her as if she was a member of their family, or how she fired off the order for the both of them like a seasoned pro.

The Formica tables were a light shade of toothpaste teal and populated by a rogues' gallery of people from all walks of life. There were just as many families hunched happily over a mountain of half-finished plates as there were bespectacled solo diners taking up a two-top by themselves with nothing but a copy of *The Sunday Times* for company. One man was passionately biting his fingernails while four forgotten wontons sat sadly in front of him in a pool of iridescent chilli oil. The white tiled floor was the same easy-clean kind you'd find in a greasy spoon, a butcher's shop or a Russian *stolovaya*, its grouting rich with the history of spilled bowls and tales of God-knows-what late-night Soho debauchery.

Almost every inch of the walls was taken up by a series of rectangular mirrors bouncing back the reflection of the also-mirrored wall opposite, giving the restaurant's downstairs the impression of a never-ending hall of mirrors. A mélange of hunger-inducing smells diffused from the open kitchen. The pucker of black vinegar seemed to cling to every corner of the room as the clang and scrape of cutlery filled it with a pleasant musical din. Walking past the kitchen as they headed to the more sedate dining area upstairs, Joel and Nina could hear the muffled scream of a hob on full whack followed by the whip-crack sizzle of oil on wok. The phone rang constantly, adding a shrill tenor to the orchestral arrangement, as orders for takeaways struggled to make themselves heard over the cacophony of pork belly caramelising in real time.

Having seen off two triangles of prawn toast each, as well as a few polite bites of some spring rolls that were still partly frozen in the middle, Joel and Nina had got quickly comfortable with showing off their appetites to one another. Beth, who sat on the vacant chair next to Nina, had a front-row seat to their mastication-heavy bonding session. She'd never enjoyed food quite as much as Joel. He was one of those people who would start thinking about lunch halfway through breakfast and be planning his dinner before he'd even finished his lunch. Beth appreciated the way food tasted. She preferred good food to bad food. But she wasn't someone who would spend their weekend seeking out the best bánh mì in the city. Nina, apparently, was.

'So it's this little hole-in-the-wall joint near Hackney Central that's open from twelve to three – I want to say, maybe, four or five times a week,' explained Nina, trying to convey the deliciousness of a pâté-laden sandwich through words alone. 'But even then you can't be guaranteed they'll actually be open. Sometimes I've been, and it's shutters down with this note that just says, 'Sorry'. Oh, and if you arrive any time later than two, they'll have run out of bread.'

Joel laughed. Nina was a natural storyteller. Unlike him, she didn't seem to be preoccupied with how her stories landed and was far less rehearsed when it came to sharing anecdotes. Joel had stories he'd told so many times – like the one where he'd got hit by a car on the way to having dinner at Alice's – that he'd got every beat and pause of them down to a fine art. If he told his hit-and-run story to someone he'd just met in front of someone like Alice or Sam, who'd each heard the story at least a dozen times, they'd be able to mime along to every moment as Joel recited the crash, bang and wallop of his encounter with a Vauxhall Corsa. Joel would even use the same exaggerated hand gestures every time. It was like having a work-in-progress comedy routine; he took internal notes each time he told that story and, with every subsequent performance, became better at telling the tale. To Nina, the telling was half the fun and she steamrolled to the end of her stories fuelled by nothing but sheer enthusiasm.

'How have you eaten a sandwich somewhere only open for three hours on a weekday if you've got a regular nine-to-five job?' asked Joel.

Nina blushed and fiddled nervously with the chunky rings she wore on her fingers.

'Promise you won't laugh?'

'I promise,' said Joel. Beth leaned back in her chair.

'I booked a day off work,' said Nina, covering her face with her hands in embarrassment. 'Is that sad? Taking annual leave so you can go and eat a pork and pâté sandwich?'

'No, I think it's incredible,' said Joel. And he meant it. He took a sip of the complimentary green tea brought in a desultory fashion to each table and tried to figure out what confession he could utter that would make Nina feel better about hers.

The caffeine that had been slowly seeping from the

tea leaves into his brain was working overtime to find some matching revelation to prove to Nina he was just as nerdy as she was, and twice as reckless with his annual holiday allowance. He thought about the day he and Beth had booked off work to see how many times they could have sex in one day before they physically couldn't do it anymore (six) but he wasn't sure bringing up a sex story about his dead ex-girlfriend while she was sitting at the table, watching him like a parole officer, was a good idea. He briefly considered telling Nina about his tactic of booking off a Friday and a Monday at the same time to get what he facetiously called a 'whole free week of holiday' before deciding it was too droll and . . . bingo. He found it.

'I once booked three days off work so I could binge-watch *Game of Thrones* in time to catch up with whatever season was on at the time,' he said, 'because I didn't want anyone at work spoiling it for me.'

'Now that is sad,' laughed Nina.

'That's not even the saddest part,' said Joel, 'I obviously couldn't tell my colleagues that's what I was doing — because, you know, it's mortifyingly embarrassing — so I told them I was going to Portugal instead.'

Nina looked up at Joel and scrunched her eyes. 'Why Portugal?'

'I don't know. I panicked. And when I came back from "Portugal"' — Joel made scare quotes in the air with his fingers — 'I had to keep answering loads of questions about where I'd been and what I'd done. To this day, people in the office still come to me if they need a recommendation of what to do in Lisbon.'

Beth knew every contour of this story. Hearing it told was like stuffing your hands into the soft, familiarly worn pockets of an old coat. But she knew Joel wouldn't tell Nina the unwritten epilogue. He wouldn't divulge how he and Beth had had flights booked to Lisbon before she died – how they'd finally been going to tie the bow on that anecdote for good – until Beth's chapter had ended too abruptly for that fairy-tale ending to ever happen.

Nina pinched a few final stragglers of rice using her chopsticks and dunked them into a crimson slick of chilli oil. 'And you still haven't been to Portugal?' she asked.

Joel shook his head. He wasn't sure if it was because of the tingle of the mapo tofu or because he felt overly comfortable with Nina already, but he started to tell her about how he had bought flights to Portugal for his anniversary with Beth. As he began to tell Nina about his problems with the Ryanair baggage system, and as she gave him a polite smile in return, he noticed Beth was shaking her head. He turned to look at her – turning to a person is usually a fairly innocuous thing to do unless it just so happens no one else can see that person, in which case you end up turning your full body to an empty chair which is . . . bizarre, to say the least – and could tell he'd done something wrong.

Nina looked on in confusion as Joel seemed to be lost for words and suddenly extremely interested in the upholstery of the chair next to hers.

'I'm sorry,' said Joel, 'do you mind if I use the toilet?'

He immediately cringed at how he'd asked her for permission to go and piss.

'No, of course not,' she said, 'I'm not your teacher.'

'Of course not,' said Joel, before adding, 'Thank you, Ms Harris.'

Nina smiled and Joel got up to head to the bathroom. Once he saw that Nina had turned back to face the other direction and had lost herself in the warm glow of her phone, he mimed at Beth to follow him to the toilet.

They walked down the stairs, past the photos of celebrities who'd eaten at the restaurant and photos of celebrity lookalikes who were just feasible enough from a distance to earn their place on the wall, and into the dinky bathroom. The toxic merger of vanilla air freshener and urine stung Joel's nostrils and caused his eyes to water, not for the first time that day.

'What's wrong?' said Beth. 'Seen another Sorolla?'

Joel didn't laugh. He didn't even crack a smile.

'I was going to ask you the same thing,' he said.

'What? That doesn't even make sense.'

'I know it doesn't make sense!' He pressed his palm against his forehead. 'But practically nothing in my life makes sense right now!'

She could see hot, salty tears starting to pool in his eyes, and any anger she'd felt towards him quickly dissipated. 'Just breathe, Joel.'

He took a deep breath in. 'I thought you were supposed to be helping me out. I thought we were on the same team but all you've done, so far, is make snide comments and look at me like I'm a . . . I don't even know what.'

'Joel. I am *trying* to help you. But it's a little difficult when all you do is constantly bring up stories about me.'

Joel frowned and hit the rewind button on some of the conversations he'd had with Nina. Okay, yeah, maybe he had brought up Beth a few times more than he should have done. But he'd always moved the chat back to another topic afterwards. Hadn't he? It was only natural Beth would crop up when she'd been such a big part of his life for years. Wasn't it?

Beth leaned back against the cool edge of the sink and pointed a loaded finger at Joel.

'That poor girl has had to play therapist with you for the last couple of hours while you've used her as a sounding board to process all of your trauma,' said Beth. She raised her voice an octave because she could. Because she knew it was the only way she'd be able to get through to Joel.

He knew she was right. He felt a litre of guilt glug into his stomach as he thought about how much he'd spoken about his grief, and how much he'd failed to ask Nina about her own. Beth was partly relieved Joel seemed to be realising his mistake, but partly torn up about it, too. There was, in truth, a large part of her that had wanted to sabotage this date. She could have butted in earlier in the day but she'd let Joel witter on about how 'my ex loved this piece' or 'my ex thought this artist was overrated' because she liked hearing proof that she'd existed. She knew it wasn't healthy Joel thought about her whenever he filled up his water bottle (saying the phrase 'my ex actually bought me this YETI' should, basically, be an arrestable offence) but she was touched by how often he thought of her.

'I've got to apologise, haven't I?'

Beth nodded. Joel nodded back, soberly, and decided he might as well use the bathroom while they were in there. Beth turned to face the wall as he emptied his bladder into the urinal. She knew he got pee-shy.

'You know how I said there was something I've got to tell you?' she asked, making eye contact with the tiles. But Joel couldn't hear her over the din of his stream.

'Give me a second,' he called out, his voice rising above the sound of sloshing water. Beth's confidence wavered. She couldn't do this to him here, in a public bathroom of all places.

The toilet gave a loud and definitive flush and Joel moved to the sink to wash his hands.

'What was it you wanted to say?' he asked.

'Oh, it's nothing,' she said with an unsure smile. 'I'll tell you later.'

Are You With Me Now?

'Sorry about that,' said Joel, as he sat back down in his chair with a gentle thud. Beth, meanwhile, sat down in her chair with the kind of silent thud only ghosts are capable of.

Nina leaned across the table, her right hand caught up in the mass of her soft curls. 'Oh, it's fine. I'm more than able to keep myself occupied,' she said.

'I'm also sorry I keep on talking about Beth,' he said.

'Your ex?' said Nina. And that was when Joel realised he hadn't even used Beth's name in front of Nina.

'Yes,' he said. 'I don't want you to think I'm talking about her to make you feel sorry for me or to make things actively weird or uncomfortable. It's just that she was a big part of my life and I think it's hard for me to separate myself from her. I still get confused sometimes about which memories are mine and which belong to her. To Beth.'

Nina reached out across the table and Joel met her hand halfway, circumventing the still-scalding pot of tea as he did.

'That's okay. I do the same thing with my mum.

Abigail. Her name was Abigail.' Nina's eyes lit up as she mentioned her mother's name.

'She was the best,' continued Nina, 'and I fucking hate that she was. I almost wish she'd have been one of those evil mothers you get in Disney films because then I'd be okay with not having her in my life. But she wasn't. And I'm not. Because she was the fucking best. And I'm never going to be able to replace her. Not properly. I guess I've got the opposite problem to you in that if anything, I don't speak about her enough. It's almost like I want to keep all those happy memories of her to myself. I know it's selfish of me but I guess I feel like telling people about her will mean that I lose a bit of her.'

'Tell her that's not true,' said Beth.

'That's not true,' said Joel.

'I know that, rationally,' said Nina, 'I'm just extremely protective of her. Of my memories of her. We used to come here all the time.'

Joel waited for Nina to continue. It was a technique he'd learned from his own therapist. Follow-up questions were helpful and showed you were an active listener, said Doctor Shah, but sometimes you had to give people the space they needed to finish their own thoughts.

'We'd sit on that table – over there in the corner,' Nina pointed out a table that was currently unoccupied and sitting in a patch of direct sunlight, 'and order way too much food. We always had to take loads back home in a doggy bag. Then, as soon as we got back in, we'd get a second wind and finish off eating at the kitchen table, straight out of the containers. Every fucking time. I think that's why the staff are so nice to me here. They remember her. And they remember how much we used to order. It's funny, I was actually terrified of being seated on that table when we arrived because I didn't want to tarnish those memories of her by having a relative stranger – no offence – take up the space where she used to sit.'

'None taken,' said Joel. And when she realised that that was all he was planning to say, Beth gave him a sharp kick under the table. As soon as her foot made contact with Joel's shin, it sent what felt like one hundred volts of unfiltered electricity shooting up his body. His knees slammed against the underside of the table and the dregs of his tea spilled all over the tablecloth.

Joel was mortally embarrassed and scrambled to mop up the mess, using the little mound of napkins he'd stained a deep shade of maroon during the meal. 'So sorry about that,' he said, giving Beth a searing look. 'I just felt an intense pain in my arse.'

Beth couldn't help but chuckle and made a note to herself that kicking someone who was alive, while not as dangerous as a hug, was still not a good idea. 'Anyway,' said Joel, regaining his composure and glancing briefly at Beth to get her consent, 'what I was going to say was that I appreciate you opening up to me about all this. It sounds like your mother was an incredible woman.'

'She was,' responded Nina, 'but I don't think she'd want me preserving her in amber. She wasn't always easy and she'd be the first to admit she certainly wasn't a saint. She could be as stubborn as a mule sometimes and, to be brutally honest, an absolute bitch when she wanted to be.'

'I think I like the sound of her even more now.' Joel smiled.

'She was brilliant. But she was also a first-generation immigrant who, for some fucking bizarre reason, felt inclined to vote for the Conservative party.' Nina laughed, looking lost in her thoughts.

'Can I ask you to do something with me?' she said.

'Shoot.'

'Will you' – and now it was Nina's turn to be embarrassed – 'sit at that table with me?'

Joel turned to look at the table where Nina and her mum had consumed more black bean sauce than most people will in a lifetime. He stood up and held her hand as he guided her towards the sun-dappled table, leaving Beth to watch this bizarre show of pageantry. A few of the staff looked up to see what was going on and used it as an opportunity to start clearing up Joel and Nina's dirtied plates.

Nina sat down on her chair and Joel descended into Abigail's regular space. He slotted in comfortably, physically speaking. It was, after all, the exact same style of chair he'd been sitting on for the last hour and ten minutes. But he knew he was doing more than simply sitting in a chair.

'Thank you, Joel,' Nina said. Her brown-butter eyes displayed a range of emotions Joel couldn't quite pin down all at once. He tongued his molars nervously.

Nearly Departed

'You're welcome, Nina,' he said.

'Should we go and get drunk now?' Nina asked. Now this, thought Joel, was an emotion he was capable of pinning down.

'You read my mind,' he said.

Beth, who had actually been reading Joel's thoughts all day long, drew in a deep breath. If he knew she'd broken her promise to stay out of his head, he'd be livid. Then again, there was a lot Joel didn't know. If she listened carefully, Beth could hear the faint murmur of her own guilt sloshing and swirling in the depths of her stomach. She was going to be in for a long night.

Karaoke

All he could taste was sambuca. His tongue felt sweet and furry, as if it had been dunked in a vat of liquorice syrup. Although it was only nine in the evening, the seedy neon lighting in the room made it feel like the dead of night. Under the violet hum of the bulbs, Nina and Joel locked eyes and their pupils went soft around the edges. They'd tried not to make eye contact with the man in army fatigues crooning 'Pour Some Sugar on Me' when they'd walked in. He was really into it and, well, it was kind of sad. Once he was done, he'd offered up a limp salute and left them with the booth to themselves.

Getting a round of shots had seemed to be in keeping with the mood of 'all you can karaoke', but Nina couldn't so much as smell sambuca without gagging – not since she'd drunk half a bottle of the stuff and got kicked out of Tiger Tiger for grinding on the manager – so Joel was left to work his way through the tray on his own.

'I'm under a bit of time pressure here,' he said, trying his best to hold in an aniseed burp and make his voice heard above Natasha Bedingfield.

Nearly Departed

'I'll put it on!' shouted Nina, who jabbed at the screen until she found the song she was looking for.

'No, I mean I'm running out of time,' said Joel. The pulse of a bassline gurgled from the speakers in a repetitive yet profoundly effective drone. Nina bit her bottom lip as she started playing an imaginary bass guitar. He couldn't help but laugh.

'I don't think this place shuts until midnight,' she replied, still confused, still strumming away.

'No, it's not that,' said Joel. He inched closer to Nina, resting his hand gently on her shoulder so he could talk right into her ear. 'I haven't got much time left to fall in love.'

Nina put the guitar down. The lyrics to 'Under Pressure', displayed over a static image of a cascading waterfall, flashed behind her head. He could tell she was trying her best not to sing along to the chorus.

'What do you mean?'

'I made a promise to myself that I'd fall in love with someone in the next five days.' He held up five of his fingers. He tried to focus on Nina but everything in the room had gone double.

'Why only five?' she asked.

'It's a long story,' Joel said as he sat down to try and stop the room from spinning. He watched with bemusement as two Ninas rose to queue up Kylie Minogue on the iPad attached to the wall.

'I've got time,' she said as she handed him a beer from the bucket in the corner.

The Second-Worst Wednesday Of Joel's Life

They sat at their usual table in the corner of The Adelaide Arms, splitting a bag of shawarmas and samosas. The grease seeped through the pale paper, softening its fibres until it became a thin, see-through membrane. The landlord didn't have an issue with anyone bringing in food from the Lebanese spot across the road, as long as they cleaned up after themselves.

'How long would you wait after I died?' asked Beth. She peeled the paper off her wrap like it was a Christmas present. Joel's mouth was already full of chicken. They weren't sober but they weren't drunk-drunk either.

'Hob lob wob I wob?'

'You're a pig,' she laughed.

He swallowed. 'How long would I what?'

'Wait. After I was dead.'

'To do what?' Joel asked, exasperated. The week before, she'd asked if he'd still date her if she was the size of a mouse.

'To move on,' she said, taking a sip of lager. 'To find someone new to fall in love with and do the whole "meeting the parents and unloading childhood trauma" thing with.'

Joel nodded, and she pressed on, 'I'm curious how long it would take you after I'm dead and buried to commit yourself to not just shagging someone new, but trying to find out what the first album they bought was and the name of their first pet.'

'Is this a test?'

Joel bit the corner of a steaming samosa and watched Beth pick up a scrap of escaped chicken from the table and fold it up carefully inside her napkin. If he'd been in the same position, he'd have plucked it straight from the sticky table into his open mouth.

'Maybe,' Beth said. She gave him a curious look. The wheels were spinning in his head.

'Okay, I'm on it. The first album you bought was Avril Lavigne's *Let Go* – which, I've got to say, was an excellent choice from ten-year-old you.'

'Thank you,' she said, acknowledging the compliment with a small nod.

'And . . . fuck. Pet is a trick question. Because there were two of them?'

'Go on.'

'And they were hamsters . . .'

'Yes.'

The sound of a one-armed bandit in the corner emptying itself of coins seemed unreasonably loud, and Joel knew he only had one shot at this. He had to make it count.

'Caramel and ginger?'

'Honey and ginger,' she said sympathetically, patting him on the arm. 'But close enough. B plus.'

He beamed like a pair of headlights. 'Thanks,' he said, and Beth tried to ignore the bits of lettuce between his teeth.

'But seriously,' Beth said. She shimmied herself forward so her arse was perched at the edge of her seat. She even put down her wrap and rested it on the table so he knew she meant business. 'Say I died. Say I got brain cancer' – Joel winced – 'or I was murdered by a gangster or something like that. How long would you wait before moving on?'

'Seriously?' he asked.

'Yes,' she said. 'Seriously.'

He gave her a searching look. He dabbed at the garlic and chilli sauce prickling his lips and crumpled the paper napkin into a ball. He thought long and hard about the words that came out of his mouth next. And those words were:

'About three years.'

He regretted it the second he said it and the argument that followed that sentence's swift journey from his brain to his lips was the worst they'd ever had. Beth had been offended. Shocked. Appalled. Horrified. Every adjective of outrage that existed that it would only take her boyfriend a measly fucking three years – 1,095 days on the planet and around 2,190 toothbrushing sessions, to be exact – to find a newer model. Someone younger. Prettier. Skinnier. Maybe someone born in the late

Nearly Departed

nineties who would like his Instagram stories less than a minute after he'd put them up.

She wouldn't let it go. For the next few weeks and months it was something she brought up at dinner parties and work events and even, on one occasion, during Sunday lunch at her parents'.

'Come on,' pleaded Joel, as he spooned a cluster of peas onto his plate. A photo of Beth, baby-toothed and decked out in a Little Mermaid T-shirt, hung lopsided behind his head. 'It's statistically very likely I would move on with my life by then.' He looked to June and Graham for solidarity but they'd both taken a sudden, and rather intense, interest in their plates.

'I don't care about the statistics,' said Beth. She spat out the word 'statistics' like it was a mouthful of sour milk. 'I just want you, for once in your life, to say something without thinking about what the most painfully reasonable response is first.'

'Even if what I'm saying is the truth?'

'Yes, okay, whatever, it might be true. But I don't always want to hear the truth. I don't always need to hear it.'

'I'm just trying to be rational. Gravy?'

'Please. But would it kill you to be fucking irrational for once?'

Graham and June exchanged a quick glance at Beth's use of the word 'fucking' but chased it with another that said, 'Let's table that for later.'

'You used to love how rational I was!'

'Joel. Honey.' Sour milk again. 'No one could ever love how *rational* someone is. That's ridiculous.'

'You said I was your rock.'

'You are my rock. But talking to a rock can be exhausting. Could you pass the carrots?'

June handed Joel the plate of carrots and he sent them down the assembly line, via Graham, to where Beth was sitting at the head of the table.

'So, what – I should have lied to you? And said something like: "No, Beth, I would never move on. I would live a sad, lonely life on my own until the day I die." Is that what you wanted me to say?'

'Yes.'

'Oh. Really?'

'Yes! Because sometimes a girl just wants to hear her boyfriend say something nice, even if it's not true. Is that really so terrible?'

'What's all this about again?' asked Graham.

'Three years,' said Beth, spearing a honey-glazed carrot with her fork. 'That's all the grief I'm going to get. All this love, affection and doing the fucking laundry and I don't even get a lie about five years of chastity in return? Typical. And you know what, Joel?' She waved the pointy end of the carrot at his head. 'If I do die and you haven't moved on with some Hannah or Ellie or – God forbid – Chloe in three years' time, then you best believe I'm going to haunt the shit out of you. That's my promise to you, and everyone at this table.'

'Beth—'

'I want you to promise me you'll do it.'

Nearly Departed

'Look, let's just—'

'Promise me.' She bit into the carrot, mashing it angrily between her molars. 'If you are so sure it's the most "statistically likely event", then I want you to promise me you will be in a statistically happy relationship three statistical years after my statistical death. You can even bring your statistically likely girlfriend round here for dinner once you're all settled in your love nest. Just for old times' sake. Wouldn't that be nice for everyone?'

Joel looked up at Beth, desperate to end the conversation. He thought she was lovely, even when she was angry. He was obsessed with the way the bunny lines on her nose bunched together when she scowled, but hated how helpless he felt in these situations. She thrived on conflict, while he would do just about anything to avoid it; their arguments would never reach a final, crashing crescendo but would get shifted to the back-right hob and put on a low heat, bubbling away like a resentment ragù. Feeling the pressure of everyone's eyes on him, Joel decided, as he often did, to take the coward's way out.

'I promise,' he said. And with that, Beth stormed out of the room.

So that was the second-worst Wednesday of his life. The worst was the Wednesday when Beth had been scooped up and mushed between tarmac and steel.

Cognitive Behavioural Therapy

'Is there anything specific you wanted to talk to me about?'

'No.'

'Then why did you come here today, Joel?'

His eyes flicked briefly to beyond Doctor Shah's chair where Beth was leaning against the bookcase, arms folded, with a bemused expression on her face. This was the closest they'd ever get to couples' therapy.

'What were you looking at just then?'

'Just when?'

'Just now.'

'No one.'

Doctor Shah narrowed her eyes. She asked him how he was feeling about approaching the three-year anniversary of Beth's death, and his gaze drifted over to the bookcase once again. Whoever had furnished the room had a real thing for the colour grey.

'I'm sorry – is there a book you'd like to borrow?'

Despite herself, Beth began to laugh.

'No, I was just . . . looking,' said Joel. He dragged his eyes back to the centre of the room. Doctor Shah was of an indeterminate age. She could have told Joel she was in her mid-twenties or mid-fifties and he'd have believed her either way. Her brown eyes were rimmed with a dark semi-circle of kohl, but it was their bright whites that were the most startling.

'Just looking? Or looking for something? Or *someone*?'

Beth stopped laughing and straightened her back. Joel was silent.

'You don't seem to be letting me in today,' said Doctor Shah, adjusting her pitch to a less friendly, more professional register. 'Every time I think we're starting to make progress, you regress to this closed-off state. You need to be open with me, Joel.'

'Ask her about ghosts,' said Beth.

'What about ghosts?' he asked.

'What about them?' said Doctor Shah. She blinked as her mouth turned downwards in the way it always did right before she was about to say something serious. Joel suspected she'd long held the suspicion he was living in a dream world, attempting to loosen himself from reality.

'Ask her if she thinks they're real,' said Beth.

'Do you think they're real?' he asked.

He imagined this wasn't the first time Doctor Shah had been asked that question, and it wouldn't be the last. He waited tensely as she placed her Montblanc fountain pen down on the table.

'You know how we've spoken a lot about intrusive thoughts, Joel?'

He nodded. The Montblanc wobbled slightly before coming to a gentle stop.

'And that those thoughts tend to stick in our heads because of the energy we expend to fight them?'

Joel nodded again. The leaflet Doctor Shah had given him after his third session of CBT had said 'IT'S NOT WHAT YOU THINK' in big yellow letters.

'I think the deceased can stick around for the same reasons. The more you try to stop yourself from forgetting someone, the more they're going to haunt you. You've used a computer before, right?'

'Yes,' said Joel, trying his best to sound serious. 'I have used a computer.'

'Okay. Stupid question, I know. But it's a bit like when you're asked to save the changes on a document before you close it. You have to trust that those documents — those memories — are going to be preserved on the hard drive, right? And you have to trust that they'll still be there when you want to open them back up on another day.

'But it's important to keep closing those documents,' Doctor Shah continued, using her hands to smooth out a couple of invisible creases from her skirt. 'Because what's going to happen to your computer if it's trying to process too many things at once?'

'It's going to overheat?'

'It's going to crash. Am I making sense here, Joel? You can't keep the Beth tab open forever. At some point, you're going to have to save your progress and close the window.'

Her answer had nothing to do with ghosts but Joel thanked her anyway and told her what she'd said about computers was incredibly insightful. Doctor Shah had seemed pleased when he said that and couldn't stop a smile from taking over the lower portion of her face.

'Do you believe in God, Joel?'

He looked at Doctor Shah and blinked twice, slowly, like a cat.

'I think so,' he said, eventually. 'But I'm not convinced he believes in me.'

The hands of the clock marked six o'clock, and then five minutes past six. It was rare for one of their sessions to run over. Doctor Shah watched Joel's eyes do a full lap of the clock before she clasped her hands together in front of her chest, readying herself for what would be her closing statement.

'You really want to know what I think about ghosts?'

'Yes,' said Joel and Beth, in unison.

'Ghosts are thoughts,' she said. 'And thoughts are just thoughts. They happen. They jump around. They don't take orders. But that's all they are. They're just in your head. You're bigger than a thought, Joel.'

I'll Cook, You Clean

'So, how did it go?' asked Sam. His thick *Sesame Street* eyebrows furrowed inquisitively and Joel couldn't help but marvel at how his naturally dark eyes looked almost black in the dimmed light of his living room. 'Yeah, how did it go?' chimed Holly from the other side of the room. She'd always had a soft spot for Joel and liked the sillier side of Sam that Joel brought out of him.

'It was good,' said Joel. He didn't tell them about the duet of Keane's 'Somewhere Only We Know' they'd performed to a crowd of five at the karaoke bar; he didn't tell them he'd already made plans to see Nina again the next weekend; and he certainly didn't tell them Beth wasn't a fan of the new Radiohead poster Holly had framed and put up in the hallway.

Their flat was small, but agreeable. They had an open kitchen which doubled as their main living space and it was in that room, enveloped in a fug of summer busy misting up the windows, that they were having their now two-month-late monthly catch-up dinner. They tried their best to stick to the monthly rota but time, as it had an awful habit of doing, had got away from them again the last couple of months. Sam had set three places at the table and Joel barely managed to stop himself from asking for a fourth when he remembered he hadn't broached the topic of alive–dead Beth. He kept schtum as Beth took a seat on the sofa and watched in amusement as Sam went about the rigmarole of carving the chicken.

'Does anyone actually know how to carve a chicken?' asked Sam of no one in particular as he attempted to violently rend the bird's breast from its spine. 'Or does everyone wing it and hope they don't get called out for it?'

'Definitely the latter,' said Joel. He took a sip from his wine glass and let the liquid glide around his mouth like silk. Holly did the same and gave Joel a knowing glance – it was identical to the 'Oh, what's he like!' glance Joel's mum would broadcast to guests whenever his dad did something that was either particularly eccentric or particularly Welsh. It reminded him of how in love they were. They had a tender relationship which, despite its sweetness, never erred into saccharine territory. Love, quite simply, suited them down to the ground.

Sam and Holly's interactions, on the other hand, would have appeared almost brusque and businesslike to an outsider if it hadn't been for the adoration you could see in their eyes. They had such a wholesome dynamic, and such an intuitive schedule of whose turn it was to wash the dishes and whose turn it was to put them away, it almost made Joel forget about the objectively unwholesome way they had met during an all-day warehouse rave.

It felt almost voyeuristic, looking back at his MDMA-drenched memory of the event, that Joel had even been present on the day when a sweaty, saucer-eyed Holly had run up to Sam and shouted something unintelligible into his ear. It was like he was peering into the window of someone's tinsel-laden living room on Christmas Day. Sam had smiled back, having not understood a word Holly had bellowed but having been charmed, regardless, by her large bush baby eyes. It turned out he'd dropped his wallet and she was simply returning it to its rightful owner. Sam had proceeded to buy Holly drinks for the rest of the night as a thank you for her kindness, and the rest, as they say, is history. Just like the weeknight when Joel had reluctantly agreed to go on a date with a girl named Beth, Sam's dropped wallet was one of those innocuous-seeming instances which had ended up totally altering the course of all their lives.

Maybe it had been fate who'd got his hands dirty and forced Sam's wallet to fall into Holly's path. Maybe Holly had simply been in the right place at the right time. Maybe everyone did have a soul mate out there in the world, waiting to be found. Maybe everyone had hundreds of them, dozens dotted on each continent, and it was all a roll of the dice as to which one you'd actually meet and spend the rest of your life with. Joel didn't have the answers, but he knew at least one of his soul mates had been erased from his life by a cement truck. Even though said soul mate was currently crouching in front of Holly and Sam's bookcase with her head tilted at an awkward 90-degree angle to check out the spines.

Holly topped up everyone's glasses as they settled down to eat. 'Do you think you'll see her again?' she asked. Joel, who had just popped a golden roast potato into his mouth, chewed frantically while he made hand gestures to indicate he would answer as soon as he was done swallowing. Holly and Sam looked at him in anticipation, waiting to hear what his verdict would be. It had been a long time since Joel had gone on multiple dates with someone and, truth be told, they were worried he wasn't doing as well as he liked to make out.

'I think so,' announced Joel, knowing he didn't just think but knew he was going to see Nina again. Holly's face broke into a smile. Sam was smiling too, but with a bit more reticence.

'Why only think?' he asked.

At that remark, Joel stole a look towards Beth. He pretended he was stretching his neck and tried to make the movement look as nonchalant as possible.

'You might as well tell them how you really feel,' said Beth, slinking from the bookcase to the comfort of the couch.

With Beth's go-ahead, Joel gushed about Nina for twenty minutes straight. He told Holly and Sam everything – the way she dressed, the way she talked, the way she laughed – not sparing them any details about the date. He described how the day had slowly bled into night like a paintbrush dipped into a glass of water and didn't feel a shred of embarrassment admitting that the only time they'd stopped talking was when they watched the sunset from the street. Was it clichéd? Yes. Did he care? No.

The two glasses of Sancerre were pulsing in his temples and he felt good. He felt alive. He even told them about his self-imposed deadline to find someone to fall in love with before the three-year anniversary of Beth's death, and they only looked relatively concerned in response. But, in spite of the Sauvignon blanc sloshing around his system, there was something nagging at the back of his consciousness he couldn't quite shake.

While he'd painted a fairly accurate picture of the day's events – minus, of course, Beth's occasional input – he felt frustrated at how he could never properly do it justice. It was like trying to explain a football game or a play to someone who hadn't been there. It didn't matter how many excited sounds you made, the person listening to your version of the narrative would always have to fill in the gaps with their imagination. Capturing the magic of a moment like that was, therefore, pretty much impossible.

Sam and Holly asked all the right questions to help them get a better picture of what the date had been like. It seemed as if Joel was pleased with how it had gone and – by the sounds of it – this Nina girl had had a good time, too. Good enough to agree to see him again, at least. The only potential red flag they'd both, separately, noticed was how Joel would keep dropping

Nearly Departed

eye contact with them while he was talking. He'd held their gazes, alternating fairly between them, but every so often he would look away entirely and stare at the cushions on the sofa. It hadn't stopped his mouth from motoring at a hundred miles an hour but it had been interesting, nonetheless, that he'd appeared to be getting consent from Holly's H&M Home cushions before divulging more information. It was almost as if he'd been asking them for permission.

As Joel rolled up his sleeves and plunged a stack of plates and bowls under the scalding tap, Holly placed an empty wine bottle into the recycling bin with a satisfying clink. It was a sound Joel would have happily ranked among life's small, perfect pleasures. It was second only to the sound those same glass bottles made when they were thrown into the black hole of a bottle bank. The slick swish as they descended, sharply, towards their fate only made the smash of them colliding into the corpses of their cousins even sweeter to Joel's ears. If he'd had a hard week at school, he'd craved nothing more desperately than a trip to the bottle bank with his dad.

When do you think they'll have kids, funnelled Beth, as Joel started to scour an enamel roasting tin in small, violent circles.

I told you to stop coming in here, thought Joel. But he couldn't fully disguise his delight that he could talk to Beth without seeming like he'd lost his marbles. It was like having someone spend the night at yours when you weren't expecting it. He hadn't tidied up the corners of his mind or made his bed before Beth came barging in. Yet, despite the mess, he couldn't deny he was glad she was there. It sure as hell beat spending the night in his head alone.

'I know,' she said, out loud this time so as not to make Joel's thoughts too congested, 'but I wanted to check in on what the plan was.'

What plan? he thought.

'The plan to get Nina to fall madly and deeply in love with you in the next three days,' said Beth.

That plan sounds a bit suspect, he thought. Like he was trying to play a Shakespearean bed trick on her. Joel plucked the roasting tin from the depths of the greying soapy water and propped it in the dish rack along with the rest of the half-dry plates.

'I didn't mean it like that,' she said. 'I just think you're still a little rusty when it comes to the whole dating thing. It wouldn't hurt to do some practice beforehand.'

Are you asking me out on a date? thought Joel.

'Maybe,' she said, arching her eyebrows into a message Joel couldn't quite decipher.

Days left to fall in love: 3

Running From The Past

'This was not what I had in mind,' panted Joel. His chest was aching. His face had started to resemble an overgrown strawberry and was covered in a layer of hot, salty sweat which stung the corners of his eyes as well as a painful spot volcanoing out of his temple. Seeing as she no longer had lungs that could burn or muscles that could cramp, Beth had suggested they go for a run to try to figure out what the best 'game plan' would be. It presented them with a chance to clear the air and see a different side of the city, she thought. In short: Beth didn't want to do endless laps around London Fields.

'You've got to get out of your comfort zone,' said Beth. Joel shot her an apprehensive look. 'I know it's not a nice thing to hear,' she continued, bouncing nimbly on the balls of her feet, 'but you've got set in your ways since I've been gone.'

'No, I haven't,' protested Joel, struggling to spit the words out as he manoeuvred less than nimbly around a postbox.

'Yes, you have. You do pretty much the exact same

thing at the exact same time, every single day. You're like a clockwork person. How do you think Nina's going to react if you tell her you don't want to pick up a pastry for breakfast because you've already planned to have a bowl of cereal instead? The exact same bowl of own-brand Shreddies you've already had every other day of the week? You need to realise that sometimes – just sometimes – things in life don't go to plan, Joel. But more importantly, some things in life don't need a plan.'

Joel's feet pounded heavily on the pavement. He could feel the shockwave from each step shoot up his thighs as his muscles asked each other how much more they could take. He eased up slightly so he had enough oxygen left to ask Beth a question. 'But I thought the whole point of today was to work out a plan for how I'm going to get Nina to continue dating me? And, by the way, I do know things don't always go to plan. I wasn't exactly planning on being widowed at the age of twenty-five.'

'For the last time, Joel: you're not a widower. And I only said we needed a game plan because I knew you couldn't resist the idea of having a checklist of things to tick off. I even considered coming up with a catchy acronym using the initials of Nina's name. I gave up at the second "N". You've got to learn how to relax again. You've got to learn to let go.'

Beth took that exact moment to shift her weight to the side and make a tight handbrake turn.

Taken by surprise, Joel stumbled, his feet slipping on

the damp grass as he tried to adjust his footing and follow her. He cursed under his breath, his heart racing as he fought to regain his balance. He thought about how he hadn't pushed himself this far, physically, in a while as he pumped the pistons of his legs to try and catch up with Beth. He couldn't deny it felt good to exhaust his body so his brain could find some peace. Why did she always have to be right about these things?

When he finally caught up with Beth, Joel tried giving her a Cool Hand Luke-like glance to let her know, 'You'll have to try harder than that to get rid of me!' But all Beth did was look back smugly at Joel's glistening face. She might have been exhausted, worn down by the battle between her desire to return to the afterlife and the guilt gnawing at her insides, but her legs kept moving, refusing to give in. This must be what it's like for people who are naturally good at running, thought Beth. Even her breasts, which had been prone to chafing painfully whenever she'd run pre-death, seemed to be absolutely fine. Her body felt like a well-oiled machine, every joint and ligament moving together in liquid harmony. The irony of only attaining this fluidity and agency over her body after it had been incinerated and scattered on Brighton beach wasn't lost on her.

Beth felt like she could go on forever but she knew she'd have to stop at some point before Joel actually keeled over. She flicked her wrist out to check on her watch, a vintage boy scout Timex that she'd taken with her into the afterlife – before realising its glass was marred by a large crack. Why hadn't she noticed that before? The watch had been a gift from her father. He'd presented it to her on her fifteenth birthday, jokingly claiming it was a present for her *quinceañera* (her family wasn't even vaguely Hispanic).

'The only thing in life you can never buy more of is time,' he'd said, the smell of his stale tobacco breath disgusting and beguiling in equal measure. Beth remembered the way he'd delicately cinched the brown leather onto her wrist and helped her set it to the correct time by nimbly twisting the watch's crown. She'd been surprised his large stubby fingers were able to make such delicate movements. The watch was the last gift he'd ever given her before he ran out on their family for good a few weeks later.

No matter how hard she searched in and around the wrinkles of her brain, Beth couldn't find the memory of when or where she might have broken that watch. As far as she could recall, it had always been in mint condition, ticking along slowly and surely until the day of her death. And that's when it hit her. It must have happened then, at that crucial moment of bone-crunching impact. Beth stopped in her tracks and Joel nearly came crashing to the ground as he tried to halt his momentum.

'Are you all right?' he gasped after he'd regained his footing. He stood in front of her with his hands on his hips, inhaling greedily through his nose and exhaling huge gusts of recycled air out of his mouth. His face had shifted along the fresh produce aisle from strawberry to a deep shade of beetroot.

Nearly Departed

'Yes,' said Beth, 'it's just my watch.' She held up her wrist so Joel could see the lightning strike fracture that was impeding her from telling the time. 'I think it must have happened when . . .'

Joel looked up at Beth with his azure eyes and tried to slow his heart rate enough to form a coherent sentence.

'It did,' he said, panting between syllables. 'Because I had it fixed afterwards.'

Now it was Beth's turn to be breathless. Why hadn't she known this? Was her omnipotence fading the longer she stayed down here? Or was this information Joel had simply pushed to the back of his consciousness so she couldn't find it? And if that was the case, what other important information could he be hiding in there, tucked away from her sight?

'You had it what?' she asked.

'Fixed,' he said. 'I'll show you.'

Watch This

Joel opened the door to his bedroom and marched towards a chest of drawers squeezed into the corner. Beth's heart raced at a hundred miles an hour. He wasn't going to do what she thought he was going to do, was he? The chest was an antique piece he'd found on Facebook Marketplace, made of dark mahogany with intricate carvings on the edges. It had four drawers, each with a brass handle that had been polished to a shine. The top of the chest was slightly scratched and it had a few other nicks here and there, but overall it was in good condition.

The drawers were packed full of Joel's clothes and various other belongings, with some items spilling out onto the floor. He tugged at the second drawer, waiting to feel the satisfying clunk as it reached the limits of how far the runners would let it go and started rooting around inside. His fingers brushed against a small leather object at the back of his bottom drawer and recoiled. The drawer used to be Joel's underwear drawer. Now, it was where he kept all of Beth's cosy winter knitwear. Beth frowned at the way her favourite cable knit jumpers and wool cardigans were loafing about in there, untouched by the outside world.

'They still smell of you,' said Joel sheepishly, when he noticed Beth was staring at the clump of sweaters and outer layers he'd moved from the drawer onto the floor so he had more room to dig. 'It's not like I get them out all the time or hold them over my face while I have a wank or anything like that,' he added. 'It's just nice to know there are still some specks of you left in the flat.'

He continued to transfer the contents of the drawer to the mound of fabric piling up on the carpet until he let out a cry of triumph. 'Here it is!' he exclaimed, his voice muffled among the thick folds of wool as he teased out a small bag filled with crumpled paper. He pulled himself to his feet, his knees clicking like castanets as he stood. He's not even thirty yet and he already makes an 'oof' noise every time he sits down, thought Beth. That cannot be good. Joel held out the bag to her, cradling it in his hands as if it were a baby bird he'd rescued from the jaws of an alley cat. Beth didn't recognise the bag. She breathed a sigh of relief.

Before she could tell him to get on with it, Joel plunged his fingers into the bag and fished out the watch. The chestnut-coloured leather was slightly frayed on one side but the face was immaculate. It looked almost brand new. Beth was impressed it was still ticking, every passing second denoted by the little hand shuffling dutifully around the dial of the watch.

'The man in the shop said he was surprised by how

little damage had actually been done. He said it must have been lucky,' said Joel, turning the watch so he could look it in the eye. 'He managed to fix the crystal – that's what they call the watch glass, apparently – in about two days.'

Beth kept switching her focus from the cracked watch on her wrist to the pristine one in Joel's hands. It was the same watch, that was certain. But she couldn't help wondering how Joel had got his hands on something that had been attached to her dead body.

'How did you get it?' she asked.

Joel closed his fist around the watch and took a deep breath. Beth watched as his nostrils flared, expanding and contracting as he tried to compose himself. 'They gave it to me after I went and identified the body,' he said. '*Your* body. They couldn't offer me any of your clothes because they were too, um, bloody. But they gave me this.' He rocked the watch slowly up and down in his palm like he was weighing a bag of money.

'Oh,' said Beth, 'I'm so sorry.' She reached out to touch the nape of his neck, to offer him a crumb of human contact, but pulled her hand back before her fingers met his skin. It was too risky. She knew he wanted nothing more than to feel the comfort of her touch and she hated herself for depriving him of that. His face was pinched with hurt but there was resignation and acceptance in his eyes. She knew he understood.

'It's okay,' he said, half believing for a second that it really was. 'I couldn't even bear to look at the watch after I'd got it fixed. Getting it fixed was something I felt I should do – maybe because it was the only thing I could do – but I felt terrible as soon as I got it back. I hated how much it reminded me of you, so I hid it in here under all your clothes. It belonged with you. Seeing it without you felt . . . wrong.'

Suddenly, with a strained sound, Joel bent his head and began to cry. He felt a wave of exhaustion come crashing down over him. He was wiped – physically and emotionally. The run had drained his body's battery, filling each limb with lactic acid, and now, faced with the object ticking faintly in his grasp, he let himself give in to his emotions. Sadness drenched him, inside and out, and his tears fell like fat raindrops onto the beige carpet. Each tick of the watch was a reminder of the guilt that weighed heavy on his soul, a haunting flicker of a past he couldn't seem to shake.

It had been ticking on Beth's wrist their whole relationship and Joel knew, deep down, he'd hidden the watch because it was proof of two painful things. One: it was a reminder that the person who used to wear it was no longer around to tell the time. That Timex had practically been an extension of Beth's body – she'd worn it when she showered, when she slept, and she'd even worn it during sex. Beth had never had an orgasm without that watch on her wrist. Seeing it lying there naked, curled up foetally in the palm of his hand, was a tangible reminder of Beth's death that Joel didn't want to accept. And two: the reflection that bounced off the now-perfect glass showed Joel exactly who he was.

He saw a man who'd try to fix every problem he

encountered; someone who'd try to find a logical solution to patch over whatever he – or anyone else – was feeling, no matter how illogical that feeling might be. There was no problem, in his mind, that couldn't be solved with a bit of level-headed thinking and enough time for action. His reaction to receiving the last thing Beth had ever worn hadn't been an emotional one, it had been cold and rational: 'This is broken, I must fix it.' Even the police officer who'd presented Joel with the watch had expected some waterworks or an overt display of grief but Joel had simply thanked them cordially and walked out of the door to find the nearest Timpson.

He was staring at a man who thought some part of Beth could be preserved if he got her favourite timepiece fixed. If he couldn't keep her heart beating then at least he could keep her watch ticking. Right? What he'd failed to realise was that by fixing Beth's watch, he'd inadvertently destroyed it. He'd turned it into something new. Something alien. Joel was disgusted with what he'd done. He threw the watch back into the bag and began covering it back up with the mound of jumpers that had kept it hidden for the last three years.

Beth stood by Joel as he started throwing her clothes back into the drawer. She watched as an olive-coloured cardigan flew in headfirst after a navy cashmere jumper she had always been too scared to wear. It was as if he was trying, and failing, to put a genie back into the bottle. She hadn't intended for any of this to happen, of course. If anything, Beth had thought she would be the one overwrought with emotion when she saw that watch again. But she hadn't been. She'd simply felt touched that Joel had gone to the effort of fixing it for her, and a bit sad he couldn't read the act as anything but a giant, wobbly metaphor.

The room was well-kept and tidy, with two tasteful framed prints on the wall and a single plant thriving on the windowsill, yet it still felt utterly cluttered with memories. Living here can't be easy, thought Beth. And it can't be healthy either. Every corner of the flat was saturated with her. Even before she'd come back and sat down on the settee, the place remained as if Beth had only just got up off it, the seat still warm from her touch. She could tell, as he let out a guttural sob, that Joel was tired of running from his feelings but had no idea how to stop. Or was simply too afraid to. He wasn't just scared of his emotions catching up to him – he was afraid they'd overtake him, forcing him to become a spectator as he watched them speed off into the distance.

'You can't run forever,' said Beth. Joel looked up through the Venetian blinds of his fingers, ashamed of how heavily he'd been ugly-crying, and tried to pull himself together. He swallowed his sobs, brushed away the tear tracks on his face using the fleshy part of his palm, and took in a few deep breaths. He hadn't been privy to any of Beth's internal monologue – or the impressive running analogy she'd come up with on the fly – but all the same, Joel was fairly confident he knew what she meant when she'd said he couldn't 'run forever'.

He'd thought by constantly moving he'd been getting on with his life. But maybe Beth was right.

All teared out, Joel was thumped with an epiphany. Yes, it was a big word but he felt it was suited to the size of the realisation he had come to. Everything was suddenly clear to him. He knew exactly what he had to do – not only to help Beth find her way back to the afterlife but also to move forward with his own life. He got onto his knees and started rifling through the jumper drawer to find what he was so desperately looking for. His fingers grasped the familiar shape of the paper bag he'd rammed to the back and he pulled hard until he'd prised it back out again. With the watch in his hand, Joel looked up and gave Beth a smile. She smiled back nervously, uncertain about what he was planning on doing, but happy to see him smiling nonetheless.

'Thank you,' said Joel, as he looked Beth right in her beautiful green eyes. For once in his life, he was ready to stop being so fucking rational. It was time to act on pure impulse.

'For what?' asked Beth. She could see a mélange of sadness and madness in his eyes she hadn't ever seen before.

'For everything,' he said, and as he did so, he ran to the window and threw out the watch as hard as he could. He watched, hypnotised by its flight, as it sailed through the air and landed with a distant crack on the pavement four floors below. He turned from the window to get a final look at Beth before she disappeared into

Nearly Departed

the ether. He got to the 'good' part of 'goodbye' before he realised she wasn't dematerialising before his eyes. Instead of slowly turning transparent or fading back into whatever form her spirit might have taken, Beth was simply standing where she'd stood fifteen seconds before with her arms folded across her body.

'And WHAT,' she shouted, 'THE FUCK DID YOU DO THAT FOR?'

Wish You Were Here

They sat on the floor, cross-legged, and let the gentle glow of the television lap at their knees. After Joel had lobbed Beth's watch out of the window and into the oncoming traffic, a good twenty minutes of confusion had ensued as Beth tried to figure out what, exactly, had been going through Joel's head. Not a lot, it turned out.

'So, just to get this straight, you thought launching my watch onto the pavement and breaking it would . . . free me from my shackles? Like a genie?'

'Yes.'

'And what was your thought process behind that?'

Joel rubbed the back of his head like a lamp. He enjoyed the Brillo pad feel of it and wondered if, maybe subconsciously, he'd adopted the same haircut as the Action Men he used to play with as a child because it gave him a feeling of comfort and nostalgia.

'You're the one who said I needed to think less and act more. I was trusting my gut.'

'I appreciate the gesture, Joel. I guess it just would have been nice if your gut could show its workings.'

Nearly Departed

'There wasn't much logic,' he admitted, 'but there's also not much logic in being able to chat to a ghost, either.'

'That's a fair point,' said Beth, who didn't avert her eyes from the screen as she spoke. She was amused at how, despite her having missed out on years of popular culture, daytime television hadn't changed. It was still full of all the same faces doing the same inane panel shows and travel programmes. Joel's phone lit up briefly before he flipped it over onto its face. 'Shouldn't you be at work right now?'

'I've got the day off,' said Joel, whose eyes were just as glued to James Martin's mum-friendly face. He'd told Sabine he'd had a death in the family last night – a grandmother he'd been 'ever so close' with – and would need a couple of days off to comfort his mother on her loss. It was, if Joel's maths was correct, the last grandparent death he'd be able to use up at work. Which was a shame considering two of his grandparents were still alive and kicking.

The sky peeping through the window was a comically bright shade of blue; the kind of perfect blue you only ever see in animated movies or on postcards. A balmy wind blew gently through the trees, causing the smaller saplings to sway their hips like hula dancers, and the sound of the television competed with the rustling and twittering of nature going about its business. It was, in many ways, the perfect day to waste inside.

'Do you still want to come up with a plan of attack for your next date with Nina?' asked Beth, as Joel fumbled around the cupboards and pulled out a sleeve of chocolate digestive biscuits.

He tilted his head towards Beth.

'Why? What did you have in mind? A Rocky Balboa training montage?'

'Something like that,' laughed Beth. And the kettle, which had been steadily chugging along for the last couple of minutes, gave a soft click and hiss to let them know it had reached its boiling point.

Tin Can Telephone

Alice sank onto her sofa and slipped off her clogs. Home. She rested her heels on the coffee table and placed her mug down, gently, on the only coaster within arm's reach. The sofa was three years old and cinnabar red, made from an eco-velvet material which an attractive sales assistant had upsold to her. The coaster was worn and smelled faintly of ale and cigarettes. James had stolen it from a pub after a big night out with his five-a-side teammates and she hadn't ever bothered to throw it out. Alice's self-pottered mug concealed most of the 'Don't Worry, Drink Guinness' slogan printed on it so it simply shouted 'Don't' at her instead. Smug coaster, she thought. She watched as the steam from the tea dissipated into the air.

Sam picked up after the third ring. He said hello, and Alice said hello back. Then silence. For a moment, Alice thought she might have called the wrong number. Sam wondered the same. Then, like a pistol, she burst into the monologue she had planned out. Sam knew it couldn't be anyone but Alice railing at him at full throttle on a school night. Alice knew it couldn't be anyone but Sam who would silently accept her tirade with nothing but the occasional putter or murmur of agreement.

'So, basically: he says they've been seeing each other again,' said Alice.

'Right. Yes. But Beth's dead.'

'Yes. Beth's dead.'

'And when you say they've been seeing each other, you don't just mean he's, like, having lucid daydreams about her?'

'No, I mean, he thinks that he's seeing her. Literally. And talking to her. Literally. And walking around with her. Literally.'

'And touching her?'

'No, no touching.' She could hear Sam frown. 'If she touches him or he touches her, he sort of . . . short-circuits.'

Sam paused. He cradled his phone between his ear and his shoulder and picked at a hangnail on his left index. He pulled the scrap of skin back, sharply, until the elastic of it snapped to unsheathe a perfectly straight, perfectly crimson strip of flesh. A dot of hot blood bubbled up and he plunged his digit into his mouth, hoping Alice couldn't hear him sucking down the phone line.

'Really?' he said, tongue still curled around his finger.

'Yes.'

'Far out.'

'Yes: far out.'

'What are you going to do about it?'

'What am *I* going to do about it?!'

'Sorry. I mean, what are *we* going to do about it?'

Alice put her hand to her stomach. 'I don't know. I'm worried about him. That's why I called. I don't know if this is a "we have to get him sectioned" kind of conversation.'

'I don't think we're quite at the sectioning stage. Yet. I saw him last night and—'

'How did he seem?'

'Fine,' said Sam.

'Fine?'

'Yeah, fine. Maybe a little distracted. But no more than normal. He didn't really mention that he'd been speaking to the dead.' Sam opened a drawer and pulled out a plaster. 'But he did say he's got to fall in love with someone in the next three days.'

'What?'

'Yeah, I know. He's set himself this deadline to – in his words, not mine – quote-unquote "move on with his life".'

'He told me that a few weeks ago but I thought he was taking the piss. Did he really say "quote-unquote"?'

'He really did.'

'I guess it's good he's set himself a goal . . .'

'Even if it's one that's completely fucking ridiculous?'

Alice picked at a piece of bulgur wheat lurking between her teeth. 'Everyone needs a hobby,' she said.

'And I'm guessing you still haven't told him about you and James?'

'God, no. I don't think it's the right time.'

'Is there ever going to be a right time?'

'No, maybe not. Maybe I'll lie to him about my relationship status for the rest of my life. In fact, maybe I'll kill James and drag his corpse around with me to parties, *Weekend at Bernie's*-style.'

Sam laughed. 'I just don't think Joel will take the news very well,' continued Alice. 'He's always talked about how he can't wait to go to our wedding and I know he made a bet with you that me and James were going to be the first ones to have a baby.'

'Twenty quid as well.'

'Exactly! So, how do I tell him we're breaking up because it's literally got to the point where we can't stand being in the same room as each other? Where even just the thought of kissing him makes my vagina wince?'

'You could probably say that exact sentence to him and it'd get the point across pretty succinctly.'

Alice sighed. 'I know, I should tell him. But he seems so . . . fragile right now. I'll tell him when he's on an upswing and hope it doesn't bring him crashing back down to thinking the world is a loveless hellscape.'

'You think awfully highly of yourself, don't you?'

'Bite me, dickhead.'

He laughed. 'I can see why James wanted to break up with you.'

'The feeling was mutual, don't worry.'

'I am sorry, though. Genuinely. It sucks.'

Sam stood up, then walked into the kitchen before forgetting why he'd even wanted to go there in the first place.

'Thanks. It does suck. But I know it won't suck forever.'

'You hope it won't suck forever.'

'It's always a real pick-me-up talking to you, Sam.'

'I mean to please. Is it weird that I miss these little emergency chats?' he asked. 'Even though they were, you know, mostly about thinking of fun and inventive ways to stop Joel from killing himself.'

'No. I miss them, too,' Alice laughed. She had once – during the peak of their intense daily phone-call phase – had a vivid sex dream about Sam. She'd woken up with the residue of his fingers still gently exploring the curve of her throat, and it had left her feeling awkward around him for a couple of days.

'Can plasters expire?' he asked, wrapping a beige-coloured one around his finger.

'Maybe. I don't know. Why are you asking me that?'

'No reason,' he mumbled, scrunching up the two discarded halves of paper plaster backing into a ball. 'So, how often is he seeing her?'

'He said he'd been seeing her every day.' Alice stared at the jet black version of herself broadcasted on her television and adjusted her fringe. 'Then she disappeared. But now I think she's back again.'

'Why do you think she's back?'

'Because the last thing he texted me was: "She's back".'

'Oh. Yeah. It sounds like she's back, in that case.'

'I just want you to promise me you'll look out for him.'

'I will,' said Sam. 'Of course I will. You know I will.'

'I know you will. I just want us to be there for him. Together. Both of us. And it's impossible for me to do that when he won't reply to any of my texts. Or answer any of my phone calls.'

Sam smiled absently. 'That sounds like Joel, all right,' he said. 'I'll send him a message later and see if I can nudge him to start speaking to some people who are actually alive. Try not to worry too much. And tell Joel about the break-up. Okay?'

'Okay.'

'Okay.'

'Okay.'

Alice put the phone down. She let it sit face down on her coffee table, nuzzled next to her now-tepid tea, for thirty seconds before she picked it up again.

Who else could she call?

Romantic Comedy

'So, what did we learn from that then?' asked Beth as Elton John warbled over the end credits.

'I've learned Andie MacDowell can't act,' said Joel, smiling his dopey smile and expecting a laugh.

'Joel, this is serious business,' said Beth. Her face flushed slightly and the corners of her mouth turned down in the opposite of a smile.

He took a deep breath. The moon was nestled in the night sky, swaddled with a blanket of stars. *Four Weddings and a Funeral* was the fifth rom-com they'd watched in a row and, despite his weakness for cheesy romance, Joel had just about hit meet-cute fatigue. Keen to get him back in touch with his romantic side, Beth had subjected Joel to what she referred to as 'the canon': Curtis, Ephron, Meyers, Reiner. Hours of hopelessly gorgeous people falling hopelessly in and out of love.

'I guess I've learned love isn't always so black and white and that, sometimes, you can end up finding the right person at the wrong time or, conversely, the wrong person at the right time,' he said, between mouthfuls, as he worked his jaw around the final biscuit from the packet. 'Also,' he added, licking the last remaining traces of chocolate from his fingers, 'I've learned weddings are a great place to meet people.'

'All right. Good,' said Beth. 'I'd say that's a pretty fair assessment. '

'Do I get a gold star now?'

'That depends.'

'On what?'

'Depends on who you thought Hugh Grant should have ended up with?'

'Kristin Scott Thomas. Obviously,' said Joel.

'Well, then,' said Beth, looking at Joel with amusement, 'I think my work here is done.'

'Really?' he asked. 'That's it? All it takes is watching a couple of rom-coms to become a master of romance?'

'Of course not,' laughed Beth. 'To be honest, I'd consider a lot of the behaviour exhibited in romantic comedies to be borderline sociopathic. Like, would you ever dump your fiancé because you've got a date with a man you've never met on top of the Empire State Building?'

Joel gave Beth's question a lot more thought than it probably deserved.

'That depends,' he said.

'On what?'

'On whether that man is Tom Hanks or not.'

'Good point,' conceded Beth. 'But I stand by my belief that rom-coms aren't a particularly useful learning tool. Unless you're trying to learn what not to do in a real relationship, that is.'

'Then why, for the love of God, did you make me sit through five of them in one go?' asked Joel, exasperated.

Beth tiptoed over the biscuit crumbs starting a conga line on the carpet and plonked herself down in front of her ex-boyfriend, blocking his view of the television. 'Look, Joel,' she said, brushing her hair away from the moon of her face, 'I'm pretty sure you owe me one after you threw my only remaining possession out of the window.'

Joel nodded. She had a point. He was also pretty sure the lesson she'd been trying to teach him all along was that he didn't need any 'training' or 'plan of attack' or floppy hair like Hugh to be prepared for another date with Nina.

That's right, funnelled Beth.

All he actually needed to do was be himself.

Bingo, funnelled Beth.

She'd either be into him, or she wouldn't. Simple as that. The heart wants what it wants, and all that jazz.

'If I was a therapist, I'd call that a breakthrough,' said Beth. Her head was silhouetted against the names of the producers and camera grips trickling down the television screen. 'Love is simple. It's about trying. But not too much – just the right amount. And as often as you can.'

She smiled. Her eyes did that frustratingly gorgeous thing they did where they glinted and crinkled at the same time and made Joel forget just about everything he'd been going to say. He could feel tears pricking at the back of his eyes, threatening to race down his face like raindrops on a car window.

'I think you've watched enough rom-coms for today,' he said.

'I think so too,' said Beth.

Tangled up in her smile, and high on a supply of Richard Curtis, he tilted towards Beth and kissed her – channelling all of his desire, anguish and desperation into his faintly dry lips. And, to his surprise, she kissed him back. Even in her low-energy state, she couldn't ignore how badly she'd missed feeling wanted. Needed. Craved. The afterlife had its advantages, but the absence of anything even vaguely kissable wasn't one of them.

The kiss lasted only a few seconds, but it was long enough for Joel to realise kissing Beth wasn't the same as it used to be. For one thing, it hurt. While he didn't have any similar experience to compare it to, the closest he could think of is that it was like licking a battery – not entirely unpleasant, but strange. Her lips were cold and faintly metallic, making the kiss both painful and addictive. His heart raced, not only with excitement but with a genuine sense of fear. Feeling lightheaded and wincing at the thought of more pain, he closed his eyes and leaned in. They kissed again, harder this time. Their lips met with a crackle, sending little sparks of electricity skittering around their tongues like popping candy. His mouth, warm and chocolatey, contrasted sharply with the coldness of hers.

For a moment, everything else faded into the background. The entire world shrank to the living room. Joel's worries seeped from his body: slowly, and then suddenly. All the anxious red dots of unanswered emails and concerns about his pension were whooshed from his brain and replaced by a low purr of contentment, as if his mind had finally sat down on something comfortable after a long day on its feet. No thoughts, just feelings, rattled around his head. And then . . . Nina. He couldn't help but picture her face – her soft Bambi-like eyes, her arched eyebrows, the way she pouted her lips like she was drinking from a straw whenever she was lost in thought. And even though she was only there for a split-second, Joel knew Beth had seen her on his brain. Beth flung her head back, ending the kiss.

Should he feel relieved? Sad? Sorry? Beth, breathless, looked at him with a mix of fury and bewilderment before pulling him in for what he could only assume was a fatal snog.

Thankfully for Joel, the kiss wasn't lethal.

He woke from his blackout about ten minutes later, dazed and confused, with the worst headache of his adult life. Rubbing the pebbly imprint of the carpet from his cheek, he pulled himself up from the floor.

'You've got a date to get ready for,' Beth said from the kitchen, watching him as if nothing had happened. As if her heart wasn't breaking.

Ablutions

Third dates are sticky territory. They are, more often than not, the fulcrum point where a situationship can turn from something casual and relaxed into something more serious. It's not where you're going to necessarily have 'the talk' or throw a 'So, what are we?' into the mix but it's where you'll probably be able to tell – even if it's just a gut feeling – whether or not you have a connection with the person you've been investing a couple of hours of your life in every now and then.

Having a shit and a shower was a big part of Joel's pre-date routine, and always had to be done in that specific order. It was cleaner, because that way you could perform your ablutions in a full-body bidet. Joel washed his hands in the sink and looked at himself in the mirror while he waited for the water to come up to the right temperature for his shvitz, appraising a face he wasn't keen on but hoped Nina could love.

Two miles as the crow flies, tucked away in a leafy enclave of Stoke Newington slowly being swallowed by nice coffee shops and organic greengrocers, Nina stared at her own reflection in the mirror. She didn't

Nearly Departed

completely hate what she saw but she wished her face was more symmetrical. She'd read that was why celebrities were so attractive to normal people; their faces were more symmetrical. Nina's left eye was slightly lazy (her dad called it her work-shy eye) but she only ever let it slump when she was either dog-tired or in the presence of someone she was immensely comfortable around. Her lips were full, a characteristic she'd inherited from her mother, and were perennially on the verge of chapping. A six-month course of Roaccutane when she was seventeen had cleared her skin but ravaged her lips in return. Now, she'd never leave the house without a little tub of Vaseline huddled in her bag under a mass of receipts and keys.

Nina's pre-date routine wasn't all that dissimilar from Joel's. It involved a matching shit and then shower but Nina, who had a thing for efficiency, one-upped Joel in the grooming department by squeezing in a quick shave while she washed. A hot shower offered the perfect amount of lubricant for Nina to glide her razor effortlessly with and against the grain of the tiny spider hairs on her legs. She was self-conscious about the cracked skin of her heels. Was it unfeminist to shave your legs before a date, she thought, taking her razor on a second lap of her right leg. No, surely not. Nina had read in an op-ed the other day that self-care was actually a radically feminist notion and shaving your legs and/or armpits was no longer considered a kick in the teeth of Emmeline Pankhurst. She liked that take, even if she wasn't completely sure she believed it.

The heat of the water had misted Nina's shower screen with a thick film of condensation. She drew an inelegant smiley face with one hand, lathering up her body with the other.

As she watched the smiley slowly fade into the newest layer of water droplets, she tried to picture Joel's smile. It was the first thing she'd properly noticed about him when they'd met. The first thing that had made him a 3D person to her. Unlike most of the men she'd dated in quick succession over the past year, Joel didn't seem embarrassed about expressing joy or delight. It'd taken him a while to get warmed up during their first date, to be sure, but after a glass of wine, he was offering her his straight but slightly coffee-stained teeth at regular intervals. She'd been having a great time in his company until he'd turned as white as a ghost and hit the deck.

'He's . . . interesting,' is what Nina had told her flatmate, Des, when she'd got back home after that first date. And although she was slightly worried about Joel's general state of health – no one should be fainting at a wine bar unless they were in their twilight years – that 'interesting' was more than she could say for most of the men who were taking up real estate in her DMs. He'd asked her questions, *plural*, and didn't just wait for his turn to talk after she'd answered them. 'But is interesting good-looking?' asked Des. 'Yes,' said Nina, and it was only when she said it out loud that she realised she was actually quite attracted to Joel.

There was nothing wrong with the way he looked but there was nothing jaw-droppingly gorgeous about it either. It was simply that, when you added them all together, his features seemed to get along well enough with each other to form a face that looked like it cared with a mouth that looked like it was accustomed to saying 'please' and 'thank you'. He was, by every metric, what her mother would have called a 'nice young man'. But Nina still wasn't sure if a 'nice young man' was exactly what she was looking for.

Hanging Around

'You're sure you don't want to come?'

Joel gave the duck egg blue workmen's shirt he was wearing a final spritz of aftershave for luck, the woody and familiar scent of a design technology workshop embedded its atoms into the fabric. Beth, meanwhile, laid on the sofa with her head on one armrest and her feet on the other. It was a therapy session pose that had its symbolism driven home by the way she rested her hands on her stomach and married her fingers together in a cross-stitch.

'I'm sure,' said Beth. She leaned her head back over the arm of the sofa until it was dangling upside down like a bat. Even with his smile flipped to a frown and his feet glued to the ceiling, Joel looked good. He'd scrubbed up nicely for his date and Beth could tell he had taken an extra fifteen minutes or so to ensure his appearance was more manicured than usual. She couldn't see his bare feet because they were encased in his favourite pair of scuffed Blundstone boots, but she was pretty sure if she were to pull off those boots and remove his socks she'd see ten recently clipped toenails.

Nearly Departed

'Do you want me to turn the TV on?' asked Joel. They still hadn't talked about the kiss, about what had happened. With every mundane conversation they substituted for the serious one, it felt increasingly likely they never would.

'That'd be great,' said Beth. And with a flick of the space commander, Joel brought the television humming back to life. It was a Lazarus moment; a miracle in miniature he enacted each and every day.

'And you're sure you're going to be fine just . . . *hanging* around here?' he said, fumbling with the buttons until he settled on a channel he thought Beth would be happy to soak in for the next couple of hours. At his audibly italicised use of the word 'hanging', Beth swivelled her head, Nosferatu-style, back to an upright position.

'Yes,' said Beth, 'I'm sure. You don't need me constantly peering over your shoulder telling you what to do anymore, Joel. You're mid-nineties Hugh Grant, remember? You've got this.'

'Right. Yes. Absolutely,' said Joel, doing his best Hugh Grant impression. It was probably a six out of ten in terms of vocal accuracy but his commitment to the jittery head movements took it up to an eight.

Beth rolled her eyes. 'Where is it you're going again?' she asked.

'Trisha's,' he said, after an agonising pause. But before Joel had even got to the last syllable, Beth was sent hurtling down memory lane to the last night she'd spent at Trisha's. She had blurry, distorted memories of singing

'Sweet Caroline' into a microphone and spilling an entire tray of tequila shots onto the already sticky floor. She had even fuzzier memories of potentially – shamefully – trying to lap up the tequila like a tabby cat.

Trisha's wasn't a bar you went to as your primary destination of the night but, rather, somewhere you ended up after having too many drinks and making too many bad decisions somewhere else. The wine was bad, the cocktails were paint-stripper strong, and you'd invariably bump into at least one person there who claimed to know the Kray twins.

Beth would almost have respected Joel for having the chutzpah to take Nina to Trisha's if she hadn't also thought he was out of his fucking mind. In all fairness, though, it was an extremely Joel thing to do.

'I guess all I can say is: good luck.'

'Thanks,' he said. 'Let's hope I don't need it.'

He grabbed his nearest tote bag, which was drooping bluebell-like off the coat hook in the hallway, and threw his keys and a battered paperback into it as he reached towards the door. Before he pulled back the handle and threw himself into the night, he turned to have a last look at Beth, who was draped on the sofa in a position resembling Ramon Casas's *Decadent young woman. After the dance* – a painting Beth had made him read about only a couple of days ago.

He was surprised his brain was so quick to make that artistic connection. Was this what being cultured was like? Could he call himself an aesthete now? His eyes found Beth's across the room and they soaked up the contact. Beth didn't even need to funnel her thoughts into his head this time; Joel knew exactly which three words her dilated pupils were trying to say and he said them back with his own. Beth offered a small, almost imperceptible, nod of her head and Joel exited the flat in a gust of energy.

Trisha's

As Nina walked up to the red pin her phone was calling 57 Greek Street, she started to get the feeling something wasn't quite right. She looked up from her device, swivelled her head like an owl, and buried her nose back into her maps to make sure she'd arrived at the right location. *Meet me at the blue door* was what Joel had texted her earlier and, sure enough, she was standing right in front of a bright blue door. But that was all there seemed to be. There were plenty of ropey-looking pubs and chain restaurants nearby, but number 57 looked like it was the entrance to someone's flat.

Putting her ear close to the door, Nina could make out the distant rabbit-foot thump of music. Joel, however, was nowhere to be seen. If this was one of those speakeasy-style places where you had to give a password or ring a special phone number so you could be led through a secret entrance behind a gimmicked bookcase or washing machine then Nina was afraid she had gravely misread how much she and Joel had in common. There was nothing worse, in her mind, than a bar that felt the need to define itself as 'an experience'.

Thankfully, after a few hour-like seconds of fretting Joel might have stood her up, Nina saw all five foot seven of him approaching from the end of the street. She hustled her phone into her pocket and offered him a little wave. He offered one back and, when he was within arm's reach, gave her a hug, too.

'I hope you haven't been here long,' he said, and she could smell the gentle scent of him, hanging in the air between them.

'No, I literally just got here.' She smiled. 'But I've got to admit, I'm not quite sure where "here" is.'

'Don't worry,' Joel said decisively. 'I haven't invited you to an escape room or anything like that.'

He winched open the door and sauntered down the stairs with the confidence of someone walking into their own living room. A middle-aged man at the bottom of the stairs was fishing in his pockets for a £2 coin to pay his entrance fee. Nina was about to do the same before they were waved through by the matron with a conspiratorial wink. Nina hated how impressed she was by the whole exchange.

The first thing Nina noticed about Trisha's, or The New Evaristo Club as it was apparently technically known, was that she wasn't the only non-white person in the room. Needless to say, that was a good sign in her books – especially as it was one she didn't come across often enough. Especially on dates with white men.

The second thing she noticed was that Trisha's was a bit of a dive. The floors were sticky and the air was thick with the smell of cheap liquor. The bar was a long, worn-out affair that looked like it had seen better days. Behind it, a row of grimy, mismatched bottles lined the shelves, each one promising a different brand of escape. She couldn't deny, despite its wear and tear, the place had character. Fairy lights twinkled benevolently above the bar, and photos of celebrities ranging from Frank Sinatra to Anthony Bourdain and Pope Benedict XVI took up residence on the walls. If only walls could talk, thought Nina, as she peeled her feet off the tequila-lacquered floor.

Although the clientele wasn't solely white, it was solely eccentric. She counted at least four pork-pie hats in the room as the music shifted its mood from bad eighties pop to bad modern jazz. A glimpse of the cramped smoking area, packed with people huddling elbow to elbow like emperor penguins, made Nina glad she'd given up. The thought of a cigarette dancing in her mind, though, made her itch for her vape. She wasn't worried about vaping in front of Joel – she'd done it pretty much non-stop during their walk from the National Gallery to Chinatown for lunch – but she'd try and hold out for as long as possible tonight. She knew once she had her first inhale of Watermelon Ice she'd be jonesing for it the rest of the night.

A group of leather-clad bikers sat around a table, their beards and tattoos a testament to their rough-and-tumble lives. Across from them, a group of young-ish yuppies chatted and sucked down beers, their beards and tattoos a testament to their significantly less rough-and-tumble lives. Nina manned the table and sat below a fading *Goodfellas* poster, tapping her rings in a steady rhythm on the plastic chequered tablecloth, while Joel queued up at the bar. There wasn't exactly a huge amount of choice, but all Nina wanted was a cold beer – preferably a lager and not some fucking Tame Impala IPA. Work had been stressful lately and she craved that first sip of something inoffensive that didn't require any footnotes or backstory to explain itself. She could almost have jumped for joy when she saw Joel making his way back from the bar with a Birra Moretti in each hand.

'So,' he said, taking a quick swig of beer that made his Adam's apple bob in time to the music, 'what do you think?'

'I think it's fun,' said Nina. She took a sip from her bottle and gave a mini shudder of pleasure as its familiar malty flavour filled her mouth and cascaded down her throat. It wasn't an immediate rush of serotonin but a fainter, simmering pleasure derived from knowing the alcohol molecules would start to crack their knuckles and loosen up the knots in her head fairly soon. 'I do have to ask though,' she said, 'how many different women have you taken on a third date here?'

A hard-to-read expression came over Joel's face, and the dim lighting certainly didn't help Nina decipher what the lines on his forehead were saying. It wasn't like reading French or German or any other language with a Roman alphabet where Nina could recognise the letters and make out the rough sounds of the sentences. It was more like trying to make out the unfamiliar scratches of Cyrillic.

'Three,' is what Joel eventually spat out.

'Three seems like quite a lot of women to take to the exact same place for a third date,' laughed Nina.

'Well,' he said, shrugging, 'let's just say those dates weren't exactly successful.'

'Then why try again?'

'Because,' said Joel, 'I like the vibe here. And if I'm going to spend time with a person, I want them to be someone who appreciates a place like this, you know?'

Nina raised her eyebrows in agreement and took another sip of beer. 'Plus,' he added, 'the drinks are cheap.'

'Amen to that,' she said, only semi-ironically, and cheers'd her bottle with Joel's to make a pleasant chime.

Days left to fall in love: 1

Countdown

There are 900 seconds in fifteen minutes. Beth knew that because she had counted every single one of them, scoring a tally mark in her mind every time the clock in Joel's living room gave a little tip-of-the-tongue tick. She'd lost interest in whatever passed for prime-time television an hour ago and had spent the rest of her time trying to keep herself occupied and – more importantly – keep her thoughts away from Joel.

Jealousy is a strangely shaped emotion. It can creep up on you when you least expect it and is capable of turning the most innocent person you know into a spitting, seething gorgon.

Sanding down the edges of her envy was something Beth had actively been working on with Doctor Shah before she died. Even as a fully grown adult, her competitive streak was something to behold. And something that generally got the better of her. Playing a game of Scrabble or Boggle or Articulate! always sounded like a great idea until Beth became overly invested in the game and said something unnecessarily cutting to someone she loved.

Casting her eyes around the room in search of something – anything – interesting to look at, Beth stared at the stack of board games collecting dust on Joel's bookcase. The last time she could recall playing any of them was the night Holly and Sam had come over for a pre-Christmas knees-up. The memory came flooding back to her in glorious technicolour. Joel had made macaroni cheese and they'd all drunk a Herculean amount of mulled wine, burning away the hours of the night with so much conversation and laughter their faces were aching when the sun came up. It was the only time in her life Beth could remember not caring about whether she won or lost. Liberate yourself from desire and you'll find everything you need. That was the kind of spiel fortune cookies sold, right?

Beth closed her eyes and tried to dive back into the pure and unadulterated contentment she'd felt that evening. She went in headfirst and swam deeper and deeper into her memory of that night, dragging herself fathoms below the surface until her lungs burned cigarette holes in her chest. If you'd sat her down the morning after and asked her whether there was anything she wanted to change about her life, she'd have said no. She would have told you she wouldn't trade what she had for anything in the world. But Joel didn't ask her that. He never asked her if there was anything she'd like to change.

Beth peeled her eyes open and came back to the surface, gasping for air. Despite how hard her brain had clutched its fists and willed itself to remember what that feeling of peace was like, she couldn't tap into that emotion anymore. The memory was lucid, but the feelings attached to it? Dulled to the point of bluntness.

Meanwhile, the clock on the mantelpiece ticked and ticked and ticked and ticked with the inevitability of a metronome. Every additional tick was like an extra proverbial blade of straw placed on Beth's proverbial back. She was glad her Timex couldn't add to the chorus and traced her index finger gently over its marred glass. The watch was still handsome in spite of its scars. If anything – she thought, holding it up to the light – they added a rugged charm to its appearance. She tapped on the face in time with the tick of the clock, each gentle tap resonating with the weight of the secret she'd carried since her return. The watch. Tap. The chest of drawers. Tap. The leather box. Tap.

From the moment she'd returned, Beth had been conscious of a nagging sensation prickling the back of her mind, like an itchy label on a T-shirt. But now, for the first time since her return from eternity, she felt confident she had the strength to do what needed to be done. She placed her hand over her mouth, her fingers gently tracing the crease of her lips. It was time to cut the tag.

Maybe it was something to do with being properly alone with her thoughts for the first time in a few days – or maybe this was simply the amount of time it took for a brain to thaw itself out after dying – but all the forgotten snatches and echoes of Beth's life, which had been seeping back into her consciousness with the slow drip of a leaky tap, were now spurting out like a fire hose. She remembered the smell of her dad's chewing tobacco. She remembered the cool feel of a cat's eye marble in her mouth. She remembered swallowing that marble and waiting at the GP's office for what felt like hours while her mother scowled next to her. She remembered what she'd had for breakfast the week before she'd died. The air was clogged with memories.

Beth stood up from where she was sitting and walked straight into Joel's bedroom. In a previous life, it had been their bedroom. Now, it was his. It was where he slept and read and never ate in the bed. Beth hadn't tried moving any objects since she'd failed so desperately to pick up a mug on her first day back but, imbued now with a greater understanding of her purpose, she felt anything was possible. She threw her fingers around the small potted plant sitting in a thirsty slouch on Joel's windowsill and lifted it up with all the force she could muster. In retrospect, she might have used a bit too much. The plant sailed through the air and landed on the carpet with a thud, spilling a pattern of soil outwards like the chalk outline of a murder victim. Satisfied with her newfound ability to interact with the real world, Beth turned her attention to the drawer.

I guess Joel was right about one thing, she thought, as she tugged on each of her fingers until they gave a gentle 'pop' and pulled back the drawer as gently as she could. Maybe I do have a bit of unfinished business here.

Small Talk

The candle flickering between Nina and Joel oscillated between catching its breath and puffing its chest out valiantly to fill the crimson glass it was trapped in. The red glow coloured Nina and Joel's conversation in a clandestine, Parisian sex hotel shade of lust. 'What happens at Trisha's, stays at Trisha's,' is what Joel said to Nina as the image of Beth licking the floor flashed briefly across his mind. The right lighting could make all the difference. As they took turns to talk, Joel and Nina admitted things to each other they would not have done had their pores been under the microscope of the fluorescent white light of a kebab shop or the over-lit kitchen of a tasteless new build. Joel told Nina about the first time he'd ever seen a pair of breasts while watching *Titanic* on a tiny portable television in his grandmother's spare bedroom and she, volleying back with panache, told him about how she used to rut her stuffed animals at night before she was old enough to realise what she was doing.

Joel told Nina about how his cousin, Tom, had always dreamed of being a rock star. It was all he'd talked about at family functions when they were growing up. Tom, now thirty-nine, was currently treading the boards as snake oil salesman Adolfo Pirelli in an amateur production of *Sweeney Todd* at the Lincoln Community Theatre. And he was happy. He might not have the mansion in LA or track-marks on his arms from years of heroin abuse but he had a wife and two beautiful children and barely even missed his daydreams of headlining the Pyramid Stage. Nina could tell from the way Joel talked about marriage and love that he had a romantic streak running through him like the white shock of a skunk. His eyes lit up when he spoke about his cousin's children; he genuinely seemed interested in what they were into.

He asked her if she'd ever heard of *Bluey*, and their conversation took a swift detour to the children's television programmes they'd watched growing up. Nina had been a big fan of *The Worst Witch*. Joel still remembered the names of *Bob the Builder*'s anthropomorphic machinery. Nina tried not to be too unsurprised. There was something inherently goofy, but charming, about Joel's lack of filter. On their first two dates, he'd been reticent about getting stuck into some of the frankly bizarre topics of discussion that interested him. But now – loosened up by a couple of beers and the safety of a place he felt comfortable in – he looked and acted much more at ease. Much more himself.

Table For One

What is chemistry but a connection between two people who can make each other laugh with the prospect of sex still on the table? Nina couldn't remember the last date she'd had where she'd laughed as much as she had with Joel. It made her somewhat anxious the sex would be equally comical. Because, yes, she was thinking about having sex with him. She couldn't keep her eyes off the horseshoe of his tricep as he reached down to pick up a bottle he'd knocked over, and she continued to stare as he returned to an upright position, her eyes tracing the lines and contours of his arm. She found herself wondering what it would feel like to touch it, to run her fingers over its smooth, taut surface. She imagined the way the muscle would flex and ripple beneath her touch, the way his skin would feel warm and alive.

Joel was a refreshing change of pace to the type of men Nina usually went for. Her dates often accused her of being overly serious – too blunt about current affairs and too unflinching in her political beliefs. It was as if she couldn't help but turn every conversation into a small debate. Joel, on the other hand, seemed to actually give a shit about what she thought. He didn't agree with her on every front but they were on the same page politically and, moreover, he respected what she had to say. They'd even talked about meeting up at Hackney Marshes the next weekend, one of those London bucket list locations Nina had never got round to visiting.

She was aware of her tendency to be a little too formal, but she didn't let that stop her from segueing their serious conversations into friendlier territory. As they traded information about their favourite gothic cemeteries in the city, Nina could see Joel's words were skirting around something larger. She hadn't known him for very long but she could tell by the way his eyes seemed to hold fire and his jokey tone had started to evaporate that there was something he wanted to say.

'Spit it out,' said Nina, brazen from the alcohol coursing through her system.

'Spit what out?' he said. Nina had interrupted his second rambling monologue, this one about the irony of paying to see Karl Marx's grave and, honestly, he was happy to be stopped from motoring on.

'Whatever it is you really want to say,' she said.

Joel smiled a closed-lip smile and scratched at the sodden label of his beer. He throttled the bottle to stop himself from peeling the whole label off; some people saw that as a sign of sexual frustration. He took a deep breath and looked Nina in the eyes.

'Okay,' he said, 'I guess what I want to know is

whether you believe there's an afterlife. That there's something, or anything, after death?'

The next twenty seconds of silence felt like an eternity. Nina held Joel's gaze. In her eyes, he could see a jumble of thoughts and feelings doing battle.

'They say that the dead live in us,' she said, slowly, choosing her words with the care one would use selecting pick 'n' mix at the cinema, 'and I don't think they – whoever "they" are – are wrong. Whether it's through the stories we tell about them or the people we become after they're gone, there's always a part of our loved ones that we carry around with us forever. Right? At least, I hope so. I'm not sure if there's a place called heaven where our souls go after our bodies are done. But memories? They're the afterlife I believe in.'

'I think that's lovely,' said Joel. He left out the bit about thinking she was lovely, too.

'Did I tell you my mum catered her own funeral?'

'No,' he said. He wasn't completely sure whether Nina was joking or not, so he gave her a look that he hoped gave off the impression of: 'but do go on'.

'Well, she did,' Nina said brightly, 'which I think tells you everything you need to know about Abigail. When she was first diagnosed with cancer – pancreas – they gave her five or six months to live. Tops. She'd lit up like a smile on her CAT scan but the last thing she wanted was for me and Dad to wallow around in those final months. She was determined we should all go on as we always had done. Stiff-upper-lip attitude. She wanted us to make the most of her being around and not walk on eggshells like she was already dead. And she was an excellent cook, right?'

Joel nodded his head as if he'd tried Abigail Harris's food for himself. He hadn't, of course, because Abigail had died years before Joel had swiped right on Nina, but he'd listened to her gush so evocatively about her mum's cooking over the last couple of hours that he'd as good as felt the rush of her warming egusi stew catwalk over his tongue.

'So, her big project for the final few months of her life was to cook up as many of her signature dishes as possible to pack up in the freezer for her funeral. That way, she said, she could be sure that the food at the wake would be up to her standards. That's classic Abigail. She was so distrustful of all of my aunties and their cooking she couldn't bear the thought of any of them catering her funeral!'

Nina was full-on cackling now, joyful tears welling in the corners of her eyes, and Joel started getting a little hysterical too. Even the man drinking alone at the table next to them appeared to be holding in a laugh that dimpled his cheeks. It was an infectious sound which rippled through the bar like a Mexican wave.

'In all honesty, it was a great comfort to have,' she said, wiping the warm tears from her face. 'Eating something she'd made with her own hands on the day of the funeral was almost like getting a final kiss goodbye. I don't even remember what we ate all that clearly, but I know I'll never have a better meal.'

Joel held Nina's hand across the table. He loved the

Nearly Departed

way she was able to fill the darkness of her memories with an orangey light of brightness. It wasn't exactly the best or most romantic moment to move in for a kiss but he thought about it anyway. He let his mind picture what it would be like to feel the soft pressure of his lips against hers and imagined what it would be like to let his tongue wander tentatively up to hers, a puppy approaching a stranger at the park.

Just as he was weighing up whether or not to make a move, his conscience gave him a sharp kick in the shin. She deserved nothing less than the truth, the whole truth and nothing but the truth. She had every right to know he was undeniably insane before he tried to kiss her.

'There's something I've got to tell you,' he said, his grip on her hand tightening just a fraction too much.

Nina's stomach dropped. Nothing good had ever followed that sentence.

'I know we're not exclusive or anything like that, but I thought I should let you know I've been, er, seeing someone. Quite a lot actually.'

A beat passed.

'If you're trying to flex here, you're going a really weird way about it,' she said, removing her hand from his grip.

'No,' said Joel, defensively, 'I'm not seeing someone like that. I'm, er, *seeing* someone. My ex. The dead one. I know it sounds crazy—'

'I don't think we're allowed to say that anymore,' snapped Nina.

'What? Crazy?'

'Yes, crazy. It perpetuates a stigma around mental health and draws on all sorts of negative stereotypes.'

'Oh, right. Sorry. But if I'm not crazy for seeing dead people, then what am I?'

'I don't know, Joel,' said Nina. 'Hopeful? Deluded? Stuck in the past? Or maybe you're setting up an overly elaborate excuse to ghost me after you've fucked me?'

'It's not like that,' Joel said. 'I'm being serious.'

'And so am I. You're a prick.'

'I'm not lying, Nina. Please. I'm . . .'

His chest tightened, and a cold sweat broke out on his forehead.

'What? You're what?'

Someone spilled a glass of syrupy wine on the floor. Joel could feel the walls closing in on him; his heart was beating wildly. His vision started to blur at the edges, like an out-of-focus photograph, and the room began to spin. A wave of nausea rose up his throat as his mind raced with thoughts he couldn't keep hold of. He knew, rationally, he was having a panic attack. But maybe he was dying? Maybe he was losing his mind?

'I don't know what I am.'

Nina narrowed her eyes. 'Right. So, let me get this straight: you wanted to take this exact moment, after I've just told you all about my mother's funeral, to tell me you've been hanging out with the ghost of your ex-girlfriend?'

He smiled, relief washing over him like the cool shade of a cloud on a hot summer's day. 'Exactly!'

Nearly Departed

Nina scowled. 'Who the fuck do you think you are?'

'God, no. Look. Shit.' The shade was gone. 'There's been a misunderstanding. I'm into you, Nina. Like, really into you. I think you're wonderful and kind and funny and I love – okay, maybe not love because that's quite intense, I'll admit – but I really, really like loads of things about you.'

Her head was whirling with confusion and lager.

'Even the way you tear apart coasters when you're angry,' he added, forcing a smile again.

Nina set down the remnants of the coaster she'd been shearing and stared at Joel. She didn't reciprocate his smile. There was a slight sheen of grease on his face and his glasses were starting to slip down the bridge of his nose. Despite the words that had left his mouth, his eyes didn't look like they'd done anything wrong. It was as if they wanted absolutely nothing to do with the loudmouth down below. For a second, she almost believed their innocence.

'You know what, Joel? You really are something else,' said Nina, picking up her bag and hurling her phone into it.

'No, no, it's not what you think,' he squeaked.

She paused. 'It's not?'

'It's not. I've been . . .'

Joel looked desperately at the chair next to Nina, willing Beth to magically apparate and help him out. Nina took one glance at Joel looking longingly at an empty leather chair and made up her mind.

She shook her head and brushed her hands on her

jeans to rid herself of whatever feelings she was starting to have for him.

'I'm done.'

She walked towards the door, hot-eyed and self-conscious, as Joel sat paralysed in his seat. A couple of heads turned as Nina left. The door swung behind her with a definitive swish and Joel could feel everyone at the bar staring at him with beady eyes. He could have sworn he heard the hollow-eyed man in a newsboy hat call him a fuckwit under his breath.

As Joel deliberated whether or not it was an awful idea to get up and chase Nina, Beth materialised at the table next to him.

'Shit,' he said, loudly. The suddenness of Beth's presence had caught him off guard, but it was more than that. For the first time since she'd reappeared in his life, Joel realised he wasn't happy to see her.

'It's about time you showed up,' Joel said, coldly. It was the best he could muster up while Beth bore holes into him from the head of the table like she was Banquo's fucking ghost.

'We need to talk,' she said.

Joel's stomach dropped. Nothing good had ever followed that sentence.

Eta

A car alarm was blaring in the distance. It wasn't close, maybe a street away, but it was loud enough to make you lose sleep. Beth and Joel walked in silence past a row of alabaster houses with imposing metal gates, the kind whose owners had shih tzus and schnauzers. Joel wasn't sure what to say, so he said nothing at all. He checked his phone for the time: 00.30. Nina would almost be home by now, he thought. He tapped out a quick text to her and hit send.

> **Joel:** Hope you got home safe. I'm so sorry about earlier. Pls let me explain. It's honestly not what you think. Looking forward to the marshes? X

He started typing THE DEAD LIVE IN US into the message bar but chickened out at the last second, deleting each letter with nineteen vicious mashes of the backspace button.

'Do they?' asked Beth, who had read the vetoed all-caps text. It was the first thing she'd said since 'Let's go home,' and Joel was startled at the hollowness of her voice. It sounded like she was speaking from the room next to him in some seedy hotel, his ear pressed against the wall with a glass.

'I don't know,' he said, drily. 'You're supposed to be the expert on that.'

An unkempt line of trees in the distance got bigger and leafier as they approached the limits of the park. The soft crunch of leaves underfoot made Joel sad that summer wasn't forever. Soon, the days would start getting shorter, the nights would get longer, and he wouldn't be able to leave the house without at least one layer with him. The nearly empty tub of vitamin D3 collecting dust on his bedside table would need to be replaced, too.

'Are you going to tell me what's going on?' said Joel as they passed a troop of drunken revellers. A fast-paced, and presumably insomniac, dog walker overtook them on the left-hand side.

'Not yet,' said Beth.

He would have admired her for her stubbornness if it hadn't been such a massive pain in the arse. He laughed grudgingly and ducked under a tree branch in his path. He couldn't do much but follow Beth's lead and hope for the best.

I Think They Call It An Epiphany

The first thing Joel did when he got through the door was flick on the kettle. Caffeine would have been a terrible decision at this time of the night but something gentle like a peppermint or chamomile tea was just what he needed to settle his nerves. He didn't even bother asking Beth if she wanted one. He was pretty accustomed by now to the dietary restrictions of the dead.

Joel decided on peppermint after a good thirty seconds of internal deliberation. He gave the tea bag a quick huff, filling his face with its sweet and piney fragrance, before plopping it into his favourite mug and drowning it with boiling water.

It was only once they were back in the flat, with Joel rustling about the kitchen in his socks, that Beth started getting nervous. A storm was coming. She knew there was going to be no way to take back what she was about to do and her stomach was filled with bats just thinking about it. What she didn't know, however, is what would happen to her after she told Joel what she needed to say. Would she disappear in a puff of smoke? Would she drop dead all over again and fill the kitchen with a decaying corpse for him to clean up? Would she simply vanish and leave him in the kitchen, alone with his thoughts? She hoped it was either the first or last option and definitely not the violently problematic prospect sandwiched in the middle.

'Are you ready to tell me what the fuck is going on?' asked Joel. He'd hunkered himself down at the kitchen table, leaning forward with his forearms pressed against the surface like a mafioso. The steam rising from the mug of hot peppermint painted heat lines in the air in front of him.

'It's over, Joel,' said Beth.

'What's over?' he said.

'This is over,' she said, throwing her hands all around the room. 'This weird happy-family bullshit we've got going on where I'm pretending to be a guardian angel giving you dating advice.'

'But I thought this is what you wanted?' he said, frustration rising in his voice. 'This' – and now it was his turn to throw his hands all around the room – 'whole thing was your idea. Is it because you're jealous or something? Or is this because of the kiss?'

A hot red carpet of a blush rolled itself out across Beth's face.

'Look, okay,' continued Joel. 'I know everything got a little weird earlier. But we can talk about it like adults. We can work it out.'

'Don't you get it?' she said, laughing, a delirious look in her eyes. 'I don't want to work things out.'

'What's so funny?'

'Nothing's funny. It's the same as it always was, Joel. It's all the fucking same.'

'What do you mean "the same as it always was"? Newsflash, Beth: you haven't always been dead.'

'What I mean is . . . Look, it's time for you to get on with your life so I can get on with my death. All right?'

'Spare me the platitudes,' he said bitterly. His eyes were burning. 'So, this is it, is it? You're going to leave me all over again? Just like that?'

'It's not like that,' she said.

'Then what is it like? Please explain to me what it's like because I don't know how you can go from kissing me one minute to abandoning me the next.'

Beth sighed, and readied herself to repeat the lines she'd been practising earlier. 'You know when you used to stay up late at a sleepover and the longer you tried to keep your eyes open, the harder it got? Like it felt as if every extra second you were awake was sapping more of your life force, but you didn't want to close your eyes because that would mean the day would be over and you'd have to wake up and return to reality in the morning?'

Joel nodded.

'That's what it's been like being back. I've had fun, I really have. But I'm tired, Joel. And I can't rest. Not here — not until you let me go back to where I belong. That's why I need you to know this is the end of the line for us. For this.'

'No it's not . . .' started Joel, before Beth gave him a stern look which made him think twice about what he was going to say.

'We're all moving towards the end. I just got there first, that's all.'

Joel shook his head. Hot tears were streaming down his face. 'This isn't fair,' he said.

'The problem is, you're acting like this is all happening to you,' she said angrily, her own tears falling now. 'Like it's some cosmic message, and I'm here to teach you a lesson or offer you closure. But here's the thing: it's happening to me, too. And I don't want to be here anymore. I'm not haunting you; you're just refusing to let go.'

Now it was Joel's turn to be angry.

'I don't know what you're suggesting,' he said. 'But it's not like I asked for you to come back. And as far as I can tell, I'm not holding you hostage here, either. I love you. I always have, and I always will. But this whole "my girlfriend's back from the dead!" situation isn't something I've orchestrated. You got to die, Beth – and you know what? You got the better fucking deal. Me? I had to live. I had to wake up and bury you every morning. Can you even imagine how hard that was?'

Beth slid into the seat in front of Joel. The anger on her face was replaced by a mix of sadness and remorse.

'What I'm trying to say is that you shouldn't still be in love with me, Joel. I'm yesterday's news. You need to move on and get yourself a newer model. Like Nina. Like my watch,' she said, trying to force a laugh.

Nearly Departed

'I didn't get a newer model,' replied Joel, who wasn't in the mood for laughing. 'I fixed the old one, remember? It was literally the same watch.'

'For fuck's sake – can you even hear yourself? It's not about the watch. It was never about the watch. Do you know how unhappy I was? How lost I felt? I might be a ghost now, sure, but I felt like one back then, too. You were so obsessed with making our relationship fit this ideal of love and security you had in your head you didn't give me any room to breathe. You never let me exist as an individual outside of "Joel and Beth" or "Beth and Joel". It was always about us, never about me or you. And that makes me so sad, Joel, because I adored you. I really did. But one day, you'll need to learn to live with yourself because it's exhausting to be with someone who has so little regard for who they are.'

She let it out, all the sadness and frustration and disappointment that had been building up for the previous few days. The sadness and frustration and disappointment that, if she was honest with herself, had been festering inside her for years. Joel listened in silence, hands wrapped around his mug, eyes screwed tight as if he was making a wish.

'You need to stop papering over the cracks of your memories,' she said. 'What we had was good – it was so good, Joel – but it stopped working. And nothing you can do will ever change that.'

'I can't believe you're trying to break up with me,' said Joel, exasperated.

'I'm not trying to break up with you. We aren't together. And I'm dead, remember?'

'It feels like you're trying to break up with me.'

'Well, I guess it's about time I was finally able to do what I didn't have the courage to do when I was alive.'

A thunderous silence sat at the table between them. Joel's brain was a whirling tornado of thoughts and feelings. He was whiplashed by what Beth had said and – maybe for the first time in his life – properly lost for words. It was like the scene at the end of a film noir where the detective has to look back and see if there were any obvious clues that his partner was double-crossing him all along. The rug had been pulled out from underneath him and, failing to place his finger on the words he needed to bring it firmly back under his feet, Joel decided to take action.

He got up from his chair, leaving his peppermint tea untouched, and marched towards the bedroom. Beth watched him move and dutifully padded after him. He made a beeline for his chest of drawers and got down on his knees in front of its mahogany face. He pulled back the handles, perhaps a little too violently for the liking of the stoppers that kept the drawers in place, and searched through the detritus inside with desperate abandon. His brow furrowed while his hands roamed the territory of the drawer, searching for something to pillage, but coming back short each time. Only once the drawer's entire contents had been thrown onto the floor, and Joel was left confused and panting with his hands on his thighs, did he think to turn around.

'Looking for this?' said Beth. She was sitting on the floor, holding up a small leather box between her finger and thumb.

'Where did you . . .' was all he managed to splutter before a sadness rose up his throat and plugged his vocal cords.

'I found it earlier tonight,' she said, rotating the box ever so slightly. 'Sort of. I only knew where to look for it because I'd already found it before. Back when I was alive.'

Beth flipped open the box to reveal the absinthe gleam of an emerald-studded ring. Trying to figure out Beth's ring size had been an ordeal. Joel had contemplated measuring her fingers while she slept, but had eventually decided on the more practical approach of measuring her rings instead. He'd visited every vintage jewellery store in town until he found something he thought she'd like.

'It was about a week before my accident,' continued Beth. A large furry moth circled the ceiling light and Joel had to restrain himself from batting at it with the nearest available T-shirt.

'I was doing an audit of your underpants to see how many pairs had holes in the crotch when I found it. I didn't know what to say or do. Because the only thing I knew for sure,' she said, looking Joel in the eyes to make sure he was listening, 'was that I didn't want to marry you.'

She had pushed aside a vast number of Joel's Emmentalled boxer briefs and orphaned socks to find it at the back of the drawer – that little maroon box, untouched for months. Beth eased it out of its hiding place and held it in her palm – it was deceptively heavy, like a lug nut – then opened it slowly. The hinges emitted a gentle creak.

It wasn't a good sign that the idea of marrying Joel had never seriously crossed her mind until that moment. It was, to be frank, a rather bad sign. Although they'd been together for five years, she'd never thought they were anywhere near getting engaged.

In a previous chapter of her life, she'd thought she'd become a world-famous artist. She'd imagined herself jetting around the globe, glad-handing wealthy art patrons and briefly showing her face at her own exhibition openings before darting off mysteriously into the night. And as much as she'd wanted to abandon those ambitions, to dedicate herself to the more realistic aim of buying a house to get on the ladder and start a family, she hadn't been able to let them go. Beth's mid-twenties had been consumed by their relationship. Every holiday, birthday and Christmas had revolved, in one way or another, around Joel, but she'd wanted to be someone people thought of as more than 'Joel's fiancée' or 'Joel's wife' or 'the mother of Joel's children'. She hadn't been ready to throw in the towel just yet.

Carefully placing the ring back where she'd found it, Beth had tiptoed to the living room where Joel was sitting, absorbed in a rerun of *Golden Balls*. She awkwardly nuzzled up next to him and he planted a warm kiss on her forehead, unaware of the terrifying glimpse she had just caught into their future.

Now, as Joel listened to Beth speak, his eyes swam with sadness and the rest of his face crumpled into embarrassment. She shimmied closer to him, dragging her bottom across the floor, so he could see she hated breaking this news to him almost as much as he hated hearing it.

'I know it's a brutal thing to say, but it's the honest truth. When I saw that ring, a siren blared in my head with big, red letters screaming: DON'T DO IT. I loved you, don't get me wrong. But there was something in the pit of my stomach telling me it wasn't right. That a commitment like marriage wouldn't be fair to either of us. I couldn't sleep properly for days afterwards because I felt so guilty and, the funny thing is, I was feeling all this guilt for something I hadn't even done yet.'

'That is extremely funny,' said Joel drolly. He was, quite obviously, devastated by what she was telling him, but Beth was glad he'd still found the energy to laugh at his own misfortune. She gave him a look that said as much.

'The longer I let that feeling fester inside me, the harder I knew it would be to say no when you did eventually propose. That's when I made the decision to break up with you before that happened and—'

'When were you going to do it,' objected Joel. He leaned forward. It was a statement, not a question.

'Honestly?' said Beth. She bit down on her bottom lip, leaving two neat semi-circles temporarily indented into the flesh. 'I was planning to do it the weekend I died.'

All the air was sucked out of the room. It was as if someone had opened the emergency door in an aeroplane. Joel's head spun like a dreidel, and he gazed up at Beth with a look of utter helplessness. He felt sick to his stomach, the vertigo of his world being turned upside down taking hold with a vengeance.

'I'm sorry, Joel,' said Beth.

Before Joel could respond, Beth's eyes closed with a zen expression and she gently tossed the ring in his direction. Instinctively, he looked down for a second, to catch it. And when he looked back up, she was gone.

Pick Yourself Up

It took about ten seconds for Joel to explode. He let out a raspy yell which had the neighbours half tempted to call the police. He deleted every photo of Beth from his phone then manically googled how to restore them. He punched the wall. He drank an entire bottle of dessert wine. He tried to find something, anything, to kick and eventually landed on his bin, which made an even bigger mess for him to clean up later. He bit down on the web between his index and thumb until he drew blood. Finally, he collapsed on the floor like a heap of laundry.

There are weeks in our lives where nothing happens at all and there are seconds where whole weeks can happen in an instant. The seconds that followed Beth tossing him the ring encompassed an entire lifetime for Joel. Every fantasy he'd ever had about living a long and happy life with Beth had been torn into tatters and thrown out of the window.

Daydreams of a garden, kids and a faithful mutt were all carried heartlessly up and away into the night by a callous gust of wind. Joel's perception of their relationship, of what they'd had together, had been permanently altered. Shifted. It turned out things had not been as peachy and perfect as he'd thought. The cracks in the foundations couldn't be caulked.

He sat on the floor for what felt like hours. In reality it was only one. But after sixty minutes of sitting, alone, the muscles in his legs started to seize up. His toes lost all feeling. Once he'd winched himself back to his feet, and the tattoo stab of pins and needles in his calves had subsided, he was left feeling more hollow than ever. Self-medicating with drugs wasn't particularly Joel's 'thing', but all he could think about doing at that exact moment in time was getting absolutely annihilated. It wasn't a call from the void or a desire for total self-destruction but, rather, a craving to separate his body from his brain for a couple of hours. Like taking your shoes off after a long day.

When was the last time he'd got high? It must have been over a year and a half ago at some techno-heavy day festival Sam had dragged him to. He'd had a good time – it was hard not to when your brain was soaked in ecstasy. But he'd run out of carrots by the time midnight had crept around and, instead of carrying on the night with the rest of the cohort at a pub that only served Carling, Joel got a long bus home on his own. He listened to a lot of Nelly Furtado on the journey back.

He searched through his WhatsApp chats until he found the number of a somewhat reliable dealer he had saved in his phone as 'Dylan'. He was pretty sure most drug dealers avoided using their real names with their clients but he couldn't, for the life of him, work out why anyone would actively want to go by 'Dylan'.

The last message Joel had got from 'Dylan' was one of the boilerplate broadcasts he sent out on a bi-weekly basis, advertising his wares. It was the textual equivalent of setting up your assortment of bric-a-brac on a gingham blanket at a car boot sale.

WELCOME TO THE 'GOLD LABEL'
   MEMBERSHIP
Price list:
POCKET ROCKET (PREMIUM)
-1c for £70
-2c for £140
-3c for £200
-4c for £250
MD
-1md for £40
-2md for £70
-3md for £100
KET
-1k for £40
-2k for £70
-3k for £100
THE MEAL DEAL
- 5c 1md 1ket for £200
Better deals for bulk orders just enquire
GET ME 5 REFERRALS GET 1C & 1MD
   FREE

The stress of procuring drugs was usually enough to put Joel off taking anything at all. Picking up gave him such a potent feeling of anxiety, somewhere between shame and agony, that all the drugs ended up doing was restoring him back to a baseline of normalcy. He usually relegated the task of securing class As to his more self-assured, attractive and less murderable friends. But tonight he thought, fuck it.

So what if it turned out 'Dylan' was actually an undercover police officer looking to sting middle-class drug users? Spending a night in a jail cell seemed like a cheerier prospect than another night in the bed he'd shared with Beth – a queen size where he'd felt safe in the love of his life partner and she, unbeknownst to him, had felt suffocated. Okay, no. That wasn't fair. He shouldn't project his anxieties onto Beth like that. He shouldn't demonise her for not wanting to be in a relationship with him. Especially considering she was dead and all.

Doctor Shah would be proud of my incredibly rational response to this situation, thought Joel, as he thumbed out a message to 'Dylan' the drug dealer.

Joel: You working around east tonight mate?

Dance Dance Revolution

Joel's hair was plastered to his forehead like the end of a wet paintbrush. His shirt was so soaked through with sweat it looked more black than light blue. He'd have worried about how he smelled but his brain wasn't focused on anything apart from dancing out as much of his sadness as possible. He felt a hundred miles from his body, as though he was looking down at himself from the wrong end of a telescope. He tugged at the strings of his limbs and they moved sluggishly with the delayed responsiveness of a marionette. Everything was in slow motion.

Images of Beth and Beth and Beth and Nina and Nina and Beth and Sam and Alice and Alice and Sam and Nina and Nina and Sam and Sam kept flashing across the projector screen inside his head. That IMAX® of Sam kept getting bigger and bigger until Joel realised he wasn't imagining him at all: Sam really was walking right up to him, getting larger and larger in his field of vision and giving Joel a crystal clear view of his big, square head.

He looked like every other person in the club, dressed in a loose corduroy shirt and faded Wrangler jeans. But the way Sam wore his outfit was more natural, and much less forced, than anyone around him. A pair of round tortoiseshell sunglasses sat flush on the bridge of his nose, protecting his dark eyes from the lights. As the music kept on going and Sam inched across the dance floor to where Joel was standing in stunned awe, he removed the glasses from his face and tucked them into his top. His arms were flailing like they had a life of their own. He looked ridiculous when he danced.

The next thing Joel knew, Sam was standing right in front of him and shouting something that sounded like 'What the fuck are you doing here?' in his ear. It sounded like 'What the fuck are you doing here?' because that was exactly what he shouted.

It took Joel's brain a couple of seconds to catch up before he embraced Sam, again not caring that his body was coated in a greasy layer of perspiration, and hollered an 'I don't know!' into his ear, before adding: 'But I think I'm exactly where I'm supposed to be.'

When their embrace ended, Sam placed his hands on Joel's shoulders and took a good look at his friend. Joel's eyes, which had been so ocean blue Sam thought he might drown in them the first time they'd met, had been overtaken by two deep and mysterious black holes. He could see desperation lurking in the darkness of his pupils.

'You're high,' said Sam, not unkindly.

'I am,' said Joel, matter-of-factly, before he felt a wave of nausea and relief wash over him as he stared at Sam's familiar face. His thick eyebrows were wild at the edges. Joel smiled sheepishly. Sam smiled back, showing off his uniform teeth and bringing Joel in for another sweaty hug.

Sam

On the long walk back to Sam's flat, Joel told him everything. Once he started talking, he couldn't stop. He knew he should be giving Sam time to digest what he was saying but it all spilled out of him like the open wound of a haemophiliac. The drugs had loosened his tongue and talking seemed to be the only way to get all the anger and confusion out of his system. So Joel talked, Sam listened, and the hustle and bustle of twenty-four-hour bagel shops and fluoro-lit corner shops eventually gave way to the gentle rustle of residential Hammersmith.

He told him all about Beth and how she'd come back into his life and how he'd been getting dating advice from her over the previous couple of weeks. 'That's how I knew so much about art,' he said. Sam did his best not to look concerned. But the more Joel spoke about what had happened to him, the less convinced Sam was that he was a complete madman. He knew he wasn't totally okay but, then again, who was?

When Joel recounted Beth handing back the ring

and him finding out she'd been planning to break up with him before her death, Sam felt a sharp pang of sympathy. It might have had something to do with the MDMA still swilling about Joel's body, but he didn't seem to be bitter about it. If anything, he seemed to have found a skewed sense of peace in having heard it from Beth herself. And, despite all of his best instincts telling him there was no such thing as ghosts, Sam found himself believing the words that came out of Joel's mouth. Or, at least, willing to believe that Joel believed he had been phantomed by his ex.

It was the same as those people who claimed they were abducted by aliens, thought Sam – just because there was no hard evidence to suggest something had occurred, that didn't mean someone's personal account of an event was inherently untrue. Because all any of us get in life is our own limited interpretation of reality, right? Who was he to tell Joel his perception of the last couple of weeks must have been some high-concept manifestation of grief? What right did he have to look him in the eye and say ghosts aren't real?

When they got back to the flat, Joel was spent. His eyes betrayed the beginning of a comedown and the sweat that had so loyally kept him cool and lubricated in the heat of the club was now making him shiver in Sam's throw-laden living room. Joel asked if Sam minded whether he had a quick shower to clean himself up. 'Of course not,' Sam said, 'but I will need to show you how to work the tap. And don't worry about waking Holly – she's out of town this week.'

Nearly Departed

The hot tap required a canny three-quarter turn anticlockwise and the cold tap a quarter turn clockwise to arrive somewhere close to the perfect water temperature. Once he was sure Joel had learned the ropes, and had firmly warned him which of Holly's shampoos and conditioners were off-limits, Sam left him to get clean. Sam hadn't expected to have anyone back at the flat tonight, so he did a quick round of his bedroom to throw any dirty underwear or clothes into his washing basket.

The next time he'd been supposed to see Joel – something he knew he should make an effort to do more often – was for drinks in a few weeks' time. 'Looks like the universe had other plans,' he muttered, closing the Find My Friends app on his phone and kicking off his shoes in the hallway.

One Giant Leap For Mankind

Sam looked up as he heard the running water slow from a torrent into a trickle. He'd never had a problem with the plumbing in his flat and was grateful he hadn't got a ghoul for a landlord like most other people he knew. Joel would probably be drying himself off by now and he tried not to linger on the thought of his best friend's naked body for too long as he padded to the kitchen and poured them each a glass of water.

'How are you feeling?' he asked, as Joel eventually re-entered the bedroom in his navy boxer briefs with a towel draped over one shoulder like he was a Roman emperor.

'Human,' said Joel. If he looked closely, Sam was sure he could see two purple-grey bags forming under Joel's eyes in real time.

'Good,' said Sam.

'Good,' said Joel. 'Oh, and I almost forgot to ask,' he added, stretching his arms behind his back, trying to pretend he wasn't as high as he was. 'Why were you there tonight?'

'Where?'

'Fabric.'

'Oh. I wasn't. Not really.'

'What do you mean "not really"?'

Sam held up his phone with a guilty shrug. 'Alice and I have been keeping an eye on your whereabouts the past few weeks.'

'You mean tracking me?'

'You could call it that. I prefer to think of it as acting like a concerned emergency task force. Anyway, we decided that hitting a club on a Wednesday night might fall into the "cry for help" category.'

'And here I was thinking it was fate,' said Joel. He gave an eye-roll of indifference but was touched by how much his friends cared.

'Maybe it was, in a way.'

They sat for five minutes in a silence only years of friendship can make bearable.

'Can I tell you something?' asked Joel eventually, breaking the spell. His fingers snagged a loose thread of towel.

'Anything.'

'Sometimes I feel like I can't – sometimes I feel like I don't know what genre I'm in.' He looked up at Sam with his backgammon-counter eyes. Joel was still beamed to the ceiling. 'It's like I've forgotten what my lines are. It's like – like I honestly have no idea what I'm supposed to be doing half the time. Like I'm always trying to gauge the mood of the scene, reading every room I walk into, just to make sure I don't ruin the moment for everyone else. Is that normal? Is that okay?'

'I think that's okay,' said Sam.

'Really?'

'Really,' replied Sam. 'I think we're all making it up as we go.'

'Right.' Joel nodded. 'Improv.' And he was going to leave it at that until he remembered what day it was. 'Do you think she'd be disappointed in me? For not falling in love yet?'

'What? Who?'

'Beth.'

Sam locked eyes with his friend. With every passing year, Joel was beginning to look more and more like his father. He supposed everyone, over time, was destined to turn into their parents.

'No,' Sam said. 'Honestly, knowing Beth, she'd probably love the idea of still being right, even when she's dead.'

Joel smiled, a small sheepish smile that still held a flicker of pain.

'I know you feel like you've let yourself down,' Sam continued. 'And I know it can feel as if you're not on the same track as everyone else because arseholes like me are going out and getting married or churning out babies but – honestly, mate – there's no rush. Half of marriages end in divorce anyways. Obviously don't tell Holly I said that.'

Joel let out a small laugh. 'I know all of that, rationally. I guess I just haven't had the most rational month.'

'You don't say?'

Joel sat down on the bed, breathing deeply and staring into space.

Nearly Departed

'Love isn't some explosion you can just set off whenever you like,' said Sam. 'It's something that happens when you're not looking. I didn't know I was properly in love with Holly until about four months after I told her I was.'

Sam was standing in the centre of the room. Joel looked up at him and his heartbeat slowed a little.

'Really?'

'Yes, really. But don't tell her I said that, either. It wasn't instant and it wasn't something I could have set a countdown for. It just . . . happened, you know? And now, even though she does my fucking head in sometimes, I can't imagine life without her. I don't want to imagine life without her.'

'It's about trying,' said Joel, remembering Beth's words and repeating them back to himself.

'Exactly! And I read this thing in the *Guardian* the other day – there was this American woman, some competitive archer or something, who fell in "love" with the Eiffel Tower. She's been married to the thing for ten years. A fucking decade! So, yeah. Love doesn't always make sense.'

'Why does her being an archer matter?'

'I don't know. It doesn't. But it fits the profile, right?'

'True.'

'Look, all I'm saying is . . . I don't even know, mate. I'm shattered. But maybe marrying an inanimate object is the only way you can ever guarantee you're always going to be in love. Because humans are basically the opposite of inanimate. They're messy, man. They're fucked up and messy. But they're the best thing about being here. About being alive. Am I making sense?'

Joel nodded.

Sam took a large gulp of water. He could see the sheen of Joel's high was starting to wear off. 'It's not easy putting your trust in someone and telling them you think about them all the time when you know, statistically, the odds are stacked against you,' he said. 'But, honestly, what else is there to do? No book or movie or pill is going to make you half as content as having someone who wants to tell you about their day as soon as you get home. If someone lets you love them, you should.'

'Because what else is there to do?'

'Exactly,' Sam smiled.

They talked about how young they had looked when they'd first met. They laughed at how round their faces had been, how they'd both ballooned from drinking too much cider, and worn jeans so tight they'd probably had an irreversible effect on their sperm counts. Sam did most of the talking as Joel struggled to steady his heart. His ears were listening but his mind was elsewhere.

'You can take the bed tonight,' said Sam, as his large hands smoothed out a wrinkle on the duvet. 'I'll sleep on the sofa.' Joel considered protesting but he didn't have a better solution to offer and so he lay down on Sam and Holly's bed. He'd never understood the point of having more than four pillows on a bed but when he nestled himself into a pile of their duck-feather cushions, he felt the fist of anxiety in his chest start to loosen its grip.

'That's very kind of you,' he said. 'Thank you, mate.' He reached out from his downy fortress to hold Sam's hand and gazed up at his gentle eyes. 'For everything.'

Sam stroked Joel's hand with his thumb. 'That's okay,' he said, before softly patting him on the cheek. 'Everyone needs a little help sometimes. Sleep tight.' The second he uttered the word 'sleep', Joel's eyes shut and he was out for the count. Sam took a long look at the man sleeping in his bed and walked quietly out of the room, closing the door behind him.

Making Amends

A thick beam of sunlight shouted at Joel's eyelids until he was compelled to force them open, shielding his face with his hand to try to mitigate the damage to his retinas. Who the fuck sleeps with the curtains open? His head felt as fragile as a cardboard box full of Christmas ornaments and Joel was unsurprised when the whole room spun on its axis as he attempted to get up and see what time it was. Squiggly dots and lines floated across his eyeballs, bouncing off the corners of his vision like a DVD screensaver.

Feeling decidedly seasick, he returned to the relative safety of lying on his back, and his eyes roamed the room to assess his surroundings. Sam was nowhere to be seen, but taking his place on the left-hand side of the bed was Holly's stuffed animal, Mr Bear – a rabbit with one glass eye whose fur was as smooth as a tumbled stone thanks to years of constant manhandling.

After a few minutes had passed, and that initial wave of nausea seemed to have subsided, Joel slowly pulled his torso up so his back was resting against the headboard of Sam's bed. All things considered, he didn't feel too bad. He felt like absolute shit, obviously – but considering what the last twenty-four hours of his life had encompassed, he'd expected to feel worse. If this was rock bottom then maybe he was okay with it. Maybe I've finally achieved a sense of zen, he thought, before a tidal wave of warm bile rose up his throat. Maybe not. He searched frantically for something to be sick in but decided to bite the bullet and swallow the liquid load instead. That was breakfast sorted.

Joel's phone, plugged in at the wall next to the bed, informed him it was eleven o'clock and exactly three years to the day since Beth had died. Fuck. He had five unread messages from Alice and zero unread messages from Nina, whom he'd both texted at around two in the morning. Double fuck. Joel didn't know how people did this every weekend. Even just the memory of seeing his own face in the mirror of the club toilet, grimacing out at him like a pantomime dame, was enough of an anti-drugs PSA to put him off taking anything else for the rest of the year.

As he considered sending a quick thank-you text to Sam, Joel noticed a piece of lined A4 folded up on the dressing table. He de-origamied the paper and read the note, written in ornate looping letters that made him immediately self-conscious about his own chicken-scratch penmanship:

Gone to the GP – not great timing I know! But help yourself to anything!!! And please reply to Alice's texts!!! Or else!!!! Speak soon.
PS – Be my best man?
S x

Joel stared at the 'x' at the end of the message while his stomach gurgled like a jacuzzi. He would have cried tears of joy if his body hadn't been as dehydrated as a sun-baked sponge. In any other circumstance, he'd have been too polite to take Sam up on his offer of free food, but his head was pounding, his mouth was arid and tasted of sick, and a slice, or maybe two, of buttered toast was the only thing he could think of that would help ease the throb inside his skull.

He padded to the kitchen and slotted the first two slices of multigrain bread he could find into the toaster. Sam's was a 'we don't refrigerate our butter' household and Joel enjoyed the kitsch aesthetic of the pink Le Creuset butter dish which kept his Kerrygold safe and sound. Waiting for the seeded slices to get an Ibiza tan, Joel thought about how Beth had always told him off for leaving toast crumbs in the butter. He started to wonder if getting out of those bad habits and being less complacent about Beth's love for him would have helped him preserve their relationship, before the satisfying spring-loaded *kaching!* of the toaster interrupted his train of thought.

'It's no good worrying about that now,' is what Joel imagined Beth telling him. And he felt reassured knowing, were she still around, that that was what she probably would have said.

He sat at the kitchen table and bit a neat crescent into his heavily buttered toast. The contrast between the crisp, almost charcoal, flavour of the toast and the sweet, salty creaminess of the butter salved some of the pain in his head. As a child, Joel had loved buttered toast but would refuse to eat it if he could physically see any bits of butter on top. Because of his fussiness, Joel's mum would have to make sure any patch of butter was fully melted onto the toast before she served it to him, turning it sunshine yellow as the butter seeped into every pore of the bread. It's the little things like that that you do for someone you love. Joel should have done more of those things for Beth – small, unasked-for acts of kindness to let her know he cared – rather than going all out on occasions like birthdays and Christmases. There was so much more he could have said or done.

He hadn't brought a change of clothes with him and shuddered slightly as he pulled the previous night's still-damp shirt onto his body. He'd make sure to change as soon as he got home, he thought, and was amazed to find his wallet and keys were already nestled together on Sam's desk. Had he done that the night before or had Sam arranged them like that for his ease this morning? Either way, it was a nice gesture and he thanked whoever had done him the solid.

Holding his keys in his fingertips, Joel dropped the set daintily into a zippable pocket of his jacket and checked his wallet to make sure he hadn't lost any of his cards. His driving licence was still there, taunting Joel with one of the most menacing black and white mugshots ever taken of him, along with his debit card. So far, so good. All he had to do now was think of some way to repay Sam's kindness and he'd be able to attain some karmic neutrality.

Fifteen minutes later and a teal-clad courier was hammering on the door to the flat. Wedged under the courier's arm was a brown paper bag containing a bundle of items Joel could recall Sam saying vaguely positive things about at some point during their friendship. Once the courier had left, Joel rummaged in the bag and unloaded the following onto the kitchen table:

A punnet of raspberries ('I used to love putting them on my fingers like little hats'); a litre of fresh orange juice ('It takes me back to summer holidays in Spain, you know?'); a bar of sustainably sourced salted caramel-flavoured chocolate ('I know it's basic but I'm horny for salted caramel'); and some chocolate digestives ('Remember when we used to hotbox my room and polish off an entire packet in under ten minutes?').

Not a bad haul, overall, but the £18 receipt did sting a little. He assembled all of the items on Sam's desk as artfully as he could and scrawled a message on a piece of paper before he picked up his things and went out the door.

Nearly Departed

Gone to see a man about a dog – thanks for everything! Again!! I hope you have a lovely day! I love you! I'll call you! And Alice! J x

Days left to fall in love: 0

Smile Because It Happened

Alice had always been fiercely independent. It was likely her autonomy had something to do with her parents' divorce – as most things about her did – but Joel believed it was just as much a reflection of who she was as a person. With how she was hardwired. Even at the age of eight, Alice would rather skip rope on her own than be forced to double-Dutch with anyone she didn't have time for. Even at the age of eight, Alice had people she didn't have time for.

'He moved out all his stuff on Saturday,' said Alice. 'Except the things he'd bought that I'd specifically picked out because, legally, they're mine. That's how it works. If you're the one who found the rattan coffee table on eBay, you're the one who gets to keep it.'

She was sitting at a sunlit table at her favourite coffee shop as she told him all this, her short hair curled up around her ears, and Joel couldn't help but look at his best friend as if she'd just been shot.

'Shit. Are you okay?'

'Yes.'

'Really? You're not just saying that?'

Nearly Departed

'No,' she said, shrugging as she took a sip of coffee.

'No, you're not just saying that or no, you're not okay?'

'No, I'm not just saying that.'

'So you are okay?'

'Yes. And I'm as surprised about that as you are.'

Joel looked at Alice with a feeling of guilt. He'd been so caught up in his grief, and so busy speaking to the dead, he'd neglected the living people in his life. The people who actually mattered. He cringed to think of the number of Alice's double, occasionally triple, texts he'd ignored over the last few weeks.

'How did it happen?' he asked.

'Gradually. There wasn't any big fight and it's not like I caught him cheating on me with his work wife or anything. It just sort of . . . ran out of steam. We just sort of ran out of steam.'

Joel gave her time to find her next sentence. He took a bite of flapjack.

'You know when you get obsessed with a new song and you want to listen to it practically every waking second of the day?' Alice asked.

'Yeah, of course.'

'And that feeling doesn't last forever, does it?'

'No,' said Joel. 'I always end up playing it so much that I get sick of it after about two weeks.'

'Always,' she said. 'And that doesn't mean you don't still like the song – it just means you need to start listening to something new, right?'

'Are you telling me or asking me?'

'Telling. And hey, James and I had a good run, didn't we? We had some fun times. Some of the best times. Just because it ended doesn't erase how good most of it was.'

'And that's it?'

'And that's it.'

Joel let out a sigh. 'Fuck.'

'Yeah, fuck.'

'I'm sorry I haven't been very . . . present lately,' he said.

'It's okay — you've had a lot of other stuff to worry about. Like, for example, the logistics of how to make out with a ghost.'

They'd already spent a solid hour on the phone discussing the haunting. Although Joel couldn't convince her any of it had actually happened, Alice seemed satisfied he had emerged from the experience having learned a vague moral lesson.

'I know,' Joel said. 'But that doesn't actually make it okay.'

'No, I suppose you're right. It doesn't.'

'So, I am sorry. I'm sorry I haven't been a good friend and I'm sorry I've been too stuck up my own arse to realise what's been going on with you,' said Joel. He reached out and rested his hand on Alice's jumpered forearm. It felt like the right thing to do. 'It's your turn to be on the worry list now, and I want you to know I'm going to be here for you no matter what. I can even be your wingman, if you want?'

'I accept your apology, Joel. But, quite honestly, there's

nothing I can think of that'd be more painful than having you by my side while I try to chat up some bassist with a choking fetish.'

'Fair enough. So, what now? After you're done shagging the bassist, of course.'

'Honestly? I don't know. And I think that's quite exciting.'

'And terrifying.'

'Yeah, that too.'

He smiled up at her. 'I love you, mate. You know that, right?'

'I know that. And you too. But enough about me,' she said, throwing up her hands in mock-protest. 'What's the latest on Nina, lover boy?'

'Well,' said Joel, leaning forward. 'I've got a plan.'

Alice groaned. 'Of course you've got a plan.'

Borrow My Doggy

A throng of people in party hats were huddled in a tight-knit testudo formation near the Chinese Pagoda. An ice cream van with a botched Mickey Mouse mural was doing good business, slinging out Mr Whippys at a frantic pace to anyone and everyone within arm's reach. Struggling to spot her in the sea of smiling, sunburned faces, Joel glanced at his phone to confirm Nina's proximity. She'd shared her location with him on Find My Friends after their second date and had unintentionally, but thankfully, left it enabled. He didn't know what she was doing in Victoria Park but he assumed it was something wholesome and hoped it was something she was doing alone.

The legion of party hats was camped out across three picnic tables. A shiny silver inflatable '2', and a lack of any other numbers in sight, suggested it was someone's second birthday. The adults slugged flat Prosecco out of plastic cups, their conversations punctuated by the shrieks of children hurtling toward one another at full tilt. Joel's gaze settled on a scrawny toddler in an expensive-looking outfit, methodically shovelling fistfuls of grass into their mouth. He only stopped staring once he realised how creepy he must look. Just as he was starting to regret not bringing a pair of sunglasses with him, a grey cloud limped across the sky, momentarily bathing the park in monochrome.

After five minutes, the sun shone again, and Joel's phone made a squawk to let him know Nina's little blue dot was coming in hot. He put his hands on the top of a bench and felt the warmth of the sun-soaked wood filtering through him. A solid brass plaque, roughly 200mm long and 50mm tall, sat below his fingertips.

In memory of Rodney Mackertitch, who loved his tea milky

Fourteen pairs of hands were now clapping because they were happy and they knew it. Joel's gaze shifted to his right shoulder and his eyes locked with hers. Nina was marching towards him with intent, dressed in short shorts and a Nike sports bra.

'Did you follow me here?' she hissed, as soon as Joel was within earshot. Her hair was tied back. Her eyes, blazing hot, revealed her anger. Joel thought for a moment she was going to hit him.

'N-no,' he stammered.

'No?'

Nina stood staring at him, her arms folded in front of the Nike logo on her chest.

'No,' said Joel, folding his own arms in rebuttal. 'I tracked you here. That's different.'

'You need to leave before I call the fucking police.'

'Wait,' said Joel, unfolding his arms with urgency, 'I think you're going to want to see this.'

The only thing Nina wanted to see was an end to the conversation but, before she could say as much, Joel stuck his fingers in his mouth and let out a shrill whistle. As soon as he did, four muscular legs attached to a hairy ribbed torso and a slobbery head came bounding over. Nina's eyes widened.

'Is that . . . is that a vizsla?' she asked.

'Yes,' said Joel, as the honey-coloured hound wrapped itself around his legs, nearly knocking him over.

'You bought me a vizsla?!'

'No. God, no. No. I *borrowed* a vizsla. On an app. But he's yours for today. His name is Gin.'

'Gin?'

Gin's ears perked up. His paws, which were comically big for his lanky body, thumped happily on the ground. 'Yes,' said Joel, ushering the lead into Nina's left hand. 'He's a good boy. Aren't you, Gin?' Gin looked up at Joel with his big wet eyes as if to say: 'Yes! Yes I am!' His long pink tongue leaked out of his mouth as Joel passed over a dog bowl, a fistful of flowers and a tidy bundle of black plastic poo bags.

'I'll have to return him to his owner by eight, but he's all yours until then.'

Despite her best efforts to keep it contained, a smile had started to work its way across Nina's face as Gin licked her fingers with his warm, sandpapery tongue. She bent down to scratch his ears; they were as soft as satin. Resting her palm gently on the top of his head, she couldn't help but feel as if his skull had been moulded to the exact shape of her hand.

'I guess this is my way of saying sorry,' said Joel. 'I know it's not going to fix anything and I'm not expecting it to, either. I just wanted to let you know I care about you. A lot. And I'd love to get the chance to make whatever this is work. Because you're wonderful. Seriously. Oh, and don't feed him chocolate. Or grapes.'

Nina wet her lips and nodded at Joel. Her thumbs worried at her rings. The flowers were her mother's favourites. Magenta peonies. She'd mentioned them on their first date but she'd assumed that was information Joel would have dumped from his brain as soon as he heard it.

'Do you always make over-the-top romantic gestures like this to women you barely know?'

'No. But I'm making one now to a woman I like to think I know a little bit.'

She couldn't help but laugh, and the sound of her accordion wheeze was music to Joel's ears.

'Where do you get these lines from?'

'I think I heard that one in a rom-com. Did it work?'

'I hate that it did.'

Joel grinned and his dimples made significant inroads into his cheeks. He was fixed like that for a solid twenty seconds before his face bent into a more serious expression. He took his hands out of his pockets. Nina looked at him to see what he was going to say. He leaned forward.

'I've got some explaining to do,' he said.

Epitaph

He stood at the side of the grave while a man walked by with a bouquet of fuchsia carnations. Have you got anything to say for yourself? His brain said. 'Not much,' he mumbled aloud. He felt drained all of a sudden, like a tube of toothpaste squeezed to within an inch of its life. He knew he shouldn't have waited this long. He knew there was no excuse for his lateness. But he hadn't understood the point, if he was being honest. Why go to the trouble of constructing a headstone for someone whose bones had been burned and ashes scattered to the winds?

Joel wished Beth was there to give his hand a reassuring squeeze and he let himself run with that fantasy, picturing himself covering her right hand with his left, gently sandwiching it between his palms as if he was trapping a butterfly. He smiled sadly. He knew every crease and divot of her palm by heart – he literally knew the back of her hand better than he knew his own – and, as he stood there and imagined the double cream softness of Beth's skin beneath the pulse of his fingertips, he was thrown back to the first night he'd held her hand.

Nearly Departed

It had been the night after their third date. They'd lain in bed, hemmed in by the cold of midnight but warm and naked under a 7.5 tog duvet, and Joel had asked Beth if it was weird they'd had sex but hadn't even held hands. Flecks of snow dandruffed the window and a wind howled dimly behind the double-glazing. A single bedside lamp lit the room in a warm glow. Joel's hand rested gently on the counter of Beth's hip bone as they stared at each other, soaking up as much of the opposite person's then-alien features as possible. Beth had reassured Joel it wasn't weird at all.

'If anything, I think holding hands is even more intimate,' she said.

'Really?' he asked.

'Yes,' she said. Then she shifted onto her back and wordlessly urged Joel to do the same with a tilt of her head.

As he stared up at the ceiling, Joel realised he'd lost track of his own conscience — the Jiminy Cricket drone of his inner monologue had all but disappeared. All he could think about was the naked woman lying next to him. He thought about the vellum of her elbow crook, the rose-bush smell of her hair and the way one of her breasts was ever so slightly larger, and heavier, than the other. He ran his thumb softly along the rungs of her ribcage. There wasn't even enough room in his head to worry about whether she was thinking of him in return. He was fully living in the moment, perhaps for the first time in his entire life.

Stevie Nicks' 'Wild Heart' swirled through the room,

wrapping around Joel like a breeze, her bluesy vibrato and delicate, yet still somewhat goat-like, pitch brimming with an unguarded expressiveness that seemed to seep straight into his chest. It was one of nine Stevie Nicks songs on Beth's playlist – a Bowie and synthesiser-heavy selection which might, to a future historian finding it hidden in an ancient catacomb, suggest the creation of new music had been made illegal in 1989. They were songs moulded to the shape of her body: songs Joel would have to turn off if he ever heard them on the radio because they reminded him too violently of her. Stevie had just arrived at the final chorus when Beth reached out to hold Joel's hand.

Her hand was slightly smaller than his and her fingers interlaced themselves snugly with his own. The moment his fingers closed around hers, Beth felt as if a weighted blanket of peace had been draped over her body. It was utterly lovely and entirely overwhelming. Beth closed her eyes and Joel closed his and they lay there together, in stasis, for what felt like forever. Neither was asleep but they weren't exactly awake either. They were suspended in a third state that hung somewhere between the two, where they were aware of their surroundings yet completely untouched by the world outside the bed.

That night, between the sheets, they'd stumbled upon their own hidden continent, unearthing the secret to immortality in the process. To stay there forever – hands clásped, eyes shut – seemed like a dream. A charmed existence. But they both knew, sooner or later, they'd have to let go. Even the best dreams have to come to an end. Joel realised in that moment he was destined to fall madly and deeply in love with the woman lying beside him. And she, in turn, knew she was going to fall head over heels for him. As their hands drifted apart, Joel's mind flooded with a million scattered thoughts, each tumbling over the next.

Overwhelmed by the sheer number of options available to him, he settled on the only word he could think of to sum up the intoxicating blend of joy and pain that comes with falling for another person. 'Shit,' he blurted out, knowing 'love' was too deranged to utter on a third date. It was the only word that even came close to capturing the laughter and ecstasy he knew was in store, as well as the inevitable heartbreak and anguish he was destined to encounter.

Beth shuffled her body round to meet Joel's gaze. Her emerald eyes mingled with his blue to make a cyan – or was it turquoise? – bit of eye contact. 'Shit,' she agreed, and they rolled into each other's embrace and didn't let go until the morning.

As the credits rolled on Joel's memory of that night, the cemetery slowly swam back into focus. Raindrops splattered against the headstone in a pointillist blur of dark grey. Summer rain. Like the flick of a light switch, Joel refocused on reality, his fingers grazing his damp cheeks to brush away the tears.

'I didn't think you'd come,' said Joel, as an anoraked figure approached from his left, their silhouette obscured by the fading light. As they drew nearer, their shoes crunching on the gravel, Joel raised his eyes to greet them.

'Of course I would,' came the reply. 'She's still my daughter. And you . . . you're still something.'

Joel smiled wryly.

'Not a very good something, mind you,' said June. 'But something nonetheless.'

June's eyes were shining in the dusk. She had Beth's eyes. Or, more accurately, Beth had her eyes. Or had had her eyes. Nice eyes, anyway, the lot of them.

Joel spoke softly, choosing his words carefully. 'I'm sorry,' he said, 'about everything.'

'It's not your fault,' she replied, almost reflexively. 'Life's not always fair,' she added, as if that were an explanation for anything.

'I know you think I'm silly for believing in things like energy and tarot and crystals,' June continued, her voice rising in desperation, 'but they help me get a handle on everything. On all . . . this. Without them, I'm not sure the world would make much sense to me.'

Joel didn't answer immediately. He turned away from her, his gaze drawn to the marble marker of Beth's resting place. 'I don't think it's supposed to,' he said, flatly.

They both stood in silence, staring down at Beth's sort-of grave, as a pair of sparrows swooped in an infinity symbol overhead. In the distance, a woman set down an oversized teddy bear next to a child-sized headstone.

'Your friend, Alice, called the other day. She told me all about what's been happening.'

'Did she now?' said Joel. He chewed on his lower lip.

June nodded. 'I've been speaking to Beth, too,' she said.

'I'm glad,' said Joel, and he looked up at June as if he

Nearly Departed

was seeing her for the very first time. He asked if Beth had anything interesting to say.

'Oh, not really,' she laughed. 'Just your classic unfinished business. She did tell me I needed to clean out her room, though.'

'Of course she did.' He smiled down at his shoes.

On the road outside the graveyard, two buggies were about to smash against each other. Joel watched through the gunmetal bars as one of the women swerved at the last second, averting the collision. An argument started between them. Their babies started screaming. They left, hastily, going in opposite directions. All this noise made it difficult to think.

'So, do you still think I'm a cursed man?' Joel asked at last.

'No, Joel,' said June, shaking her head, 'and I'm sorry I ever said that. I think you've simply been dealt a bad hand.'

She let the sentence hang in the air. He turned it over in his mind and tried it on for size, pulling it over his ankles and up to his waist, but it didn't quite fit. It was too loose around the middle. Too baggy.

'I used to think that, too,' he murmured, tracing his finger over the bold capitals of Beth's name. He admired how it began with the gentle curves of the B, inviting you in under false pretences, before transforming into the clean, steady resolve of the straight lines that anchored the rest of her name. Beth would have approved of the symbolism, regardless of whatever the hell it was meant to symbolise. 'But you know what? I think I'm actually pretty fucking lucky. Lucky to have met her in a world where so many never even got the chance.'

June rolled her eyes dramatically and leaned her head on Joel's shoulder. He tilted his head to meet hers with a soft thud.

'Did she make you watch *Sleepless in Seattle*?' she asked.
'Yep.'
'What about *Four Weddings*?'
'We watched that one, too.'

'Figures,' said June. She grabbed Joel gently by the wrist and slipped a smooth card into his palm. He looked down and saw the Ten of Swords staring back up at him.

'What am I supposed to do with this?'

'Whatever you want,' June said. She gave his shoulder a reassuring squeeze and plodded off in the direction of the treeline.

Joel took a deep breath and tore the card up into halves, quarters and then eighths until it resembled wedding confetti. He held up the little pieces of his destiny in his hand, letting the wind pick them up and carry them away.

'And Joel,' shouted June from fifty metres away, 'let me know when I'm going to get to meet my new daughter-in-law!'

He could hear her smile echo through the trees.

'I promise, I'm on it.'

Epilogue

'I don't get people who are late for flights,' said Nina. 'Like, you've paid so much money for the privilege of flying to another country, you should at least have the good grace to arrive on time.' Nina had a green crossbody bag slung over one shoulder and was wielding a half-empty latte in her right hand. A combination of lack of sleep and a general fear of flying meant she was feeling especially tetchy. She hoped the caffeine would settle her nerves before they boarded the plane.

'Me neither,' said Joel as a family of four came running past at top speed, their oversized backpacks crashing down on their backs with every elongated stride they took. It reminded Nina of those scenes in *The Empire Strikes Back* where Luke has to do all of his Jedi training with Yoda strapped to his back. She said as much to Joel and he laughed in agreement.

It had been almost a year now since the first time Joel and Nina had had sex and eight months since they'd decided, mutually, to not see other people. Nina had got into the routine of referring to Joel as her 'partner' at work because she couldn't stand how sentences like 'Oh, my boyfriend loves that band' sounded out loud. She couldn't put her finger on it but there was something inherently embarrassing about admitting you had a boyfriend. It was probably the 'boy' bit that made it feel so infantilising. Partner, however, sounded much more adult, more serious; like you could be lovers who lived together but also – potentially – that this was merely a person who worked closely with you at the detective bureau.

Joel and Nina agreed arriving at least three hours before their flight was an extraordinarily good idea. Neither understood the need for the terminal to have four WHSmiths. 'I'm going to use the loo before we have to get to the gate,' said Nina. She stretched her arms up, revealing a delicious slice of midriff between her T-shirt and her leggings.

'Okay,' said Joel, reaching out to give her hand a quick squeeze. 'Have fun!'

'I will,' she laughed, giving his hand a small kiss before beginning her trek to the nearest women's bathroom where a queue was already snaking out of the door. Joel watched as her green bag bobbed along and disappeared into the crowd.

There's something banally and beautifully British about an airport Pret A Manger, thought Joel, as he suctioned up a pastry crumb precariously positioned on the tip of his thumb like a boulder in a Road Runner vignette. Sure, it's just hordes of hungry, uncaffeinated people queuing up to tap their card and pay £18 for a skinny latte, plain croissant and ham sandwich. But there's an energy there.

Nearly Departed

It's a bit like the saucer-eyed lines for water refills you get at festivals – a communal feeling of anticipation mixed with a resignation that everyone's in it together and, guess what, you've got no other option anyway. The money you're spending isn't real because it never is in airports and, besides, you've got an easyJet flight to somewhere sunny in three hours and 'you're on holiday'. You've earned it. The coffee doesn't even do its job at properly waking you up because – like money – caffeine isn't real in an airport, either. You're simply drinking it to feel something and to forget, for fifteen minutes or so, you're in fucking Luton.

Nina returned from the bathroom with a fully filled-up water bottle and what looked to be an extra spring in her step. She walked tall and her feet seemed to know exactly where they wanted to go, eating up the floor in front of her in big bites until she reached the table Joel was sitting at. He knew she had given herself a pep talk in front of the bathroom mirror while she was gone and he loved how visible its effect was on her demeanour.

'Are you ready?' asked Joel.

'I am,' Nina said, sounding – to all intents and purposes – extremely ready indeed.

After double – and triple-checking they had both of their passports and other essentials, they joined the cluster of people squinting up at the flight information emblazoned on a large electronic display board and searched for their flight and its corresponding gate number.

'Gate 26,' said Nina, pointing up to the screen. Joel

followed the direction of her finger to confirm the information for himself. Sure enough, the flight was boarding in thirty minutes and the gate was about a fifteen-minute walk away. Joel tried, and failed, to hide that he was turned on by Nina's excellent time management skills. He siphoned that arousal into a light touch of her tricep that said something along the lines of: 'God, you're good.' She responded with a friendly pat on his arse which was shorthand for: 'And don't I know it.'

Packing light had never been Joel's strong suit but Nina had been cutthroat in the amount of clothing he was allowed to take to the wedding. 'Joel,' she'd said, as he sat on the floor surrounded by a mosaic made of every pair of pants and socks he owned, 'it's going to be, what, thirty degrees? You do not need to take a fleece with you.' He'd heeded her advice and, marching towards the gate, felt a stirring sense of freedom in his lack of baggage. He was a regular Robinson Crusoe.

Nina could see Joel was smiling slyly at whatever it was he was thinking about, and a smile slowly but surely unpacked itself on her face, too. She knew they'd pull up to the beachfront guest house Holly and Sam had booked for the wedding party in about five hours, and without hesitation, tumble into the sort of feral, slightly clumsy sex that only ever seems to happen in hotel rooms.

'Passengers with Speedy Boarding for the seven-thirty flight to Paphos, please line up at the departures desk at gate twenty-six.'

Joel was ninety-nine per cent sure he hadn't paid

Nearly Departed

extra for Speedy Boarding, but he looked down at the PDF of the boarding pass he had on his phone anyway, just to be sure. Nina did the same, along with five other people sitting in the waiting area, and laughed at the predictability of that action. They both watched, smirking, as two men in matching Ralph Lauren polo shirts wrestled to be the first in line.

'I mean, we're all literally going to get on the same plane,' whispered Nina. 'Who cares if you're the first one on it?'

'I have no idea,' shrugged Joel. 'Americans?'

Another fifteen minutes passed – of what Nina assumed was expensively peaceful and pointless bliss for the Speedy Boarders sitting in a mostly empty plane – before the announcement was made for everyone else to board the flight. Nina unzipped her bag to pull out her passport and Joel fished his own out of the light jacket she had said he could wear on the plane if he was so fucking intent on taking it with him.

As Joel joined the queue, the strap of his bag started to dig the edge of its polypropylene teeth into his shoulder. He knew from the ant-bite feeling tingling under his shirt that the strap had already left a maroon imprint of itself on his body. He placed the bag on the floor and picked it back up with his left hand to give his right a break. It was when he went about the process of clunkily clean and jerking his bag onto his shoulder that he saw her.

She was standing at the window, looking out at the tarmac. Even from one hundred metres away, Joel could recognise the back of Beth's head. He felt a tennis-ball-sized lump form in his throat.

Her hair fell down her back like fresh pasta on a drying rack and Joel knew if he got close enough to touch it he'd be able to smell the purple of the synthetic violets used to flavour her shampoo. Joel nearly dropped his bag in shock but caught it at the last second – a rapid, harried, slapstick motion which was successful in startling the balding man before him and grabbing Nina's attention.

'What are you fussing about?' she said to Joel, swivelling to face the same direction as him. Joel, lost for words, simply stood and stared out at Beth's back while Nina craned her head to see what he was looking at. Before he could think of what to say, Joel watched Beth turn around, raise an arm and wave. She did it sadly and kindly like a mother waving off their child on their first day of school, rather than sadly and sadly like a wife waving off their husband before they go to war. Unsure of what other options were available to him, Joel waved back. It seemed like the polite thing to do. And from the corner of his eye, he noticed Nina was waving, too.

'Who is that?' asked Nina. She'd seen photos of Beth before but – from this distance, and with her less than stellar eyesight – Nina couldn't make out anything apart from the general shape of the person who was waving. It was a fine shape, to be sure, but not one that instilled any emotion in her aside from confusion.

'A friend,' said Joel, slowly lowering his arm back down to his side.

'Right,' said Nina, who could feel the anxiety of being suspended 12,000 metres in the air inside a large metal bird creeping up on her. 'Should we quickly go and say hi . . . and goodbye?'

'No,' said Joel, smiling faintly as he slowly turned his back on Beth – knowing it was likely he would never see her again and praying he had the strength not to regret his decision.

He looked Nina squarely in her eyes. He loved the way they seemed to dance with emotion, reflecting every thought and feeling that passed through her mind. He didn't know they would break up in four months' time following an argument over what takeaway to have for dinner, before promptly rekindling their romance a week later. Because as Joel stood there, lost in Nina's gaze while the Border Force officer at the desk started getting justifiably irate, he knew he would do just about anything to make her smile. And that, for now, was more than enough.

He placed his hand on the side of her face and took one last look into her eyes before shutting his own and letting himself melt into a kiss.

'It's time to get on with it,' he said, as they moved apart again. He took Nina's hand, and they were swiftly ushered through the gates and into the plane, leaving the world behind to eat their dust.

Acknowledgements

I'm forever indebted to my agent, Barbara Levy, for taking a chance on me and all my friends and family who have supported me over the years. A vast and cosmic thanks to my parents Ron and Julie for raising me with love, care, laughter, and an endless supply of books. I wouldn't be the man I am today without you. A big bloodline-based thank you also goes out to Toby for being the best brother anyone could ask for.

I've stolen a great deal of the characteristics, clothes, and haircuts of the characters in this novel from the people in my life I care about the most, so if you see even the faintest glimpse of yourself in here – or recognise a phrase you once told me at the pub – I owe you a pint. I can't list everyone but thanks go out especially to: Wilf, Jo, Charlotte, Josh, Holly, Joe, Jamie, Liv, and Matt. You're all the best. Don't let anyone tell you otherwise.

A large gushing thanks to my publisher Carolyn Mays and the entire team at Bedford Square Publishers for helping to bring this novel to life and into actual bookshops. Which still feels surreal, to be honest. Thanks also go to Joanna Dingley for her vital work on the big picture edits and Amber Burlison for her equally important work on the copy edits – this became a much better book because of your patience and direction.

Thank you to all the readers who were kind (and mad) enough to read early drafts: Megan Carroll, Olivia Davies, and Dominic Wakeford. Each of you offered invaluable advice and reassured me that my efforts in writing this weren't totally wasted. It would be remiss of me not to mention coffee at this point, too. Coffee was there for me through every stage of turning this from a manic Google Doc into a finished manuscript. And when I say I couldn't have done it without it, I mean it.

Of course, this book wouldn't exist without Katherine, who is the best thing about me. I would have binned this idea long ago if I hadn't had you by my side. You never gave up on me, even when I had given up on myself, and I hope one day I can repay that kindness. Thankfully, we've got the rest of our lives for me to work on that. I love you. I always will.

And finally a special thanks to you, the reader, for making it this far. I can't believe you've read this entire thing. Have you got nothing better to do with your time?

About the Author

Image credit © Sophie Davidson

Lucas Oakeley is a writer and journalist. He has written for a range of publications including – but not limited to – *GQ*, *Vogue*, *National Geographic*, the *Economist*, *Esquire* and *VICE*. He was shortlisted as a finalist for the Guild of Food Writer's Food Writing award in 2020.

@lucasoakeley
@LucasOakeley

Bedford Square Publishers

Bedford Square Publishers is an independent publisher of fiction and non-fiction, founded in 2022 in the historic streets of Bedford Square London and the sea mist shrouded green of Bedford Square Brighton.

Our goal is to discover irresistible stories and voices that illuminate our world.

We are passionate about connecting our authors to readers across the globe and our independence allows us to do this in original and nimble ways.

The team at Bedford Square Publishers has years of experience and we aim to use that knowledge and creative insight, alongside evolving technology, to reach the right readers for our books. From the ones who read a lot, to the ones who don't consider themselves readers, we aim to find those who will love our books and talk about them as much as we do.

We are hunting for vital new voices from all backgrounds – with books that take the reader to new places and transform perceptions of the world we live in.

Follow us on social media for the latest Bedford Square Publishers news.

@bedsqpublishers
facebook.com/bedfordsq.publishers/
@bedfordsq.publishers

https://bedfordsquarepublishers.co.uk/